Praise for Jack Cady:

"Like John Steinbeck, [Cady] is an accomplished storyteller. His works resonate with the passions and foibles of ordinary people, and he makes his readers care for them."
— Tor.com

"A remarkable talent for translating familiar life rhythms of ordinary people into moving and meaningful writing . . . his style is direct, simple, and natural."
— *Publishers Weekly*

"Jack Cady's knack for golden sentences is an alchemy any other writer has to admire."
—Ivan Doig

"An exceptional writer."
— Joyce Carol Oates

"A writer of great, unmistakable integrity and profound feeling."
— Peter Straub

"[Jack Cady is] a lasting voice in modern American literature."
— *The Atlanta Constitution*

THE CADY COLLECTION

NOVELS

The Hauntings of Hood Canal
Inagehi
The Jonah Watch
McDowell's Ghost
The Man Who Could Make Things Vanish
The Off Season
Singleton
Street

Dark Dreaming [with Carol Orlock, as Pat Franklin]
Embrace of the Wolf [with Carol Orlock, as Pat Franklin]

OTHER WRITINGS

Phantoms
Fathoms
Ephemera
The American Writer

Ephemera

Collected Writings, Volume 3

Jack Cady

FAIRWOOD PRESS
Bonney Lake, WA

EPHEMERA
A Fairwood Press Book
November 2025
Copyright © 2025 by the Estate of Jack Cady

Fairwood Press
21528 104th Street Court East
Bonney Lake, WA 98391
www.fairwoodpress.com

Series Cover Design by Jennifer Tough
Collection Editorial Direction by Mark Teppo

ISBN: 978-1-933846-28-9
First Fairwood Press Edition: November 2025
Printed in the United States of America

Contents

Introduction

Mark Teppo

I NEVER MET JACK CADY. I WAS A YOUNG SPRAT IN the last of the nineties, eagerly attending my first science fiction conventions. Norwescon. Westercon. That one up in Bellingham that one year. I suppose Jack attended those too, but, well, I was young and full of myself and there were many grizzled editors wandering about (and I say this with all the humility that age brings, realizing that I'm on the cusp of that grizzledness myself). And he was gone by the time I got into publishing.

Now, publishing. I came to it earnestly, laughing off the old joke that circulated among the cynics and world-weary ("How do you make a small fortune in publishing? Start with a large one."), but one of the projects I wanted to undertake was the preservation of a body of work that was otherwise being overlooked. There's a steep cliff once you get past the classics and the moderately well-known. The occasional genre influencer will have a title or two that crops up repeatedly in the offerings from the exclusive and fine press, but for the rest? Well, those books sink and are forgotten, which is a shame.

That's how Jack's oeuvre came to me. There were (and still are, frankly) a generation of genre writers who were taught by him (Fairwood's dedicated publisher being one of them), his stories and books won a few awards, and he was a part of the

1

Pacific Northwest literary landscape. And—rather critically—his papers were readily available at the Pacific Lutheran University archive, which were a half hour's drive or so from my house.

I didn't know Jack, but the idea of putting together a unified collection of Jack's work seemed like an idea very worth undertaking.

I wrote an email to Carol Orlock, Jack's widow and literary executor, and she was polite enough to take me seriously and hear out my pitch. Not only would we reissue each of his novels, but we'd also gather up all the short fiction, the relevant non-fiction, and whatever else might strike our fancy as being pertinent to the man's career, and put together a shelf of Jack. Each novel would be accompanied by stories or non-fiction Jack had written that would embellish or contextualize the work to some degree. Carol said yes, and I went and made friends with the archivists at PLU.

This is how we found an article that Jack had written for the U. S. Coast Guard magazine in 1956, an article which gave an oddly autobiographical note to *The Jonah Watch*, Jack's first novel. It seemed prudent to include Jack's piece "On Writing the Ghost Story" with *The Off Season*. And his long article "Transcendentalism and the American Highway," which was first published in *Tattoo*, a collection issued by Circinatum in 1978, was, again, a bit of autobiographical non-fiction that cast the fictional nature of *Singleton* in a different light.

These, and other bits of connective tissue, were how we built a legacy for Jack that would allow those of us who came late to Jack to know him a little better. It was—and is—a good goal for a project like this, and I'm delighted that we are here at *Ephemera*, the third collection of assorted stories and non-fiction.

I published the first portion of this project, but when I moved from Washington to Oregon, there was a bit of nonsense regarding business names and one state recognizing the validity of business in another state. There was an opportunity to hand off this project to Patrick Swenson and Fairwood Press, which was—in many ways—the right place for the project to be. Patrick had, after all, actually been a student of Jack's, during Jack's time at PLU.

All of this would not have been possible without the grace and calm resolution of Carol Orlock, who gave both Patrick and me a great deal of room to rummage about in Jack's past. She let us find our way, lightly guided us when we wandered away from the core spirt of Jack's work, and steadfastly maintained her guardianship of Jack's work. Thank you, Carol.

Ephemera was intended to be the final book in the collection, following *Fathoms* and *Phantoms*, but as we did a final sweep through the archives to assemble this book, we stumbled upon more material. I thought we had been thorough, back in the day, but like all projects that involve rooting around in a writer's brain, more stuff keeps percolating to the surface. There's a novel that was never finished, as well as a non-fiction book that was meant as a follow-up to *The American Writer,* focusing on what Jack saw as the underpinning and origin of the American mindset toward the fantastic.

This is how I came to know Jack.

And, as to whether or not Jack and I were ever in the same room, here's an anecdote. As I was going through his correspondence, I ran across handwritten notes scrawled across a letter from Kristine Kathryn Rusch. She had bought his story, "The Curious Candy Store" and wanted it for issue seven of Pulphouse. He was, according to the scrawl, making a trip down to Eugene to visit Rusch and the gang at Pulphouse. The scrawl read: "I94 OR 95 exit to Eugene. City Center. Coburg Road. Over a green bridge. Honda Dealership. Immediate left. Building behind Bavarian. Mark is guy at Pulphouse." [Periods added for clarity; this is, after all, a scrawl laid out more like poetry than proper sentences.]

It's hard to say when Jack wrote those notes. Whether that letter was the most recent letter he'd received from Rusch, or if it had merely been the most handy piece of paper when he was taking down directions. Either way, there was a brief moment around this time when the guy working in that downstairs office would have been me.

So, maybe, I did meet Jack. Though, after a decade of puttering about with the phantoms and ephemera of his career, it's possible that my memory of that summer is thoroughly compromised. Haunted, if you will. I'm sure Jack would approve.

—Mark Teppo
September 2025

Ephemera

The Sons of Noah

And the fear of you and the dread of you shall be upon every beast of the earth, and upon all fowl of the air, upon all that moveth upon the earth, and upon all the fishes of the sea; into your hand are they delivered.

—Genesis 9:2

WHEN DARKNESS EDGES THROUGH THIS VALLEY, SHADING SLOW figures of cattle moving toward milking barns, last light falls on the weathered steeple of Sons Of Noah Church. The church stands on stilts beside Troublesome Creek, as do all our barns and houses. The valley is a flood plain.

Visitors to our Northwest valley always ask why we, the country people, stay in a place bound to flood every seven years. Why do we choose to live in houses foundationed on twenty-foot timbers hewn from ancient cedars. Why live where cattle climb ramps to elevated barns. We reply that floods renew the soil and make good pasture. Our milk and produce are the purest in the world. What we say is not false.

What we do not say is that this valley casts a spell. It is shadowed by eight-thousand-foot mountains. The valley is twenty miles long, seventeen miles wide. Weather systems bred in the Aleutians bring rain nine months each year. Darkness often covers the land, even in daylight, and not all darkness is threatening. The mountains are protectors, because the world beyond these mountains is beset by demons.

From this mountain valley our sons sometimes go away to the Army. Those who survive always return, and they tell crazy tales. They speak of endless streams of automobiles, and of demonic voices chattering from television screens. They speak of billboards and politicians, wars, suicides, whoring, rape, drugs, satanic worship.

Visitors describe us as 'peculiar', and maybe that is true. On the other hand, we hear of the outside world and describe it as insane. We do not mind if the rest of the world chooses insanity, as long as that world leaves us alone. At least, we have not minded until now.

I am elected to write of this. My name is Thaddeus Morris, which of course means little, although around here the name carries weight. I am not the oldest man in the valley—the oldest is our preacher, Jubal Petersen—but I'm old enough. My fingers are crabbed around the pen as I write, and lamplight, fueled by finely rendered sheep fat, glows smoky and slick across these pages which aim at your salvation. We do not want to harm you. We wish to be known as builders, not destroyers. We hope you will be warned.

Allow me to show how life is with us, then tell the sad story of a terrible destruction which has caused us to become troubled. I must recount a bit of history.

Our ancestors came to this Pacific Northwest from upper New York State in the 1860s, following the Oregon Trail. They had strong leadership and holy purpose. From their very beginnings they called themselves The Sons Of Noah. Their beliefs centered around the mistakes and sins of Noah after The Flood. They saw themselves as quiet people who would eventually reclaim the world through decent behavior and piety. Old diaries kept by womenfolk tell of that harsh trek, of worn-out Conestogas, of privation, of dying oxen, of Indian raiders.

Our people found coastal Oregon over-populated. Trees fell before pioneer ambitions. Log houses sometimes stood no more than a thousand rods apart. Indians wearing seal skins, or colorfully dyed cedar bark robes, clustered around settlements. They traded furs for guns and whiskey. The world seemed filled with bustle.

The leader in those days was a man named Aaron Schmidt. In prayers Schmidt received solace, and in dreams he received direction. There was a Northwest valley, he was told, avoided even by the Indians. In written records the harsh journey northward to the Olympic Peninsula is known as 'The Pilgrimage'.

This valley finally lay revealed. It lies two thousand feet above sea level, and above a mighty rainforest. Our pastures are vibrant and lush, and the darkness of this valley is a good thing. With more sun the pastures' growth would carry frenzy.

A road now runs part way in, but the last two miles are corduroy road, suited only to ox carts. These days we sell produce and cheese to merchants who monthly send trucks to the head of the road.

That original congregation arrived, and first built a church and a graveyard. The long pilgrimage took its toll on older members, including Schmidt. The earliest grave markers were simple stones from the mountainside. To this day they sit as squat reminders of faith among the multitude of carved markers. In a hundred years many are born, and many die.

The original congregation looked about in wonder. Grass grew lush, and a constant supply of pure water ran in Troublesome Creek. The valley spawned life. Our forefathers took two-hundred-pound fish from the creek, fish so bizarre that they seemed ancient as creation. Fish with teeth like the canines of wolves. Fish with wing-like fins—that when tanned became fine leather—and walking fish with appendages stiff as legs. Bear and cougar and elk shuffled and stalked and ran through the valley. Beaver and possum, weasels, foxes and wolverine contested for food and life. Our people gave thanks in prayer, but they were also mystified.

These days we have more knowledge, because we are not averse to new ideas. We learn a great deal, because we take in more of the world's coin than we can possibly spend. Our only purchases from that outside world are salt and books. We study books of today and books of the past. In this way we figure out our world.

Our valley sits atop a great fissure. When these mountains were created, the rock structure split, then tumbled back on itself. Beneath our feet lies a primeval lake. Troublesome Creek, which seldom runs more than forty feet wide, is also bottomless. Living water from melting snow in the mountains runs along the surface of the creek. It passes over water that may be two thousand feet deep, or more. The rock is impermeable. The entire fissure holds water as old as the original creation. We do not know everything that lives down there, but sometimes we get indications. It works this way.

Every seventh year the valley floods. There are Biblical explanations for this, but none are scientific. As flood spreads across our fields we check our boats. Water does not often rise more than ten or twelve feet, while our houses are twenty feet above ground. Only twice in this century has water risen to cover the floors of our houses. In 1917 it rose to twenty-one feet. In 1942 it rose to twenty-three. Flood covers the graveyard like a protecting hand, and no grave is ever disturbed. Even the upright markers do not tilt.

For those years of highest water we have flatboats to carry our horses, oxen, cattle, sheep, fowl, and swine. Ordinarily we pass between houses and barns and church in rowboats. Water rises quickly. Flood replenishes the land, and the flood seems driven by a mind of its own. Waters flow, then concentrate. Some years they may greatly enrich the Jensen acres, sometimes the Petersens', or other farms. The valley lies for forty days beneath flood, then water slides away, down the mountains or into the fissure of Troublesome Creek.

The water level sometimes drops quickly. Huge shapes flee across fields, dashing back to the safety of deep water. Silver streaks intermix. They are flashes of light sparkling above the drowned pasture. When water drops too quickly, strange fish are stranded in the fields, although there is a type of fish that is never stranded. The variety is fleet and many-colored, like shooting rainbows through the torrent. These fish have nearly human eyes, but larger, seeing wider than do we. It is a busy time for our whole community.

Men harness horses and oxen to huge mud sleds. The sleds skid to the fields, and a process of selection begins. We try to protect the original creation. Those fishes still living get dumped back in the creek. Then the men use pitchforks to load the rest onto the sleds. There is no waste of the creation. Men dress out the fish, and women dry them. We have never had seven lean years here, but are prepared should they occur. Twice there have been fish that had to be towed by two oxen.

And so we live, living among the primal forces and original fury that brought this planet into being. Power grows. We walk beside great waters.

On Sundays, after services, we gather in front of Sons Of Noah Church: the Andersens, the Jensens, Adams, Schmidts, and two dozen other families. Traditionally, it is a time of quiet joy.

Beside the church, the churchyard with its gravestones becomes a living presence. Our ancestors lie at our very elbows, so to speak. Children, who have learned to sit patiently through morning services, romp among the graves. They are like flitting butterflies, brightly colored, dancing in games of hide-and-seek behind tombstones.

We talk among ourselves, the way our people have sought truth since the 1860s. We used to discuss crops and ideas. Unhappy I am to report that these days we are forced to speak of power.

A demonic world presses close. Aircraft sometimes pass overhead, where once passed only the birds of the air. More beasts of the field, deer and elk and wolves, are driven to our high valley as a demonic world logs the rainforest. We are careful in our speech.

"We do not command these waters. To think we command is the sin of pride." Our preacher, Jubal Petersen, says this. He was once a man of immense strength, and even in his age he still drives oxen. His shoulders are square, and his hair is a cloud of white above a high and furrowed brow.

The children play. Here and there young wives and husbands whisper together. One girl's waist has grown. In a few months there will be birth and christening. The generations are intact.

Men stand in silence, waiting for the spirit of truth to guide their words. We are not a hasty people. The men are fair of face. Their suits are subdued colors of gray, blue, brown. Work-hardened hands hang restful at their sides. The men stand like protecting trees of the mountain forests.

"Do we serve at the threshold of divine power?" one says. His name is Lars Landstrup, his father was Eric, his grandfather was Sven. Lars' strength is great, and, of all of us, he worries most about right and wrong. "Maybe," he says, "we protect the creation."

"The waters protect us," a woman murmurs. Mercy Adams is a grandmother now, but there is that about her which recalls the beauty of her youth. If our women have a leader, then surely Mercy leads. "We are in delicate balance," she says. She glances toward the younger women, toward the young wife who is with child.

The graveyard lies silent, except for children's play. Our women stand like flowers. They dress in gowns showing the many colors of natural dyes. Above the graveyard the steeple rises like a benediction.

"Our cause is just," another woman murmurs.

"We do none of this for gain," a man says. "We are not engaged in spurious adventures."

Our disputations rise because some men from that outside world are most hideously dead. We fear that we had a hand in matters. We do not yet question the tenets of our faith, but clearly something is askew. Our ancestors believed that their quiet ways and piety would overcome the world. They believed in the power of reverence, not the power of force.

And yet great forces aid us. Power accumulates. I must now record the manner of those terrible deaths.

We did not immediately understand that the man was insane. Perhaps we might have helped him. One cannot hate the insane, only pity them. At the same time, if a wolverine gets loose in your streets it must be contained.

On an April morning last year, when sun glowed like a blessed spirit through mountain mist, the solitary figure of a man appeared at the head of the road. His outfit exceeded his need. Perhaps such waste should have warned us. He wore wool knickers, tall boots with much lacing, and a down parka quilted like a sleeping bag. His rolled pack rode on heavy shoulders, a pack filled with enough implements and supplies to last—if he knew what he was doing— for many months in the forest wilderness. Yet he had only hiked in two miles from the paved road where he left his truck.

And the truck, itself, was another mark of insanity, had we been clever enough to read its meaning. One of our sons who has been outside described it as an all-terrain vehicle. The truck proved capable of driving over rough country but was too small to haul anything. We thought it rather silly.

We have always welcomed our few visitors to this valley. We've hoped they would feel the serenity of this place, thus learn to be serene. Our message of piety would go with them when they returned to the outside world.

The man was bluff, but friendly. At the same time, he at first spoke to us as if we were children. He was a man accustomed to commanding others. In the grand illusion of his power he regarded us as simple, ignorant folk. We have had other visitors who thought us simpleminded. We always tolerate their pride, knowing they will leave.

For three days he camped at the head of the valley. The Jensen family invited him to supper and offered him a bed in the large room used by their sons. The man Hamilton, "Joe Hamilton to my friends," he said, took supper but refused the bed. He pitched his tent at the far edge of Jensen's western pasture. The tent stood as a glowing spot of unnatural blue among the gray and blue mist of our valley. Hamilton spent three days walking the lower reaches of the mountains. In April, Troublesome Creek runs swift from melting snows. People who live at the far end of the valley carry goods to market on rafts.

On Sunday Hamilton attended church. He joined in hymns, singing in a strained and nearly boyish voice that was most unlike his speaking voice. We know now that either eagerness or tension pinched his song. We enjoyed his presence, thinking him a willing and possibly able man. We have never, in this century, had a convert.

After services matters took an unsettling turn. We stood in groups after church. Muted sunlight washed across the churchyard, casting pale shadows behind gravestones. Muted breezes touched spring grass around graves where tulips grew in thick patches of yellow and red. A few crocus remained.

Hamilton stood among Landstrups and Jensens, as our minister, Jubal Petersen, approached. Hamilton's voice did not carry. He seemed trying to cooperate with the quiet of Sunday service, but was awkward with quietness. His large shoulders huddled inside the down jacket. We thought him shy, not manipulative.

"This must be the most peaceful place in the world," he said to Lars, "although you work very hard." His face was roundish, like a painting of a Dutch sea captain. Blond hair receded above a high forehead. His lips were thick, his speech precise. His large hands were unmarked and carried no callus. The high-laced boots shone with mink oil. He was somehow aggressive, although he seemed shy.

"Tibet," Lars said. "I expect Tibetan monasteries are the most peaceful places in the world. We could probably learn something from them."

"I have means," Hamilton murmured. "What a convenience it would be if this valley had a water system." He said this with a straight face, and we tried to receive it with straight faces. "For the convenience," he said.

"Troublesome Creek is convenient," Lars told him. "That's why we live beside it."

"For sanitation purposes."

"Our people solved those problems a hundred years ago." Jubal Petersen joined the group. He looked uneasily toward the graveyard, then toward hitching rails where horses stood waiting to pull wagons home. Children ran among the horses, clambered over wagons and carriages. They laughed and shouted after being freed from Sunday sermon, but on this Sunday they did not go near the graveyard.

"Perhaps a stranger might come to belong here," Hamilton said quietly. "If he required no land and paid his way."

It was a strange statement. It would be difficult to pay one's way around here without working the land. Even our minister is a farmer who earns his family's keep.

"It would make life easier," he said, "if your roads were paved." He looked at the creek and the towpath. "A man could build flatboats engined with a drive on each end. It would be easier to get to church." His voice did not conceal a sort of boyish excitement. Nor did it conceal the notion that he wished to show us his version of salvation.

We've heard it all before. Bring bulldozers to the head of the road. Install electric plants. Bring in oil, gasoline, fire engines, tractors, flush toilets, chainsaws. Life would be easy, then. Idyllic. We've heard it from visitors, and occasionally even from our sons who have just returned. After our sons have been home for a year or two they regain their senses. Still, we had never heard it said with the missionary zeal of Hamilton. He spoke with the fervency of a disciple of 'progress'. His fingers tapped, tapped, tapped at air as he attempted to drive home his points.

"It is true that we work hard," Lars told him. "Whether it's a virtue or not, hard work is the price we pay for the peacefulness you admire." Lars also looked uneasily toward the graveyard. He was a head shorter than Hamilton, but he seemed as tall. He has the blue eyes and thin lips of a Dane, but his voice is always gentle. "You've been here for three days," he said, "and you've heard no sounds of engines. Listen."

Children's voices tinkled joyfully across Sunday silence. Above the mist a hawk circled, and the faded shadow of the hawk slid across fields. The liquid murmur of Troublesome Creek blended beneath the far off crowing of a cock. Horses snuffled, shifted in lightly creaking harness. From the Petersen place a new calf bawled for its mother.

And then silence deepened. For moments even the voices of children seemed muted. From the graveyard came a lack of sound that we had never heard before. The best description would say that it was active silence. Always before, our forefathers have lain passive and tranquil. Their message to us is a message of faith.

Jubal Petersen looked at Lars, then at Hamilton. If the rest of us heard only active silence, it may be that Jubal heard more. "Of all the sins available," he said to Hamilton, "perhaps the sin of pride is most dangerous. Zealousness is often a form of pride." His voice was kind but firm. "We are aware of something happening here that you are not. I must excuse myself."

Jubal turned to the churchyard and walked slowly among the graves. We stood in wonder. Our minister was obviously communing with the dead. His dark-suited figure moved easily, and he occasionally murmured as if answering questions. At first his wrinkled face showed sadness, and then a sort of fear. Jubal is not a man to fear anything, and he especially would not fear our dead.

When he returned he spoke quietly, first to us, and then to Hamilton. "Do not underestimate the eternal power of the human spirit," he told us. To Lars he said, "There's a mystery here, and what I've just said has naught to do with pride." To Hamilton he said, "You are welcome as a guest. Confine yourself to being a guest. If you do that, all will be well."

He raised his hand, not to bless us but to dismiss us. There was plenty of excited talk among the families during the ride home, and during the following week.

During that week madness overcame Hamilton. To his credit he tried to remain respectful, yet his insanity compelled him toward destruction. It seemed that, because he had the power to change things, he could not deny use of the power. We forgive him because of his insanity, but we do not forgive the power that corrupted him.

On Monday morning he folded his tent and disappeared down the road to the outside world. We supposed we were quit of him and were greatly relieved. At the same time we felt loss. Had the man remained among us for a few months his urgency would fade. A good, strong man is never a burden. We knew he was ambitious, did not know that in the world's terms he was rich.

On Friday the distant sound of truck engines came faintly across fields nearest the head of the road. Shortly afterward we heard the chip, chip, chip of a helicopter, and we looked toward the pass where Troublesome Creek begins its slide down the mountain in its rush to the sea. A large silver box hung beneath the helicopter. It proved to be a house trailer. One of the Jorgensen sons went to investigate.

He found Hamilton consulting with surveyors, workmen, and an engineer. The house trailer sat on a ledge and was used as a field office. The men immediately set to work. Through habit, perhaps, they wore hardhats as they climbed along the mountainside at the head of the road. Ancient trees have not survived at that elevation because warm winds sometimes blow in winter. There are many avalanches. Orange hardhats moved through the light-green branches, and surveyors broke or cut young trees to take sights. The snarl of a small chainsaw echoed like a stream of curses.

April is a busy time. Work continued in the fields, but at our backs we felt Troublesome Creek turn from rapid flow to subdued violence. Waters rolled as dark shapes moved just beneath the surface. Occasionally huge, blade-like fins hovered in thin sunlight, then disappeared. This was not a seventh year, a year of flood. Yet Troublesome Creek grew active. Against all custom we quit work two hours before dark. After supper everyone assembled at Sons Of Noah Church.

Families lingered before the church. Soon we would climb the many steps to the church, but at first it seemed necessary to remain clustered before the churchyard. If our ancestors had a say in this matter, as we reverently hoped they did, we wanted ears that would hear.

What we heard caused a strange combination of emotions. We were both soothed and made to fear, although we feared not for ourselves.

It is hard to say whether the voices came from the graves or from Troublesome Creek. The murmuring was vast, as if it rose from creek and fields, from barns, silos, graves; as if it rose with controlled energy from sloping sides of mountains, from the steeple of the church, from the darkening sky. Power rose midst murmurs of peace, a power fantastic, a power that was fabulous.

In our quiet lives there is no equation for such power. There can only be sin in such power. We did not know what we had wrought. The voices assured us that all would be well. The voices were serene with power.

We entered our church. There are many steps, and a railed balcony. One of our sons says it reminds him of a ship's bridge. The church is thriftily made, with clear windows that allow sunlight and starlight.

"You must tell us everything the man said." Jubal talked to Billy Jorgensen, who at fifteen is still awkward, but who can already do a man's work. Billy will soon be known as William, and will take his place among our men.

"Mr. Hamilton has a plan," Billy said quietly. "He schemes a special kind of lodge. I told him about avalanche. He talked about retaining walls."

I am compelled to report that a spirit of fierce and possessive pride overtook our congregation. We watched Billy, listened to his straightforward speech, and each of us no doubt thought of him as our son.

"He plans to sell peace," Billy told us.

Noble thought. But peace cannot be sold, only earned. It developed that Hamilton would treat our way of life as a commodity.

He would build a lodge for the use of those who suffer too much fame. It would be a haven for politicians and generals and movie stars, a place where guests registered only by their first names. He would build a lodge where, if one guest recognized another, it would be the height of discourtesy to acknowledge the other's fame, a place where those who suffered limelight could retreat and for a while become anonymous.

"He means it as a compliment," Billy said. "At least he told me that."

Any man or woman even reasonably sane would understand that Hamilton's plan was a deadly insult. However, insult was not the threat. We have handled insults and misunderstanding since the 1860s.

"He will change what he touches. We must reason with him." Lars is slow to anger, but should he ever turn to anger it would show itself as cold and deliberate fury.

People spoke quickly, agitated, and younger men urged action. Beyond darkened windows wind carried a quick storm of mist, like mighty clouds sweeping the valley. Candles flanked the altar, and candles stood in torchères beside the aisles. We suddenly felt small and helpless, but not helpless before the ambitions of Hamilton. A torrent of rain began to walk the valley, and rain drummed on the roof of Sons Of Noah Church. The voice of Troublesome Creek deepened. Storm pounded, throwing gales of wind like cannon. We knew what was happening in all the streams and tributaries of the mountains.

"Hamilton and his dreams are removed from our hands," Jubal said, and he was sad. "He is delivered unto other hands." For a moment Jubal looked tenderly at his congregation. "We have lived beside the forces of creation," he said, "and we have underestimated them. We thought, no doubt, that because we are patient, they are patient as well. See to your beasts and your boats. Dawn will light over mighty waters."

Our lanterns gave light unto our feet as we brought beasts to the barns, and yet were we aided by powerful forces. We are accustomed to rain, but on this night where we traveled—to barns, fields, storage sheds—rain only feathered around us. Our swinging lanterns were washed by mist, while everywhere beyond us in the fields and mountains rain pounded like the trump card of heaven.

A clear dawn displayed our well-washed valley where Troublesome Creek ran boiling. Before we ever lifted our eyes toward the end of the valley, we knew that the laws of nature were set aside by nature's God. Troublesome Creek stood three feet above its banks, but it did not flood beyond the banks. It ran like a compressed road of water, standing above the surface of the ground. Great fishes streaked flashes of light. Some of the fishes were dark, but others were cast in luminous colors. Through the years there are more fishes with nearly human eyes. These now dominated the waters. They twisted, dove, then rose to crest in sunlight.

At the end of the valley, the creek no longer discharged down the mountain. It built higher and higher, the voice of water like the sounds of thunder. It rose, as though an ocean were being upended. The turmoil of water echoed like surf. The flood rose as if the great fishes themselves pushed the water, and we could not distinguish crashing waves from the flash of silvery backs. The waters surged here, there, rose and fell in a grand orchestration. The waters sped according to their own designs, or on the commands of unbreachable power.

Water sealed the entrance to the valley, and it steadily rose toward Hamilton's camp. The trucks and house trailer were red and silver dots among the trees, and the wall of water reached forth.

Voices sounded in the distance, but they were not the voices of Hamilton and his men. These voices were ancestral. They were commanding, but serene. They directed the waters, while above the waters sea eagles screamed, dove, beat the air, rose high, only to again dive toward Hamilton's camp, where frightened men scampered like mice.

We clustered beside our church as our young men unhitched horses from carriages. They prepared to ride in an attempt to aid

Hamilton. Our young men yelled to each other, and they planned to cast ropes by which men might be drawn to salvation. Our men were desperate in their Godly aim of saving lives.

Jubal stood among us, our rock about which the stream of life swirls. He listened more than he watched, but he also watched our men. "Useless," he muttered, "but of course they must try." He turned to a group of us. "This is not about one man with shabby dreams," he muttered. "This is a message to us, and we do well to observe carefully. We'll have to understand the message."

I could see his point. That chaos of water could overwhelm great cities. It did not flow forth simply because of Hamilton, who might be destroyed by a small particle of such enormous energy.

Clouds, of a kind not seen since the creation, formed along ridges of the mountains. There were towering clouds of fire, and equally high clouds of ice; yet the fires did not consume and the ice did not destroy. Fires rumbled upward, darkly smoking, swirling toward the heavens, and sunlight glinted from cascades of shattered ice. Sunlight penetrated black columns of smoke. Light winds swept the valley, interleaving cold and heat, while massive chunks of ice, ripped from glaciers, appeared in Troublesome Creek. Then great winds began to howl, twisting in the high heaven, as if they blew through space from distant stars.

Frightened animals screamed from the safety of barns, and the creek rose steadily until it was a wall of water. The wall stood high, then higher. First it was above our heads, then rapidly grew until it stood above our rooftops, but it still did not flood. Giant trees torn from mountainsides began to twist and turn in Troublesome Creek. Voices rose serenely above the tumult.

I heard the saddened voice of my mother, long dead, and the firm voice of my father, long dead. The ancestry strode invisible among those waters, and we heard the congregated voices of our people. They spoke without hate, only sadness. Yet they commanded the waters.

Hamilton died as men on horses pounded through the valley in an attempt to aid him. He outlasted his cohorts. After all, the surveyors and workmen and engineer were only men doing a job. Their last sight of this world was a rain of glacial ice that killed instantly; and then the bodies were tumbled into the waters and devoured by fishes. Hamilton's death, however, was prolonged.

For a while the creek flowed backward. Then it ceased to flow in any direction and simply stood as a gigantic wall of water. Clouds black as the soul of night stood overhead as lightning crashed, jumped between clouds, illuminated a shadowed landscape that lay beneath volcanic shocks of thunder. Within the wall of water silver flashes streaked, and the flashes echoed human voices. The ancestry rode in those flashes, the eternal human spirit rising to protect—or warn—or teach—we know not which.

Not everything in the creation is beautiful. That which raised its head above the surface, and clasped Hamilton, caused even the bravest of our young men to rein back their horses. Even when the water-form expanded, becoming elongated over half the length of the creek, we could not tell whether it fed with mouths or eyes; for what we took to be mouths were also lidded. They blinked in unaccustomed sunlight, and smoke, and hail. Darkness and light shifted, as if color were liquid, and the creature carried all colors and all darkness.

Hamilton was carried, his round face distorted by screams, just above the surface. The creature of the flood drove the flood, and the flood roared above the tiny voice of Hamilton. This strong man, so filled with pride, but also filled with possibility, thrashed amidst his screams. He called to us, beckoned, and whether he screamed curses or apologies we do not know. His voice garbled with fear, perhaps with repentance, and then his voice was instantly silent. In the enormity of water, the great shape dove into the crevasse, sliding into darkness and the pressure of two thousand feet. Hamilton was only a small spot of color from his expensive clothes as he disappeared into eternal night.

We do not know. We do not know. Mystery surrounds us. We walk in fear of ourselves. To such power we have no right.

With the death of Hamilton the flood receded. Waters sucked into the earth, returned to the crevasse, but no fish were stranded. Troublesome Creek resumed its normal course. Clouds whipped past, then dissolved like echoes. We stood anticipating the eternal promise, the rainbow which stands as sign from the Almighty that He will never again destroy the world by flood. The rainbow appeared, but it brought small comfort.

We returned to our families, our fields, and our beasts. Spring calves romped beside their mothers, and cattle moved fed and content in new grass. The steeple of Sons Of Noah Church rose beside the creek, a loved and familiar silhouette against the surrounding mountains. We have always treasured peace and quiet ways.

Yet we have memories. The first ugly sound of the helicopter, chip, chip, chipping away, like a tiny hatchet attacking a giant tree. We remember the easy confidence of Hamilton, the blindness of his power. He had the money and the equipment and the men that would allow him to alter the very peace he yearned for. He could not deny using his power, nor so, we fear, can we.

Another spring is at hand. Our congregation has met in fear and question for nearly a year. I need explain carefully what troubles us.

The world encroaches. Sometimes, even in this far place, the skies carry a hint of muddy color. On days when winds stand exactly in the mouth of our valley, distant sounds of engines live on the very edge of hearing. More beasts of the field flee here. Deer have always grazed among our cattle, but now the most shy of all large creatures, the elk, gather among our herds. As forests decrease we become sanctuary for wild beasts—bear and cougar and wolves. We control them, these dying generations of animals. We light bonfires in our fields against the wolf. We bear no grievance toward the beasts, who must, after all, pursue life and habitat.

And we bear no grievance against the world of men. After all, perhaps we are 'peculiar' people. Our way is holy to us, but we allow that each man must follow his own path. If that path is one of destruction, then who are we to say it nay? We cannot oppose madness with madness.

But we now understand that Hamilton was a symbol. His death forecasts what may be the death of the world that spawned him. He died in a clash of powers. Against such forces he never had a chance.

Thus do we congregate in fear. Even our children become quiet after service, for children are wise in their ways. They know something is wrong. They sense that we—or our ancestry—or all of us together—control the original, primal energy.

We fear our power. We fear it. Although there is eternal promise that the Creator will not destroy the world by flood, there is no promise that Man will not. We feel tributaries rising in the mountains, and sense the rolling of distant thunder. We feel the rivers of the earth turn quarrelsome. The waters of the earth pulse before our feet. Take heed. Take heed. We feel the oceans bulge.

The Bride

IF THE SCULPTURE STILL STANDS IT MAY STAND FOREVER—A marker of deepest import, a warning to all that even lives of quiet can erupt with extraordinary revisions. The neighborhood feels both loss and lost; and the neighborhood does not know whether to fuss or feel foolish.

One quiet life belonged to a very plain Jerome _____—the last name does not matter. It is not a name ever used by a cavalry-man or an acrobat. It is more the name of a pedant, or a book-keeper, or, as was the actual case, the owner of a hardware store. Jerome_____ seemed the least likely person in the world to be attacked by abstract ideas, and certainly not by abstractions of art.

That the sculpture actually was art was mildly debated by those who know little of such things. Had the neighborhood thought the debate important, trouble might have passed harmless by. There would have been no misunderstandings, no cruel revenge. Citizens could still look each other in the eye instead of walking with gaze downcast.

The sculpture appeared in a small park that stood before Je-rome's hardware store, and the store stood on a quiet shopping street in a medium-sized northwest city. The sculpture manifest-ed one night as if on wings of magic. The quiet man, Jerome, had closed his hardware that evening, locked the door, rattled the knob, and walked away as on a thousand other evenings. No least thought of art intercepted his senses. He thought largely of cup hooks and framing squares.

And lo, on the following morning, when mist still clung around street lights and when businessmen loitered at the counters of diners, the sculpture had appeared not sixty feet from the front of Jerome's store.

It stood among tendrils of mist and beneath golden leaves in an astonishingly beautiful autumn. October light crept through mist and fell first upon exquisitely sculpted feet and lower legs, then increased to display unclothed thighs, torso and breasts in perfect proportion of an idealized female form. She was not the thinish woman of fashion magazines, nor did she infer the fecundity of a goddess. She seemed, instead, the ideal mate of lonely men accustomed to hiding desires for happiness known only in dreams.

As day increased in diminishing mist, perfect shapes became perfectly defined beneath raw rock that perched above rounded shoulders. The sculpture showed no face. The rock stood naked, undressed, untouched, unpolished. It seemed at first an insult, certainly a contradiction. Why, above such a perfect form, had the sculptor refused to finish the work? Why, in the name of all that was wonderful, had some arts commission or other bureaucratic force chosen to ornament a public park with a woman who had less face than a brick? And why, by all that was holy, including holy matrimony, had the sculptor titled the piece, *The Bride*?

Conjecture spread among patrons of the park, and among Jerome's customers, even as Jerome remained puzzled; and puzzlement was a fairly new experience for the man. If he gave outward sign, it was only the sign of speech. This quiet man became less quiet.

"I expect," he told a young housewife who visited the store for batteries and staples, "that the fellow who does the work will come by in a day or two and finish it up. That statue might even be a little bit fast for a neighborhood park."

He believed as he said this that he would be proved wrong. There was mild fascination in the idea. He was not used to being often wrong.

The young matron, willowy of mind as well as frame, agreed that something should be done. "It's not the nudity," she pointed out, "but the chubbiness. The statue is distinctly unmodern in what is distinctly an upscale neighborhood. Head or no head, the lady is clearly not a tennis player."

And Jerome, who feared he would become even more puzzled, became so. He believed he understood his customers, but either he or this customer missed some sort of point. He told himself that the young matron was very, very young.

As autumn moved its leaf-falling way across the park, and as old men and women came later in the day to sit and reminisce, the sculpture displayed a new magic. It had first appeared on wings of mist. Now it gained presence among falling leaves of red and yellow. Beneath certain patterns of sunlight and leaves, it nearly seemed to move.

As trees discarded robes of green, surroundings of the sculpture became stark. Instead of a soft and arboreal backdrop the sculpture appeared standing before a wrought iron fence bordering the back of the park. Brick buildings rose like red canvas in the background. Bare trees stood like phone poles, and benches in the park carried patches of rust where summer's activities had worn or scraped away paint. The park seemed shabby, a bit hostile, and too well used.

"A naked trollop," an elderly person told Jerome. "Next it will be drugs and gunfights. You may depend on that."

"Perhaps if the statue were finished," Jerome murmured, and silently concluded that he deceived himself; and that self-deception was not practical. When the elderly person departed, carrying sixty watt bulbs and a closet hinge, Jerome turned from gazing at the park and looked down the narrow tunnel of his store; a tunnel, some would say, that in every way resembled his life.

Along one wall ranged tools of every ordinary variety, for little that was esoteric was in demand in that neighborhood where piety announced itself as a normal condition. Wrenches and chisels and rakes and shovels, together with wheelbarrows and ladders, stood, or hung, or lay waiting for work. In the center aisle ranged pumps and utensils and small appliances: fans and toasters, radios, and camping gear. The other wall carried hardware of every common variety, nails and screws and pipe fittings, screens and filters, tarps and faucets. Beneath fluorescent lighting the store, being three times longer than it was wide, seemed like an extended thought, an abstraction concerning things terribly concrete.

The store, first installed by Jerome's father, sat in the center of a neighborhood that had once been wealthy, had deteriorated to near bedlam, and then been reclaimed as a haven for the well-to--do; who—because of their places in the celestial scheme—felt extremely well about themselves.

The store now neared its sixtieth anniversary, and Jerome, who was fiftyish, looked down the tunnel and remembered his father, remembered his mother, and for the first time in many years admitted that he was both single and lonely. He had not meant for life to be thus, not in his dreams. Perhaps that simple admission returned his gaze to the sculpture, and to the fact of its difference.

There appeared—assuming it was not some trick of autumn light—a definite change in the rock where, proportionally, one would expect to see the chin and lower lip of an idealized face. The change was vague, a few chips of rock, perhaps, but to Jerome most shocking. He did not dismiss the change as a trick of autumn light. He did allow to himself that someone might be working on that face. He told himself to be more observant, for he realized he had been taking much in the way of certainty for granted.

The Bride changed little in the following weeks, although the park went through normal change. City crews raked leaves, swept walks, and left the park clean and bare and open to the chilling winds of early November. The Bride stood as a focal point of warmth in a rapidly decaying autumn.

And then a first breath of snow swirled through three-A.M. darkness when, in that neighborhood, only policemen and cats were known to roam. Snow dusted streets and made tiny windrifts in gutters. It was dryish snow flickering across cones cast by street-lights, and it filled the morning—once the cafes opened—with opportunity for cliches about snow, and memories from elders who spoke of past and virulent winters. The park stood deserted. At daylight Jerome was first to see what he instantly regarded as an abomination.

The sculpture stood lightly clad in a garish bikini. A knitted wool hat ornamented that shapeless block where Jerome had constantly imagined a soft and gentle face. The bikini, worn by a living woman, would have been orange and red and daring. On the sculpture it was only grotesque. The genius of the artist gave feelings of warmth and softness to the stone, while the pliable and flagrant fabric only denied those feelings. Jerome did not analyze, nor did he have the background to do so. He only knew that what he saw was vulgar.

The man felt deeply offended, the offense driving him back into his normal quiet. The offense lay not against art, about which he knew little. It was offense given against imagination, illusion, and an offense against himself; for it threatened to drive him back into a state of quiet loneliness.

Finally (and it was not until midafternoon that he understood his feelings) it was an offense against the woman, The Bride; against her youthful hopes and dreams. His quietness temporarily deepened, and at the seat of quietness he discovered anger. How dare some vandal disrupt dreams?

To the neighborhood no offense was taken. A certain low humor prevailed.

"From the neck up she reminds me of my third wife." This from an architectural type, who, except for his number of former wives, greatly resembled Jerome. The architectural type stood before the hardware counter where he made estimates for the rehabilitation of a cottage. His square, though not bulky frame, stood solid beneath a face of blue eyes, full lips, and a head of brown and thinning hair. "From the neck down she reminds me of my first."

"I would think," said Jerome after the architect departed, "that if a man had a wife he would regard the matter as rather more important than that." He watched with detestation as the architect disappeared.

A woman of substance, a woman who gave both funds and advice to the 'deserving' poor, held to the opinion that "The statue has finally collected its due. Because," the woman of substance argued, "what that thing cost might have fed a family of thirteen for as much as a month."

And Jerome, while insisting on the courteous quiet of the correct businessman, noted quietly to himself that the woman of substance carried a good deal of that substance on her posterior as well as in her purse.

It became a tedious afternoon. Wags suggested suntan lotion. Perhaps, some guessed, The Bride had won a honeymoon to Hawaii. A churchy-sort spoke of Adam, but especially of Eve; but even more especially of Eve's blighted apple.

Always before Jerome had anticipated mild displeasure with certain customers. That was bound to be part of any job. On this afternoon, however, he began to see that ignorance was an ugly thing; although he could not yet say that it was dangerous.

When he closed the store and rattled the knob before walking home, he turned compelled toward the sculpture. Garish fabric shone bold as a stoplight in the winter evening. As daylight faded, insult seemed to deepen. The sculpture somehow seemed on the brink of movement, as if the faceless woman whose young body stood so expressive of hope, called for aid. Had she been a real woman in distress, and had Jerome been a true man of action, his response would have been immediate.

Instead, he walked home muttering as darkness fell across the neighborhood. He muttered through the long evening. He muttered at T.V. anchors on the eleven o'clock news, and at commercials which coupled great passions of love with the use of deodorant. He muttered as he dressed warmly and left his house.

His steps held the certainty of the realistic man, but also the lightness of a thief. There was, practically speaking, no reason to choose a shadowed passage avoiding streetlights. He was a stable fixture in the neighborhood, a most unlikely suspect in any sort of crime or debauch. Indignation drove him, but indignation strode softly on toes of caution. He was not accustomed to being abroad at midnight.

Arrived at the park, he discovered himself without a plan. Cold air moved through leafless trees. Across the street his store stood dark and elongated, like a coffin for adventurous dreams. Jerome sat on a bench, hugged his coat about him, and nerved for action. Never, except in dreams, had he assisted a woman in her disrobing. The man had never unhooked a brassiere, never intimately viewed the lovely curve of a shoulder. To him, sitting in darkness, what he was about to attempt bordered on assault. That The Bride, so degraded by fabric, might wish his aid did nothing to lighten an act he felt barely capable of imagining.

Shadows cast by empty tree branches lay like dark webs in the snow. His breath came in anxious puffs and he momentarily heard his heart chugging in his chest. He had no great experience with curiosity, yet now he momentarily wondered if he were sane.

A low murmur moved like a subdued breath mixing with cold air; a murmur of welcome—the sort of loving voice that some most fortunate of men must hear upon returning home—a voice of a long-loved woman, the voice of a friend. The murmur lingered, then moved away on a light breeze.

He behaved as awkwardly as his worst fear. The vandal who had disfigured the sculpture had effectively knotted the swimsuit top, and even more effectively knotted the bottom. Jerome's cold fingers plucked at fabric, working at first in haste—and then, because he was otherwise sensible—plucked methodically.

For a moment the warm murmur returned, then departed as headlights of an auto appeared. Jerome, struck with no small amount of terror, watched as a police car moved slowly toward him.

He stood poised to flee. Then courage and necessity kept him from hiding in shadows or behind a tree. He knew that what he attempted was necessary, and, finally, decent.

If a car could amble this police car did. A searchlight made routine sweeps of store fronts. It probed the tunnel of Jerome's store. The policeman continued on his way, and the searchlight did not enter the park. In that quiet neighborhood, the searchlight assured the sanctity of property.

When the police car disappeared around a corner, Jerome continued his careful work. The offending clothing came away. It was flimsy stuff that barely made a lump as he thrust it into a pocket of his overcoat. He did so while discovering that he was quite out of breath.

He peered carefully in all directions, then walked across the street and entered his darkened store. His stock contained folding cots and sleeping bags. He felt reckless, a man of adventure, perhaps something of a rascal who need not walk home through empty streets; but a rascal of means, and of kindly intent. In darkness he walked the familiar aisle to nudge a thermostat. As heat arrived he returned to the front of the store to stare through the window at The Bride.

This quiet man understood duty and obedience. His store was, in its way, a public trust. People depended on it to be open. People depended on him to know about ells and tees and traps. They relied on his judgment when painting houses, or when running irrigation for gardens. Duty and obedience were stern companions, but ones that offered reward. He was an important force in the neighborhood, a valued man.

Now, staring into the darkened park, he felt something beyond duty, obedience, or even rascality. The feeling was new and he could give it no name, at least not at first.

He felt loved, somehow, although his experience gave him little to work with. Yet, he understood the serenity displayed by some of his customers. Not all men who came for goods were successful householders, husbandmen of growing gardens and growing families, but some small few of them were. He understood the quiet but powerful presence of men who loved, were loved; men of character who would protect both lives and souls beyond all question of cost.

We may think kindly of him as he stood there, and we may guess at wonderment and magic that swept his mind like a breeze perfumed with flowers. He was not an expressive man, and he daily worked in a world that spoke of 'love' and 'romance' in commercial terms. For him, all useful words had been pre-empted. Standing in that darkened and quiet store, he had feelings but no language.

The Bride gave warmth to the bare park and the bare street. Leafless trees cast no flickers among shadows. There could be no illusion, no false guesses or explanations depending on the cast or slant of light. The Bride's posture portrayed a young woman at ease. Gone was the formal stance, the pose, the overt display of romance. In mechanical terms her stance had scarcely changed, yet now she stood gently. Jerome knew her too well, had seen her in every kind of light. He told himself he should be alarmed. Instead, he unrolled a sleeping bag, slept for five hours, and woke feeling as optimistic as a young boy.

Above rounded shoulders of The Bride, winter dawn revealed the semblance of a face. Uncut stone had given way to vague out-lines of brow, nose, and cascades of hair. A pert and well-formed chin supported the suggestion of a mouth, the further suggestion of a smile. The stone seemed alive with potential for almost any sort of future. The youthful body radiated self-confidence that, perhaps, had somewhat to do with romance; but also to do with experience. As gray dawn illuminated the park, and blown snow whirled before light winter wind, Jerome viewed The Bride and felt—although he certainly did not understand—the contentment of a man who has faithfully served old-fashioned but honorable codes.

The neighborhood, having grown accustomed to the sculpture, remained largely uninterested during that first winter as patterns developed between Jerome and The Bride. Jerome slowly became attached to the sculpture, and to the small park, while the neighbor-hood held other concerns. Winter work and winter entertainments, together with a holiday season and a coming new year, occupied most conversations. Basketball season bounced across the week-ends, and children wished for snow, or felt gypped concerning the lack of enough for sledding. In the hardware store, interests dealt with holiday lighting, or the thawing of frozen pipes. Few people noticed The Bride, and no one seemed to notice change.

Indifference seemed a blessing. Jerome soon wished that every-one would remain indifferent.

The blow-up came as two electricians strutted their humors be-fore other customers. These were men of youngish middle age, cer-tainly old enough to know better, and—Jerome told himself—the rough conversation passing between them was about what he ex-pected from electricians. The men compared The Bride's physique to women they claimed to have known. They jokingly preferred The Bride, although with reservations about frigidity.

"Take your business elsewhere," Jerome said to them. He spoke almost off-handedly as he bagged an ornamental trivet and an extension cord. "There's a shopping center two miles down the road." He turned from them and toward another customer, an el-derly lady.

The two men stood momentarily perplexed, then traded confu-sion for indignation. The short one, a beefy type who might have made a good truck driver, offered the opinion that Jerome's proper place was in hell. The other, athletic and tattooed, swore in a general way that included a good portion of the civilized world.

"There are bars and gutters that will tolerate you," Jerome told them quietly. "Goodbye." He watched them leave, and felt a certain satisfaction. The men had been good customers, but what did that have to do with anything? "I will not tolerate such language in my store," he said to the elderly lady.

"They sounded about like my bridge club," she told Jerome as she departed. "I've kind of gotten used to it."

A man in love, and who is inexperienced with love, will be driven by illusion. A man in the flush of a first love, and the re-sulting realizations of manhood, will almost surely exhibit zealotry which—although it eventually passes—is tedious while present.

That he was in love there can be no doubt. Quiet enthusiasm filled his days. For a while in midwinter he became a prude, so in-sistent on proper forms that customers sometimes whispered in his presence. Gossip asserted that Jerome had converted to one of the lesser religions, or was mentioned in a rich uncle's will to the sum of millions if he sought purity; and gossip had it that Jerome's cor-rect demeanor was prelude to a run for public office. The gossip remained cheap and secondary. The neighborhood had many mat-ters of concern: den decoration and diets, furnace filters and dance lessons. The adventures of a hardware store owner did not weigh heavily in a neighborhood that bragged of gas mileage.

During this difficult time, when customers entered on tiptoe or did not enter at all, The Bride changed in subtle ways unnoticed by the neighborhood. If a face began to appear on a sculpture standing in a cold and deserted park, any passerby would assume the work as being in process of completion. No doubt some people remembered her as the 'blockhead' she had once been. Now those same people, had they bothered to observe, might have been enchanted. The face gradually firmed and, although unfinished, became smooth-cheeked, vaguely pretty (but with every appearance of practicality); while still appearing caressed.

As winter sniffled its way through the calendar, and as spring announced a single crocus glowing yellowly from light snow in the park, innate good sense returned. Jerome's bigotry reformed into sound judgment, and kindness danced ahead like a pup exploring new trails.

He gave every evidence of sterling sanity, and his customers thought him a most attractive man. They did not know that in his private thought he referred to himself as a husband, a householder, a man with a wife. The neighborhood knew only standard delusions; the fantasy of status conferred by snazzy automobiles, or the romance of blue chip stocks.

It was not that he thought himself married to The Bride. The man had enough common sense to discuss plumbing, and enough to know that one does not sit down to dinner with a sculpture. On a different level though—say the level of poetic romance—he understood The Bride as a symbol of fulfilled need.

Recall that the man had no experience with women. He could remember no high school sweetheart. He had never been a military man listening to boundless exaggerations by recruits, or a player of sports exposed to the banter of locker rooms. Jerome was not a hermit, but in modern terms he could serve that need until a hermit could be found.

Yes, he turned to kindness. And yes, he thought himself a husband, a man trusted, loved, the companion of someone who pictured a future beside him. In the realm of modern fantasies, Jerome's seem awfully mild, and decent by any standard. One could not use such fantasies to sell goods. In order to sell small beer one needs a man in lust. This man was in love.

As spring stretched like a waking cat, and as new buds cracked on trees in the park, Jerome's quiet passion made itself evident. On warm days he ventured from his store when customers were absent. He walked in the small park, and those who observed him claimed that he talked to himself a good deal—or to passing dogs, to trees, and to beds of early flowers. That he might be speaking a brand of poetry, his own brand and thus mawkish since he knew nothing of poetic form, occurred to no one. In his great concentration he became forgetful. Customers had to cross the street and fetch him to the store in order to satisfy their wants.

In this springtime beside The Bride he was so taken with new emotions as to forget possible future structures. When birds began to nest he recognized a missed opportunity, and he watched nesting patterns to see which birds fitted where in the park. He made notes. He kept a journal.

That entire year was a year of arranging, although he did not use that word to describe his actions. When a few curious customers asked about the attraction of the park, he simply said that he thought of expanding the garden section of his store. The indirect answer told customers nothing, but the customers nodded wisely and agreed. With his actions, though, Jerome hid his love in plain sight of a busy world, and his love remained invisible.

As he arranged the future placement of birds by charting where he would hang birdhouses, he also saw to the maintenance of furniture. As days lengthened he spent time after his store closed, sanding rust patches on benches and trash containers, or lightly greasing hinges on a wrought iron gate. Park crews, on their weekly visits, found little to occupy them. In a single summer crews learned to take tidiness of this particular park for granted. Somewhere, a supervisor decreed the park but lightly used. Maintenance crews visited only to mow grass and haul away refuse.

Jerome became unofficial master of the park, spending more and more time awkwardly speaking poems while expertly handling tools. If he was conscious that the sculpture changed he still did not realize that the sculpture created the artist, and that he, the created artist, in turn created the sculpture. The divine process of art took place in that small park—taking place in the middle of an abiding love affair—and no one, except possibly The Bride, had the foggiest notion that anything huge was happening.

She blossomed during that summer. She seemed to fill out,

if only a little. Her breasts grew a trifle fuller, and her hands became strong features. A hint of secrecy dwelt about her lips, and her stance grew serene. She seemed not contented, merely, but very, very happy.

It was, on the surface, an ideal climate. In that Eden of a neighborhood one expected no serpents. One expected baby carriages, children, dogs, and superannuated souls toddling behind canes. Young lovers might stroll, but rarely hand in hand. Passion, where it existed, was expressed but covertly; for it was the general opinion that passion belonged in lesser parts of the city, or on the voluble lips of southern Europeans. In that neighborhood pigeons seemed expressly hired to clean up spilled popcorn, while teenagers were expected to do their carousing in the back seats of autos parked out of sight.

Yet, in that seemingly ideal climate, the first small chill of propriety seemed to purse the lips of leaves along the summer paths. The neighborhood, believing itself well educated and a master of contemporary graces, viewed change in the park and felt a hint of dread, a token of discontent, a trifle, even, of fear. Something artistic (most everyone agreed) was going on over there, and it was something that could not be healthy. The neighborhood told itself that it subscribed to the symphony, for God's sake, and held memberships in the museum. Was that not enough, in anyone's view, to ask of people? Because something out-of-place in that park caused discomfort to good folk for whom discomfort constituted a burden.

The spirit of ignorance lies behind most desolation. Vandalism rises because the young, too ignorant and unskilled to create, must create something; even if that something is chaos. The vandal grows, becomes adult, and with increasing skill is capable of creating hell. This, with few elaborations, is a general explanation of human history.

In Jerome's case the spirit of ignorance moved lightly against him on the breath of rumor. It was said of him that he had always been a bit peculiar, but that he now straddled a fence that ran somewhere between strange and downright odd. In consequence, his business fell off.

Perhaps he did not notice, so rapt was he in the discoveries that surround emerging forms; patterns of groomed grass, and the possibilities of glancing sunlight distributed from carefully placed sprinkler heads. He discovered how brick walls had their own lustres, and how the chalky-red brick of old walls could serve as canvas against which one encouraged the growth of leaves. To Jerome, and to a few small children who—through parental neglect—had retained some fragment of imagination, the park became as familiar and friendly as a well-used living room.

And, no doubt, Jerome discovered some of the deeper and more serene qualities of proven love. The Bride became his companion during that summer, and he became hers. It was not a speaking acquaintance, but a murmuring acquaintance. It was an affair of delicacy, consideration, and listening. No one, and especially Jerome who knew her best, expected a sculpture to speak; and, of course, she did not. And yet, somehow, she listened; and somehow so did he. This communication, which on the surface stinks of cheap romance, did not seem cheap to him; a man so new to love.

And thus the summer passed and leaves once more blew in golden cascades before a chilling wind. Customers began to think of the appurtenances of winter. Snow accumulated in the nearby mountains, and Jerome did good business in ski racks and tire chains. As northwest mist swirled through the park Jerome was aware, and his customers aware but vaguely, that the park retained much of the warmth and glow of summer; and that helped cause a problem.

For it is not true that all the world loves a lover, and it is even less true that the world loves a happy and contented man. Human insecurity being what it is, and human desire being vigorous, it is a terrible thing for the discontented to view another's happiness.

And perhaps a happy woman is even more threatening, even if that woman is literally carved from stone. We may suppose this is the case, and we may be certain an attack by the craven will always and only be leveled against the helpless.

She stood in the warmth of the park where branches of sycamore displayed seed pods like the decorations of a Christmas tree. She also stood as the focus for private talk, for a covert citizens' committee, for a carefully worded editorial in the neighborhood's *Shopping News*.

It began as a whispering campaign. Something affected the children, because some of the children now seemed befuddled when viewing normal hypocrisy. Even worse, some made friends with The Bride. Children were known to sit at her feet as if rapt from tales of frogs who were princes; children feeding crumbs to birds at a season when there should be no birds, pigeons excepted. Something awfully motherly attached to people's mental picture of The Bride. Something homelike attended that park.

Real mothers—mothers who had honestly bred and who could tell tales of suffering—rapidly understood that a nude statue constituted an assault against family, against femininity, and against anything one might conceivably think of as sacred. Real fathers—fathers who traded shares and paid for the best orthodontists—accepted the nudity but feared the frogs and princes.

It was, the neighborhood agreed, too much. It was just plain over the line, beyond the reef, out of the pasture, and down the road. The committee visited various churches. Petitions circulated. And then, as if some cruel judgment dwelt along those quiet streets, weather swooped in from northern climes. It snowed. It snowed a bundle.

There were not enough snow shovels, and the nearest snow blower chugged beyond the mountains 200 miles to the east. Pavements and sidewalks lay slickery from lack of salt. Nervous householders saw lawsuits on the horizon as pedestrians skidded. Snow rushed from the north while dogs scampered among children let loose from school, children playing in a park where snow seemed different from snow on the street. The children might have been those in a Currier and Ives print, the dogs with changed characters, like the good, good dogs in fatuous movies. The streets filled with curses, dinged fenders, occasional heart attacks, and delay, delay, delay. There were not enough baby sitters. Working moms and working dads lost days of work. They skidded, felt frustration, demanded snow shovels.

Jerome struggled heroically, and with no small desperation. He raided wholesalers by calling in favors. He pressed tools and supplies into woeful and indignant hands, and received a blistering when his hastily assembled inventory faltered. He was told—and rightly as far as the neighborhood was concerned—that if he paid attention to business and quit causing trouble in the park, he would have enough shovels. He was told that people were more important than statues, and finally, that he had better watch out, because some people, some Very Important People, had about gotten their fill of his shenanigans.

If a man is privileged to hold a great love, then he must also be prepared to defend it. If Jerome had been living in a dream, the dream now arrived at that celestial point where artistic conception turns toward its inevitable conclusion.

Former customers still wonder about his motives. Even now they occasionally mutter to each other—"How did he do it? Just how, in the middle of snow tail deep to a tall giraffe, did he do it?"—and customers then shuffle away from each other, for each bears some small burden of—what?—remorse?

Because Jerome now realized that his task no longer lay in the distribution of hardware. A perhaps fatal step must be taken, the Rubicon crossed. His was not an easy decision, but it was made easier by the anger thrown against him. He realized he had little time.

No one knew him as a man of action. He did not know himself as such. No one dreamed that a man his age, with a secure existence and a store so established that it was bragged on as an institution; no one could imagine him engaged in totally irrational behavior. The neighborhood, in its covenant with respectability, felt about that store as it felt about the steeples on churches—not as a finger pointing to heaven, but as a finger pointing all criticism away from them.

And yet, he acted, and there was a lesson in his action for anyone clever enough to read. The great authority of art stems from its presence, and the memory of its presence, for it does not own the authority of a police baton. Its very survival (and sometimes the seed of its destruction) lies in its truth. When truth is plainly shown it has been known to spread wings, which may here have been the case.

Some people maintain that Jerome rented a crane and a truck, although he had little time to scheme. Most likely, though, in that romantic confabulation that had gone on between them, the two simply plotted a successful escape through the air.

The sculpture had appeared as if on wings of mist and now departed on wings of snow.

Because on a morning even more snowy than usual, the neighborhood woke to the fact that The Bride was departed, the park deserted; and—had the neighborhood time for lesser concerns—might have speculated that art, too, had fled. Such would turn out not to be the case.

Most alarming was not an empty park, but a full hardware store. Customers found the store open and unattended. An index card stood before the cash register. It read: 'Thank you. When you leave, please turn out the lights'.

The neighborhood staggered before the realism of event. People needed tools, vacuum cleaner bags, paint remover, and needed someone to whom it could give money. The neighborhood took pride in 'paying its way', in self-sufficiency, in 'a day's work for a day's pay', in professionalism, and in 'the bottom line'. The neighborhood passionately wanted to pay someone. It wanted to consume reams and reams of insulation for water pipe. It truly needed drain opener.

On that first day customers entered timidly. They searched the aisles, found needed objects, then stood confused before the cash register. Some, more methodical than others, figured price and sales tax. Then, lacking change, they left approximate amounts. Such customers usually made it almost to the door before remembering that they were in the presence of their peers. When that realization hit, they returned to the counter and picked up their cash. A few scratched their heads, and then wrote IOU only to recall, as they approached the doorway, that an IOU was a promise to pay, enforceable in any court, and endorsable, probably depositable, legally the same as cash. At which time the customer returned to the counter and picked up his IOU. After all, who knew what might happen to legal tender just left lying about.

On that first day some customers made a great show of entering amounts in notebooks, in keeping their own accounts, and even making out charge invoices. They would then step timidly onto snowy sidewalks, hugging purchases beneath their coats while giving every appearance of honest intent.

On the second day the situation deteriorated. A lust for possession captured every decent citizen. Red wheelbarrows aglitter with goods disappeared in white clouds of driving snow. Green lawnmowers thumped along icy streets. A regular torrent of tools and supplies flowed beside snow-capped houses which seemed vague and insubstantial in the face of storm.

And worse, that night when all should have been peaceful and the police in absolute control, a vandal entered the store. He painted in small but firm letters across the cash register the single word 'Repent'. On the third day people could not bring themselves to look at the cash register.

By then the neighborhood writhed in the throes of hell. Every man's hand seemed raised against every man. To say that the store was looted would not be exactly correct—because no one actually trucked away all of the fixtures, and the cash register, until the fourth day. The effect, however, was one of looting. By eventide the shelves were clean.

A solemn procession had moved through that store as neighbors bore away loot, but bore it always beneath the guise of purchase. The lure of merchandise overcame the lure of respectability. Politeness became at first difficult, and then a real achievement. The neighborhood's collective cheeks burned, and guilt seared those rationalizations about clearing the place out before it attracted criminals; and such other perfectly logical reasons for otherwise unwarranted behavior. Darkness fell over houses filled with shame, and winter clasped the streets.

In February rain cleansed the Northwest. The neighborhood trudged through rain, and the neighborhood was exhausted, confused, and uncertain. Evil—or at least the specter of sin—seemed to hover in northwest mist, and the storms of February crossed the land on sable wings. 'For Sale' signs appeared before a few houses. The neighborhood, everyone agreed, had been going downhill. It became the fashion to curse the memory of Jerome.

And then Jerome's second gift arrived as spring burst forth on the voices of birds.

Not all birds nested, and not all nesting birds stayed in the cleverly hung and cleverly concealed birdhouses, but it seemed that all birds visited. Spring opened with an invocation by birds. Birds who were simply passing through stopped by the park in order to sing. Nightingales warbled and whistled and chirked through warm spring evenings. Mist flashed like silver ornaments along blue wings, red wings, wings of green, brown, purple and orange; and there sounded the certain quack of ducks. What might have seemed an invasion was never perceived that way even by the very, very bitter. Jerome's choreography displayed perfect control and perfect conception. The birds knew where to go, how long to sing, and when to depart the stage.

For theater occurred in that park, theater bespeaking love and life, theater talking of beauty and the drama of renewal. Crocus flew open before daffodils so bold that the voices of birds were mistaken for the voices of flowers. Trees rapidly budded, then threw cascades of blossom into springtime mist. Squirrels as fat as sausages, and as smart-mouthed as juvenile delinquents, postured from branches and sassed the neighborhood cats.

It was spring, you say. That sort of thing happens in every spring, does it not?

In this spring, orchestrated by Jerome, it happened in abundance. Winds blew with great certainty, and, although gentle, knew exactly when, and where, and for how long new leaves should rattle; and for how long the nests of birds should rock in a cradle of wind. Banks of flowers rolled like waves of a many-colored sea. A small stream appeared, rising from the back of the park and running until it disappeared beneath a small hill. Fingerlings flashed blue and silver and emerald in that stream. The very light of heaven proclaimed spring. Subdued sunrises brought lights up on the stage, and clouds walked the sky allowing the spotlight of the sun to search here, there, illuminating backdrops of red brick walls.

The neighborhood might have missed the show, except, by then, a combination antique store and coffee house opened in what had once been a hardware store. Customers sat at small tables and sipped from small cups. They watched the park from afar, afraid to enter.

For the neighborhood knew, somehow, that it had something yet to deserve, some penance before it was worthy; and the neighborhood became bitter because it did not know what to do. When children entered the park they changed, became happier, but were secretive about what they saw. If frogs and princes and trolls and fairies dwelt beside the running waters of that small stream, the children kept the knowledge to themselves.

By June the main show ended and park crews were in strong control, but memory remained. To this day the neighborhood is uncertain what was lost—or, as the neighborhood defines it—stolen from them—but the loss is severely felt. Life these days seems brittle.

For a grim sentence accompanied that spring, a sentence which says that henceforth the life of the neighborhood will be lived in the chatter of coffee houses. There will be, most likely, little in the way of art; although the coffee houses will sell clever greeting cards. No great snows will fill the streets, and there will be no storms. Drama in the heavens, thunder, wind, rolling clouds and gorgeous dawns will move to other climes. The neighborhood will receive enough sunshine for children's play, but not enough to raise property values.

*

And the fleeing lovers, what of them?

A small museum resides in a small library in an old and very small town. The town lies east of the mountains in a region holding foothills and high desert. It is a town that, in some long distant past, displayed self-satisfaction and pretense; but it is a town that has seen weather shred the best house paint, has seen ivy clamber and spread along the south wall of the courthouse, and has seen birth—death—Model T Fords—horses—Sunday school picnics—a town no longer pretending sophistication, and resigned to being what it is, if not exactly satisfied.

One descends from the mountains on a busy freeway, then drifts onto a cloverleaf and drives on two-lane for better than twenty miles. Weeds and grasses beside the road are cut once a year, and fencerows disappear beneath brush, sage, occasional morning glory. The road eventually tops a small rise, the town is revealed below—the steeple to your left is the Baptist church, the one to the right is Methodist. The tiny museum sits kitty-corner between Methodists and the grade school.

An aging man tends the place which is locally famous, renowned, in fact, throughout the town. Trees whisper above the brick museum, and a pond walled in brick and stone is a-burp with carp; the fish orange and white and purply-bespeckled as they glide in the shadows of ferns. Jerome, having solved some of the problems of artistic form, has created a sculpture here: trees, building, a weather system driving from the mountains, plants, and the tranquil voices of townspeople all folding into a statement of quiet praise.

He came as a stranger but did not remain one for long. The natural suspicions of a small town met him, looked him over, judged that he 'would do'. If he appeared as if by magic, and if he seemed somehow to have always been a fixture at the museum, the town was wise enough not to bother itself with reasons.

And if his great love—that love who formed him—appeared as well, then that suits the town. She stands in the museum among the mementos of a century, standing gently beside cases containing antique tools, glassware, paintings, fabrics, yellowed sheets of music on the rack of an old fashioned harpsichord; standing among the familiar and treasured objects of home. She has changed from her former public self. Her upper arms seem a bit more fleshy, her breasts sag a little, and her hips are no longer slender as in her youth. As she has formed her man, so she has been formed. She stands at rest, her face tranquil, perfectly shaped, smiling; a face reflecting her man's devotion, her beauty inexpressible—and not even the Baptists, finally, can find cause to complain. The Bride's nudity is no longer all that noticeable, because one's gaze always and forever moves only to her face.

The Burning

Sunlight gleamed as Singleton and I walked down the hill to the charred wreckage of what had been a truck. Gates was dead, and the breeze lifted sooty material that mixed with the valley smells of weeds, flowers, and diesel stink. Manny was in jail. Nothing more could be done for Gates, but now Manny was sitting in his own fire, burning because he was kind, because he was gentle.

Traffic was moving as usual on the long slopes; only an occasional car slowed, its occupants looking over the scene of last night's fire. The truck drivers would know all about the trouble, and they did not want to see. Besides, there was a hill to climb on either side of the valley. They could not afford to lose speed. I knew that by now the word of the burning had spread at least a hundred miles. As far as Lexington, drivers would be leaning against counters listening, with wildness spreading in them. Singleton and I had not slept through the long night. We revisited the scene because we felt it was the final thing we could do for both men.

Close up the sunlight played on bright runs of metal where someone had pulled the cab apart hoping to recover enough of Gates's remains for burial. An oil fire, when the oil is pouring on a man, doesn't leave much. Only the frame and other heavy structural members of the truck remained.

"If he had only been knocked out or killed before the fire got to him...." We were both thinking the words. Either might have said them.

"His company's sending an investigator," Singleton told me. "But since we're here, let's go over it. They'll be sure to ask."

"Are you going to pull?"

"No." He shook his head and ran his hand across his face. "No. Next week maybe or the week after. I'm not steady. I called for three drivers. That's one for your rig too."

"Thanks. I've got vacation coming. I'm taking it."

The road surface along the wreck was blackened, and the asphalt waved and sagged. It was a bad spot. The state should have put up signs. Forty-seven feet of power and payload; now it seemed little there in the ditch, its unimportance turning my stomach. I wanted to retch. I felt lonely and useless.

We walked to the far hill to look at the tire marks. Narrow little lines which swung wide across the other lane and then back in, suddenly breaking and spinning up the roadway. Heavy black lines were laid beside them where the driver of the car being passed had ridden his brakes and then gone on up the hill. Coming down were the marks Gates made, and they showed that he had done what a trucker is supposed to do. He had avoided at all costs. The marks ran off the road.

I never knew him. Manny, tall, sandy-haired, and laughing, was my good friend, but I did not know Gates. I did not know until later that Singleton knew him.

We had picked Gates up twenty miles back on the narrow two-lane that ran through the Kentucky hills. We rode behind him figuring to pass when he got a chance to let us around. It was early, around 3 A.M., but there was still heavy vacation-season traffic. Manny was out front behind Gates. My rig was second behind him, and Singleton was behind me. Our three freights were grossing less than fifty thousand so we could go.

Gates's tanker must have scaled at around sixty thousand. Even with that weight you can usually go, but his gas-powered tractor was too light.

It slowed us to be laying back, but there was no reason to dog it. He was making the best time he could. He topped the hill by June's Stop and ran fast after he crested on the long slope down. He had Manny by maybe two hundred yards because Manny had signaled into June's.

When he signaled I checked my mirrors. Singleton kept pulling so I kept pulling. When he saw us coming on, Manny canceled the signal and went over the top behind Gates. It allowed enough of a lag for Gates to get out front, and it kept Manny from being killed.

We took the hill fast. You have to climb out the other side. I was a quarter mile back, running at forty-five and gaining speed, when I saw the headlights of the little car swing into the lane ahead of Gates's tanker. The driver had incorrectly estimated the truck's speed or the car's passing power.

It was quick and not bad at first. The tanker went into the ditch. The car cut back in, broke traction, and spun directly up the road-way. It came to a stop next to Manny's rig, almost brushing against his drive axle and not even bending sheet metal, a fluke. The car it had passed went onto the shoulder and recovered. The driver took it on up the hill to get away from the wreck and involvement.

Manny was closer. He had perhaps a second more to anticipate the wreck. He had stopped quicker than I believed possible. It was about a minute before the fire started. I was running with my extin-guisher when I saw it, and knew I would be too late.

"I wish he'd exploded," Singleton said. He kicked up dust along the roadway. He was too old for this, and he was beat-out and shak-en. The calmness of resignation was trying to take him, and I hoped it would. I wondered to myself if those clear eyes that had looked down a million and a half miles of road had ever looked at anything like this.

"Exploded? Yes, either that or got out."

"He was hurt. I think he was hurt bad." He looked at me almost helplessly. "No sense wishing; let's go back up. "

After the wreck Singleton had backed his rig over the narrow two-lane, following the gradual bend of the road in the dark. He had taken the two girls from the small car into his cab.

I had stayed a little longer until Gates's burning got really bad. Then I brought the little car in, feeling the way I feel in any car: na-ked, unprotected, and nearly blind. I was shaking from weakness. The road was blocked above. There was no oncoming beyond the pot flares. The cop with the flashlight had arrived ten or fifteen min-utes after the wreck. Behind me the fire rose against the summer blackness and blanketed the valley with the acrid smell of number-two diesel. Because of the distance, Manny's rig seemed almost in the middle of the fire and silhouetted against the burning, though I knew he had stopped nearly fifty yards up the roadway. My own rig was pulled in behind him; its markers stood pale beside the bigger glow. As I was about to go past the cop, he waved me over.

"Where you taking it?"

"Just to the top," I told him. "The girls were pretty shaken up. Don't worry, they won't go anywhere."

"Think they need an ambulance?" He paused, uncertain. "Christ," he said. "Will that other cruiser ever get here?"

"What about Manny?" I asked.

"In there." He nodded to where Manny sat in the cruiser. The lights were out inside. He could not be seen. "I'll take a statement at the top. You'll see him at the top."

I wanted to call to Manny, but there was nothing I could do. I took the car on to June's Stop. Rigs were starting to pile in, even stacking up along the roadway. Cars were parked around and between them, blacked out and gleaming small and dull in the lights from the truck markers. Most of the guys had cut their engines. It would be a long wait.

Singleton's truck was down by the restaurant. Inside around the counter, which formed a kind of box, drivers were sitting and talking. A few were standing around. They were excited and walked back and forth. I wanted coffee, needed it, but I could not go in. At least not then. A driver came up behind me.

"You Wakefield?" he asked. He meant did I drive for Wakefield. My name is Arnold.

I told him yes.

"Your buddy took the girls to Number Twelve. He said to come."

"As if we didn't have enough trouble...."

"He's got the door open." The guy grinned. He was short with a light build and was in too good a mood. I disliked him right away.

"Listen," he said. "They say there's going to be a shakedown."

"Who says?"

"Who knows? That's just the word. If you left anything back there, you'd better get it out. Check it with June."

He meant guns and pills. A lot of companies require them in spite of the law. A lot of guys carry them on their own, the guns I mean. Pills are Benzedrine, Bennies, or a stronger kind called footballs. Only drivers who don't know any better use them to stay awake or get high on.

"I've got it right here," I told him, and patted my side pocket. "I'll hang onto it myself."

"Your funeral," he said, grinning. He gave me a sick feeling. He was a guy with nose trouble, one who spreads his manure up and down the road, a show-off to impress waitresses. "Thanks," I said, and turned to go to the motel room.

"Hey," he yelled, "what do you think will happen to him?"

"You figure it out." I went over to the motel, found Twelve, and went inside.

The room had twin beds. Singleton was sitting on one, facing the two girls on the other. One was kind of curled up. The other was leaning forward still crying. Vassar, I thought. No, nothing like that on 25 South; University of Kentucky likely, but the same sorry type. I edged down beside Singleton. "Why do you bother?" I asked him. "To hell with them." The girl bawling looked up hard for a moment and started bawling worse.

"I had room," she bawled.

We were all under a strain. The diesel smell was bad, but the other smell that I would never forget had been worse. Even away from the fire I seemed still to smell it.

"You thought you had room!" I yelled at her.

"No, really. I was all right. I had room." She was convinced, almost righteous. At some other time she might have been pretty. Both were twenty or twenty-one. The curled-up one was sort of mousy-looking. The one who was bawling was tall with long hair. I thought of her as a thing.

"No—really," I yelled at her; "you had no room, but keep lying to yourself. Pretty soon that'll make everything OK."

"Leave it, Arn," Singleton told me. "You're not doing any good."

He went to the sink to wet a towel, bringing it to the girl. "Wipe your face," he told her. Then he turned to me. "Did you bring their car?"

"I brought it—just a minute. You can have them in just a minute." I was still blind angry. "Old, young, men, women, we've seen too many of their kind. I just want to say it once." I looked directly at her. "How much have you driven?"

For a moment it didn't take; then she understood. "Five years."

"Not years. Miles."

"Why—I guess—I don't know. Five years."

"Five thousand a year? Ten thousand? That would be plenty; you haven't driven that much. Five years times ten is fifty thousand. That's six to eight months' work for those guys down there. You had no room!" I bit it out at her. She just looked confused, and I felt weak. "I'm ready to leave it now," I told Singleton. "I should have known. Remember, we've got a friend down there."

"I've got two."

He looked different than ever before. He sat slouched on the bed and leaned forward a little. His hands were in his lap, and the lines and creases in his face were shadowed in the half-light from the floor lamp.

"Who was he?" I asked.

He looked at me. I realized with a shock that he had been fighting back tears, but his eyes were gray and clear as always. The silver hair that had been crossed with dark streaks as long as I had known him now seemed a dull gray. The hands in his lap were steady. He reached into a pocket.

"Get coffee." He looked at the girls. "Get two apiece for everybody."

"Who was it, Singleton?"

"Get the coffee. We'll talk later." He looked at the girl who was curled up. "She's not good."

"Shock?"

"Real light. If it was going to get worse, I think it would have. Maybe you'd better bring June." He got up again and tried to straighten the curled-up girl. He asked her to turn on her back. She looked OK. She tried to fight him. "Help him," I told the one who had been bawling.

The restaurant was better than a hundred yards off. A hillbilly voice was deviling a truck song. June was in the kitchen, I told her I needed help, and she came right away. Business is one thing, people are another. She has always been that way. She brought a Silex with her, and we walked back across the lot. In the distance there was the sound of two sirens crossing against each other.

"The other police car."

"That and a fire truck," she told me.

June is a fine woman, once very pretty but now careless of her appearance and too heavy. It is always sad and a little strange to see a nice-looking woman allow herself to slide. There must be reasons, but not the kind that bear thinking about. She had a good hand with people, a good way. She ran a straight business. When we came to the room, she asked us to leave and started mothering the girls. We went outside with the coffee and sat on the step.

"I'm sorry," I told him. "I shouldn't have blown up, but for a minute I could have killed them. I hate every fool like them."

"It's their road too."

"I know."

"Everybody makes mistakes. You—me—nobody has perfect judgment."

"But not like that."

"No. No, we're not like that, but she won't ever be again either. She has to live with that."

I understood a little more about him. He was good in his judgment. It was suddenly not a matter for us to forgive. There was the law. It had nothing to do with us.

"Manny never held those brakes against you," he told me.

Once I had checked his truck for him, and he had a failure. I wanted to say that it was different.

We sat listening to the muffled sounds from the room behind us. Soon, off at the downhill corner of the lot, headlights appeared coming from the wreck. The state car cruised across the lot. It stopped at the end of the motel row. Singleton stood up and motioned to him. The car moved toward us, rolling in gently. The cop got out. Manny was sitting in the back seat. He was slumped over and quiet. When the cop slammed the door, he did not look up.

He was an older cop, too old to be riding a cruiser. In the darkness and excitement there had been no way to tell much about him. He was tired and walked to us unofficially. We made room for him on the step. He sat between us, letdown, his hands shaking with either fatigue or nervousness.

"Charles," he said to Singleton, "who was he?"

"You'd better have some coffee," Singleton told him. He reached over and put his hand on the cop's shoulder. I poured coffee from the Silex, and he drank it fast.

"Gates," said Singleton. "Island Oil. When Haber went broke, I pulled tanks for two years." He stopped as if reflecting. "He was pretty good. I broke him in."

The cop pointed to the car. "Him?"

"Manley, Johnny Manley."

"You're taking him in," I said. "What's the charge?"

"I don't know," the cop told me. "I wouldn't even know what would stick. His rig's half out in one lane. If you're going to say I need a charge, then I'll take him in for obstructing the road."

"I didn't mean that. I'm not trying to push you. I just wanted to see how you felt."

"Then ask straight out. I don't know what I think myself till I get the whole story."

Singleton walked to the car. He leaned through the window to call softly to Manny. Manny did not move, and Singleton leaned against the car for a little while as the cop and I sat and watched. A couple of drivers came by, curious but respectfully silent, and the cop ran them off. June came out with a chair and sat beside the steps. The two girls came out and stood quietly. I looked at them. They were both young, pretty, and in the present circumstances useless and destructively ignorant. I could no longer hate them.

"Is that him?" one of them whispered.

"Yes." I felt like whispering myself. It seemed wrong to be talking about him when he was no more than ten yards off, but I doubted that he was listening to anyone. He was looking down, his long body slumped forward and his hair astray. His face, which was never very good-looking, was drawn tight around his fixed eyes, and his hands were not visible. Perhaps he held them in his lap.

"They can't prove nothing," the cop said. "I bet he gets off." He stood up. "Let's get it over with; we've wasted time."

Singleton came back then. "Tell me," the cop said to him.

"He won't be driving again. I don't know what the law will do, but I know what Manny can't do. He won't take another one out. You can take her statement on the accident"—he pointed at one of the girls—"and his"—he pointed at me. "I was just over the crest—couldn't see it very well. What I can tell you about is afterward, but"—he turned to the girls—"I want to tell you something first because maybe you ought to know. I've known that man yonder seven, eight years. He's a quiet guy. Doesn't say much; really not hard to get to know. He likes people, has patience with them. Sometimes you think he'd be more sociable if he just knew how to start." He hesitated as if searching for words.

"I don't know exactly how to tell it. Instead of talking, he does nice things. Always has extra equipment to spare if the scales are open and the ICC's checking, or maybe puts a bag of apples in your cab before you leave out. Kid stuff—yes, that's it, kid stuff a lot of the time. Sometimes guys don't understand and joke him.

"When he finally got married, it was to a girl who started the whole thing, not him. She was wild. Silly, you know, not especially bad but not the best either. She worked at a stop in Tennessee and quit work after she married instead of going back like she planned.

The guy has something. He did good for that girl. I don't know what's going to happen to them now, and it's none of our business I guess, but I just thought you ought to know."

He turned back to the cop. "I came over the crest and saw Manny's and Arnie's stoplights and saw Arnie's trailer jump and pitch sideways till he corrected and got it stopped. I pulled in behind them, and they were both already out and running. Before I got there, I saw the fire. He could tell you more about how it started." He looked at me. I was thinking about it. I nodded for him to go on because it was very real to me, still happening. I wondered if maybe I could get out of having to describe it. I knew there would have to be a corroborative statement, so as Singleton told it I thought along with him.

He did a good job of the telling. He had gotten there only a minute or so after Manny and I were on the scene. Manny jumped from his cab, dodged around the car with the girls in it, and ran to the wreck. I took only enough time to grab my extinguisher. When I got there, Manny was on top of the wreck trying to pull Gates out and holding the door up at the same time.

The tanker had gone in hitting the ditch fast but stretching out the way you want to try to hit a ditch. It had made no motion to jack-knife. The ditch had been too deep, and instead it had lain over on its side. All along there—for that matter, all through those hills—the roadside is usually an outcropping of limestone, slate, and coal. In the cuts and even in the valleys there is rock. Until the truck was pulled off, there would be no way to know. It was likely that the tank and maybe his saddle tank had been opened up on an outcrop of rock. There was a little flicker of fire forward of the cab. Gasoline, I had thought, but it did not grow quick like gasoline. The diesel from his tank was running down the ditch and muffled it some at first.

I went for it with the extinguisher, but it was growing and the extinguisher was a popgun. Manny started yelling to come help him, and I whirled and climbed up over the jutting wheel. Singleton was suddenly there, grabbing me, boosting me up. I took the cab door and held it up, and Gates started to yell.

Manny had him under the shoulders pulling hard, had him about halfway out, but he was hung up. I believe Gates's leg was pinched or held by the wheel. Otherwise Manny would not have gotten him out that far. Manny knew though. He knelt down beside him staring into the wrecked cab.

The fire was getting big behind me, building with a roar. It was flowing down the ditch but gaining backward over the surface rapidly. I gave Manny a little shove and closed the door over Gates's head so we could both reach him through the window. He was a small chunky man—hard to grasp. We got him under the arms and pulled hard, and he screamed again. The heat was close now. I was terrified, confused. We could not pull harder. There was no way to get him out.

Then I was suddenly alone. Manny jumped down, stumbling against Singleton, who tried to climb up and was driven back, his face lined and desperate in the fire glow. Manny disappeared running into the darkness. Where I was above the cab, the air was getting unbearably hot. The fire had not yet worked in under the wreck. I tugged hopelessly until I could no longer bear the heat and jumped down and rolled away. Singleton helped me up and pulled me back just as screams changed from hurt to fear; high weeping, desperate and unbelieving cries as the heat but not the fire got to him.

I was held in horrified disbelief of what was happening. Outside the cab and in front of it were heavy oil flames. Gates, his head and neck and one hand outside the window, was leaning back away from them, screaming another kind of cry because the fire that had been getting close had arrived. The muscles of his neck and face were cast bronze in the fire glow, and his mouth was a wide black circle issuing cries. His eyes were closed tight, and his straining hand tried to pull himself away.

Then there was a noise, and he fell back and disappeared into the fire, quietly sinking to cremation with no further sound, and we turned to look behind us. Manny was standing helplessly, his pistol dropping from his shaking hand to the ground, and then he too was falling to the ground, covering his eyes with his hands and rolling on his side away from us.

"If I'd known, I wouldn't have stopped him," Singleton told the cop. "Of all the men I know, he's the only one who could have done that much."

He hesitated, running his hand through his graying hair. "I didn't help, you understand—didn't help." He looked pleading. "Nothing I could do, no use—Arn didn't help. Only Manny."

The girls and June were sobbing. The sky to the eastward was coming alive with light. The cop who was too old to be riding a cruiser looked blanched and even older in the beginning dawn. I felt as I had once felt at sea after battling an all-night storm. Only Singleton seemed capable of further speech, his almost ancient features passive but alive.

He looked at the patrol car where Manny still slumped. "They can't prove he killed a man. There's nothing to prove it with. They can't even prove the bullet didn't miss, and in a way that's the worst thing that can happen. You see, I know him. You think maybe he'll change after a while—maybe it will dull down and let him live normal. It won't. I sat with him before you came and did what I could, and it was nothing. Do they electrocute in this state or use gas? If they were kind, the way he is kind, they'd do one or the other."

I Take Care of Things

IT WAS LATE BEYOND THE USUAL TIME OF THE SIRENS. I SAT ON the driver's side of the cruiser waiting for Frank to quit heaving. Our light was flashing a circular beacon into the blackness of the surrounding trees. We were just inside the park. The light made a changing red glow in the trees and pulled darkness behind it like a vacuum. The trees were moving in a light wind and spitting a few leaves. The light ticked, rotating. My hands were tense. There had been a wreck. Two kids on a motorcycle had missed a curve at speed. One was a girl. She had been thrown against a guy wire. They must have rapped into the curve at sixty-plus. It had been a big bike.

Fire equipment was parked fifty yards down the road. A fireman in a yellow slicker leaned hard on the straight stream nozzle that could whip the hose like snapping steel cable if it got loose. The water hit the pavement and bounced into a spray of red from the emergency lights.

Between us and the fire truck another fireman came from behind some trees. His face seemed paler in the flash of red than in the darkness. He steadied himself against a tree. Then he stepped onto the road. I eased back in the seat and watched. Pretty soon we could go.

Frank was getting quiet. He sat with the car door open and his feet in the road. He raised his head like he was testing himself. Then he wiped his mouth with his shirt sleeve. He touched his hand to his shirt front and dropped his hand fast. He had pulled the boy out from the broken frame of the motorcycle.

"I will," I told him. I reached to unbutton the shirt which had a lot of blood on front. The blood was cold and slick. It is always a strange feeling. I opened the buttons down to his belt. He pulled the tail out of his pants and got the rest. He jerked the shirt off and balled it up, throwing it on the floor in back.

"Your badge," I told him.

"Screw the badge," he said, "and you, too." His voice was close to hysteria. He got out of the wet undershirt by pulling up and holding it away from his face. His hair was pushed around. He was getting bald toward the front. The thin side hair tangled and stood up. His brows were heavy and looked messed. Probably they looked like that because his eyes were wild. He was only thirty-three or four, but he looked like a crazy man of sixty.

"I'll get the badge," I told him.

"And the rest of the world."

"Everybody, huh."

"Them, too. Leave me alone."

He is older than I am by a couple of years. In some ways he is younger because he never learns. At least his feelings never learn. I saw him break up once before. Cops are wrong to break up.

"Be back," I told him and climbed from the car. The ambulance was being loaded. They were about finished. I walked to the back of the ambulance. The guys were not careful.

The driver was an old man, very tall if he would straighten up, but he was stooped. His gray hair was streaked red and black in the lights. His helper was a kid. The kid looked wrong. Almost like a head. He looked high.

"You ready?" Their job was bad. You could tell about the body. Across the bridge of her nose there was a scrape that was nearly bloodless.

The driver looked at me. He was about to close the door. "Nearly ready. You want to check it?"

"No need."

"No need to hurry either," the kid said, and grinned. He was tall like the driver. His hair was too long. It was black and was slicked against his head. His hands were manicured. A homosexual maybe, or something different. All kinds of perversion hang around death. Up close you could tell he was high. He giggled.

"You like it." I watched him. He stopped giggling. His eyes looked all right except that they were excited. He was not high on drugs.

"No," he said. His voice was trying to go low and serious. He could not quite get it down there.

"Sure he does," the driver said. He was old and looked old. Ambulance guys working a big city are usually losers. Paid by the shift. Sleep in.

"Come over here," I told him. We walked away from the ambulance and toward the cruiser. About midway I stopped. There was no reason to let him see Frank.

"Make an inventory?"

"Didn't you?" He looked indignant. I gave him a leaf of paper from my book because the forms were in the car. He began scribbling, using the back of the book. They had custody of a couple of watches, a billfold, and a few bucks currency. "He doesn't steal," the old man said, "and I don't need to." He was hot. It was my job.

"He ride in back?" I pointed to the kid.

"Sometimes. He don't always ride with me."

"With live ones?"

"I ride with the live ones. He don't go with me all the time. I don't know what he does with other guys." He knew trouble, that old man. He signed the paper and gave it to me. There was a kicked look in his eyes. He wanted to say something and either did not know how or did not know what.

"Sorry about the list," I told him. He turned and walked back to the ambulance. The helper climbed in the riding side and they pulled away. Before they were around the curve the old man secured his light.

It was about wrapped up. The firemen had pressure off the hose. I was going to ask them to shoot under our car but it was too late. Instead, I walked to where the girl had hit. A human has a lot of blood. The pavement was clean under the lights. Beside the road the gravel was gone. It had been washed back into the grass. The roadside was slick with mud. Grass was beaten down and washed out in one big area. There is a lot of pressure on those hoses. Later on the park crews would come around and sod. Maybe they would not even know why the grass was washed out. Maybe they would bitch. It was clean. A good job.

I waved to the nearest fireman and went back to the car. When I climbed in Frank looked better. He was still not good but he seemed to have some control. He was sitting straight, not slumped over. His arms were muscular but his chest was kind of puny and thin. His chest was heaving. It looked like a contradiction after seeing his arms.

"I'm sorry," he said. He looked straight ahead.

"Sorry is for kids," I told him. "I'll take you home. They don't need for you to check in naked."

"Taking a chance."

"Can't you tell the difference? Taking no chance. The shift's out in an hour anyway." I drove to the edge of our sector before calling in to report the scene clear. Then I took us out of service. It was past four-thirty Thursday morning. A loose time. Even if I was seen I could explain.

"Coffee," I told Frank. I pulled beyond an all-night restaurant and walked back. The counterman was sitting and reading a magazine. I have known him for a couple of years. He can guess things, the way guys can sometimes when they are used to being alone. He looked up when I walked in.

"Hi, Burns," he said. "You had a bad one." He stood up and poured coffee in two paper cups. He did it slow. Rheumatism.

"Bad enough." I leaned on the counter. The walk-boards in back of the counter looked greasy and slick.

"I heard the noise." He is not a nosy guy. He was just asking if I needed anything besides coffee.

"Make it black," I told him. "You ought to wipe this counter." I had leaned in a spot of mustard or some kind of slop. The counter was cracked linoleum, dark green where it was not peeling.

He passed me the coffee. "What a crappy job," he said. By the time I was through the doorway he was reading the magazine again.

Frank spilled some of the coffee in his lap. It scalded and he sat still. Probably it helped steady him. Then he started drinking the coffee and that helped more. A pretty fair cop, Frank. But, wrongheaded. He relates. Takes it personal. When he first saw that body I know he thought of his daughter. She is thirteen and healthy and does not ride on motorcycles. He thinks muddled. He gets one thing on his mind and it means something else. At first I thought it was morals. He would lose his temper. I've seen him beat a pusher into the hospital and the guy was only dealing in pot. It is not morals. He relates.

"I got something to tell you," he said. His voice still sounded lousy. There was a tremble like someone who was crying.

"I probably don't want to hear." I drank off the rest of my coffee and pulled away. It was true. I did not want to hear because he gave me an uneasy feeling. Something he had done had made no sense. Fooling around.

When we got to the scene we had checked the kids out fast. I went to run traffic by and chase the ghouls off. When they did not leave I put our spotlight on the girl and that got rid of some of them. Frank had been in the bushes freeing the boy's body. The ambulance guys could have done that.

"I got to tell you," he said.

"Save it."

"Now." The more he talked the worse his voice got.

We rode for a while. It was less dark. Not light really. It was the way it looks just before you get the first far-off suggestion of dawn. Frank leaned forward like he was completely exhausted.

"Listen," he said, "put yourself in my place."

"There ain't no amount of money."

His voice got on a low monotone. Probably he figured to control it that way.

"I looked at the boy," he said, "and you went out to the road. Then I went and looked at the girl. Clean cut. Surgical."

"Forget it."

"I got mad. Cars backed up. People walking off to puke and then coming back for another look. Just a little girl."

"Everything dead looks little." I looked at him because I was hearing something. His hands were out of control. His eyes were wild again. His mouth hung open. He was panting like a dog. That was what I was hearing. A dog pant. His control was gone and suddenly, right there, I hated him. It was a strange feeling.

"Get it over," I told him. I could not remember hating anyone like that before.

"Went back to the boy. Big hump of stuff in the bushes. Part human and part iron. Wedged into the bushes getting madder. That girl. Hating. Crying. Started to swear. Felt for a pulse."

"Found one, didn't you?"

He turned to me, shocked out of his panting. I had him cut from under. "Yes, light pulse."

"Thanks." I looked out at the street. We were near his house. "So you got mad and turned the whole mess upside down like you were pulling out a body. That what you wanted to tell me?" I was ahead of him. It wrecked his climax.

"His back was broken. It twisted and then there wasn't any more pulse." He was gasping so hard he could hardly breathe. He could not say anything more. I drove. It was only a couple of blocks.

Death. You work with it. Sometimes it's dirty like when a drunk goes out in an alley. Sometimes it's painful. Old people with heart attacks. Automobile injuries that bleed them white and cold before you can get it stopped. Gas. Fire. Drowning.

I pulled up to his house. He did not move.

"You want me to decide," I told him. "You want me to make it right by doing something. Make up your mind for you." I hated him.

"You know what it is."

"Well, the hell with you. Get the coroner's report."

"You know the word. You know what it is."

"Sure, the word is that it's five-thirty in the morning and I need sleep." I turned to him. "Okay, give me your gun."

He passed it over like he was glad. He was actually breathing better. I dropped the gun between the seat and the door on my side. "Get out," I told him. He got out like he did not understand. I reached over and slammed the door.

"Get some sleep," I told him. I shoved it in gear and got away before he could answer. The gun was beside the seat. He could not shoot himself. Instead, he was going to have to stand in the growing light without a shirt. The whole world chases itself in an eighty-mile-an-hour frenzy. He could match his mind to that along with whatever he called a conscience. He could walk to the nearest precinct or he could damned well go in the house to his wife, take a shower, and go to bed.

There was the beginning traffic. Milkmen and other route guys. I felt better than I had for an hour. Leaving Frank like that was a help. It had been uncomfortable when I hated him.

The Lady with the Blind Dog

SHE MAY HAVE ONCE BEEN A LADY, AND SO JILL AND I CHOOSE to think of her that way. I was first to meet her. She seemed a miserable old woman who tugged a panting dog through crowded streets, beneath blue sky and sun. We met during summer when light lay across San Francisco like the gaze of Mediterranean gods. Jill and I were, and still are, warmed by that sun; but now sometimes feel held in place; pinioned.

When Jill met her, Jill said, "She makes me feel so old, and I'm not ready. Only the blush of the rose, that's only what I want. I don't want to be old. I don't." Her voice almost hysterical.

That was quite some years ago. Jill is now old, but can't get accustomed.

The Lady grew no younger; but not a day older, either. The dog still pants, unchanged.

The dog is a mixture of small, fluffy breeds with white fur, and with feet callused and clumsy. The callus comes from a constant round of padding along sidewalks. The nose is flat like a pug, and the eyes are pop-eyed like a Boston bull terrier. The eyes vary; chalk white, fish-belly white, dead white, and they contrast with the red tongue, always panting.

It's got a red collar, too big for a dog that can't weigh more than five pounds. It's got a temper, because it will snap at anything or anybody. The lady drags it on a leash stout enough to hang a man. There are chew marks on the leash, but the dog's teeth are worn flat. It never barks. It never growls, or not exactly. It makes a low sound, a rumble, a noise that somehow sounds like fire racing before wind.

If the dog actually growled, I think people would flee.

Flee from a five-pound monster? Probably. With monsters, size doesn't matter much.

"Our monster," Jill says. "Does everybody have one, or are we just lucky?" She's still a lovely lady. The blush of the rose has long faded, but the high forehead has no more wrinkles than in her youth. Her hands remain lovely, her figure slim, and her neurosis only wild enough to make her interesting.

When young she wanted to be an actress, which is half of why we came to San Francisco. At the time the city owned a reputation for experimental theater.

The other half: I wanted to be a landscape architect drawing graceful lines of leaves across the world; make the world beautiful. I had other wants as well. I wanted to be warm. We were in Boston where outside-work is a frigid five-month sentence during winters. You have to let your hair grow to protect your neck. Your hands are never warm, nor your feet. I spent my last two winters there with a tree company, pruning and snow removal.

When we got to San Francisco I didn't even need to get a haircut; just walked into the office of the nearest landscape construction company, and walked out with a job. At the same time, in Cleveland and Chicago, there were riots and looting. In those days I paid little attention to the news. My attention focused on the job.

In the downtown financial district, where the old lady first showed up, there was a well-established pocket-park. The park sort of dwelt between tall buildings. People from the offices took their lunches on good days. They sat on lush grass and chatted, chewed sandwiches, sipped thermos coffee, and for a few minutes quit pretending that what they did was especially important.

As the business district grew, and as more buildings rose, the park became crowded. My first assignment was foreman of construction for a new park. My crew and I built it right across the street.

The architect designed the place with seven little hills, because San Francisco is built on seven hills. It was a routine design, nothing exotic, but green and functional. Our machine operator piled and carved soil. A subcontractor put in sidewalks. My guys installed irrigation and pine trees, and then seeded grass. After which, I went sort of crazy.

It wasn't an ordinary job, or ordinary conditions; at least not to someone with experience. The irrigation heads were placed in a way that, with the touch of a button, I could light off enough water to cover seven little hills and better than an acre of ground; silver arcing flashes crashing above raw soil.

And, it was the middle of summer. Cloudless days. Overflooding sun. Grass seed down. What I did made no sense, except—ask any gardener.

Grass seed dies if it dries once wetted. A constant sheen of water is wanted. I made a bet with myself. I bet that I could bring that job in so fast it would go in the record books. And I did, from first water to first cutting in seven days.

Water crashing silver through sunlight, strong as creation, beautiful as hope. I dodged here and there, wet half the time while adjusting irrigation heads. Turn off the water, let the soil heat beneath that sun. When the first spot of gray showed surface dryness; time to light 'em off for another five minutes.

Crazy old lady. She first appeared on a sidewalk in the park across the street. From a distance she moved like a dark blotch against green grass, and beside loads of people dressed for business; gaily colored dresses, summer suits of tan.

The dog half-walked, was half-dragged beside her. The old bat could have allowed the dog to walk on grass, but she short-leashed it. The dog couldn't stray an inch. It had to walk on hot concrete. Even from across the street, you could tell it was blind.

The lady dressed witchery. Her darkish dress hung near shoe tops, thin ankles; dress of dark maroon but faded to sort of red—shabby where it almost touched her shoe tops. The dress looked made of velvet, and the lady wore a ragged fur jacket, but she shivered beneath that sun. Her face looked like someone or something had taken a normal human head and twisted it. Her lips sagged and could not quite close. Her face was smooth around the eyes, but it seemed like one eye rode a good bit higher than the other. Her face sagged everywhere else. Her eyes were closer to black than gray. Small slobber occasionally dripped.

"They wonder about you," she whispered. "All of them. They watch you scamper, and they wonder." Her voice sounded metrical as a harsh poem.

"You're gonna burn up in that coat," I told her. "You're gonna get heat stroke." Crazy old lady. I looked across at the other park, from which no one paid the least attention. "Nice dog. What's its name?"

She shivered. Beside her the dog panted. The eyes seemed to

change in the sunlight, from milky to wheyish, sometimes marble-white. The dog did not rest on its haunches, or lie down; it never has. It is always ready to spring.

"Are you okay?" I asked. Sun already had me burned brown, and my hair bleached. Now the sun lay between my shoulders like a hot iron. The lady shivered. I thought she might pass out.

"Torment," she said, and I did not know whether she spoke of herself or the dog. "Don't come close.... Nothing wrong with his nose."

The dog's nose was crusted, the way dogs get in the last stages of distemper. Bald patches lay scabbed in the wavy fur. Its tail hung thin and ratlike.

I remember thinking she was cruel not to have the animal killed. Then I thought maybe the dog was her only companion, and she was so old.

Around us, I could feel the first stirring of life as seed germinated. It was like the soil began to breathe. Life, then death. Turmoil, then darkness. Regeneration, then life.

"Don't you mind them," she said. "And don't you worry. You can make the world beautiful. I've got my eye on you." She tugged at the leash. The dog snapped at air, snap, snap, clicks of flat teeth. White-popping eyes.

I watched her leave, dark ruby splotch against the gleaming white of the city. She walked less than a half block and then sort of faded. It didn't happen fast, and there were people going to and fro on the sidewalk. She might have stepped into a doorway, but that seemed unlikely. I told myself I wasn't scared. Later on, I told Jill I wasn't scared. What a liar.

I told Jill during one of our little dust-ups. We fussed at each other because of the job. She didn't understand why grass was important.

Seed hit the red stage in three days. The red stage is crucial. It's when the seed has to stay constantly wet. If you can bring it from red to green, and keep it green for thirty or forty hours, the job is home free.

What happened was, I parked at the job and slept in my car. I woke from time to time, like a mother with a new baby. Hit the irrigation for a couple of minutes, then go back to uneasy sleep. Jill spent nights at home, trying to persuade herself that I was not out with another woman. She tried to stay nailed in place, but paranoia got the best of her.

She wanted to be an actress, but what she needed was acting lessons. She showed up at the job around ten at night: a snazzy-looking young woman, riding a bus, then walking the empty streets of San Francisco; a young woman bearing sandwiches. Pretending love, and not paranoia.

"You didn't have to, but thanks." I actually sort of treasured the sandwiches, even if she was nuts. I could, back then, be as phony as she. Then I paused, realizing she was scared. If she was not scared, she would have checked me out from a distance, then gone back home.

"I'll give you a ride, then come back."

The old lady appeared beneath street lights as we climbed in the Ford. I wondered if the lady patrolled that park across the street. I wondered how somebody that old could constantly walk, day and night. The dog shone as a small white spot beneath street lights. The lady moved slow as befitted her age, but she dragged the dog most firmly. The leash tied them together, tighter, at the time, than Jill and I were tied. I started the car.

"Drive roundabout," Jill said. "Don't go the direction she went." Then she said, "Please."

"Problem?"

"I don't want to be old," she whispered. "There's stuff I got to do. Ingénue, that's me."

Jill was never little-girl pretty. She had the face and body to play Shakespeare's Portia, not some comic twinky. Her face and body are as far as matters ever went. She pretended she knew it all. She figured talent doesn't need training. Jill can pretend to perfection, but it's always Jill pretending. She never learned to act.

Driving her home, in that night long ago, it took less than a minute to find that she too had met the old lady. It happened on a deserted street; deserted because the San Francisco business district lay like a black and abandoned tomb after dark. Jill had seen the lady and dog from a block away. They crossed paths because who could imagine danger from an old lady and a tiny mutt?

"She told me not to worry," Jill whispered. "She said to examine my skills. What skills? I can type. She said she was keeping an eye on me." Jill's voice came as close to sounding 'little-girl' as I've ever heard. She was totally scared, dry-mouthed and spitless.

What I didn't tell Jill, or at least didn't tell her for some years, is that the old lady said, "Don't worry. I've got my eye on you," to lots of people. Mostly, she was ignored, which is the standard in San Francisco. The city is, or used to be, proud that people can be as weird as they want, as long as they don't cause trouble.

My grass came in (I thought of it as mine), and the maintenance crew arrived with lawn mowers. I left the park for other installation jobs, running as far north as San Rafael, and south to San Jose. The company landscaped freeways, power transfer stations, business and industrial parks, The Cow Palace, universities, and BART, the rapid transit system. Then, in three years, the company went broke. Too many Chiefs, not enough Indians.

And, during those years, all hell broke loose. Riots and burning in Atlanta and Boston, Buffalo and Cincinnati, Tampa, Newark, Detroit. The newspapers reported a war going on in the far east, but I had my own troubles.

Unemployment happened. I found myself back on the streets in autumn. Landscape outfits cut back against the coming winter rains. Jill worked as a temp secretary and started hanging out with little theatre groups. I looked for any kind of work.

It was a thin time, but had its points. I job-hunted from early morning to mid-afternoon, then, discouraged, loafed. For the first time in a long time, I was able to watch what went on. I learned to like the scurrying of shoppers in the west end. I liked the mixtures of colors and languages and oriental faces; plus Irish and Italians, Russians, Hebrews, a sprinkling of Spaniards.

The old lady appeared one afternoon near the bandstand in Golden Gate Park. I saw her from a way off, saw mostly the white spot of dog, and faded velvet dress. I loitered on a park bench, like a bum in a two-bit movie. Seagulls squawked overhead, circling, but they stayed away from her; or maybe away from the dog.

"Torment," I said when she approached. "He's looking well." I moved to one end of the bench, making space. "Take a break." Scared yes, but I was interested. Anything that can impress a seagull . . .

"He looks the same," she said, and she actually took a seat. I had the uncanny feeling that she was there, but really wasn't. I felt that if I touched her, my finger would go right through. Like, maybe, spectral.

The dog stood short-leashed, and two feet from my ankle. "Such a lovely city," she murmured. "Such a pretty day. By the time I'm free to know it..." She paused as the leash tightened, and the dog tried for my ankle. She held it most firmly. The dog rumbled, panted; red tongue, white fur, scabby and blind.

I felt sorry for her. She spent her days, even her nights, walking around tied to a dog that should be dead of old age. There had to be something better for her than that. "If you let him run, he couldn't go far."

"The last time he ran," she said, "quite a few ended in a graveyard." Her voice sounded honestly sad, like she honestly spoke the truth.

I didn't mind if she was crazy. After all, I lived with Jill who was nutsy. I wasn't all that bright myself; stupid enough to work, when I worked, at dead-end jobs that offered only plants and trees as benefits. Plus, half of the people on the streets seemed screwy. One more Crazy didn't matter.

"He enjoys suicides and mayhem," she whispered, as much to herself as to me. "Decimation is his nature. Decimation is his right." She sat wrapped in the fur jacket, sitting in sunlight and shivering. A little slobber hung as a droplet in one corner of her mouth. "When he runs, people make fatal jumps. They destroy others, destroy things. They kill what they say they love." The dog stood on thin legs. It looked like it could hardly walk, leave alone run.

"I must go," she said. "I have my work." She stood. "You can weather hard times. I've got my eye on you. Don't worry."

At that time, in Los Angeles, people were scared because of something called the Tate-Bianca murders. It had something to do with cults. Whatever.

I got a job driving city bus. Half of the guys driving those things were splow-heads, freaks, junkies, jerk-offs; and generally on their way to rehab or a cemetery. The other half were guys worth knowing. I tooled bus for fifteen years.

For a while I kept hunting something better. Took a couple of night classes at community college; agronomy and botany. Actually designed and installed a Japanese garden in the tiny yard in back of our apartment. Could have done more.

Should have done more. Could have been an architect. But, a day's shift of driving sends a guy home tired. The pay was okay, it became easier to work than think.

Jill hung out at little theater, helped paint sets. Caught an occasional walk-on. Never really studied. She depended on a scant and untrained talent.

It came to me, as I wore out brakes by the truckload, that something magical happened in the streets of San Francisco. Tons and tons of people, lots of whom didn't even speak English, managed to get along and not kill each other.

They fought traffic that ran like demented weapons. Hysteria should, and maybe did, lie just beneath the surface, but mass murder didn't happen.

What did happen is the skyline changed. The city grew upward, suburbs expanded, and craziness of a different sort lurked on every corner. Too many people, too much money, and too much desperation to make the rent. And, yet, no mass murder. Murder, when it happened, remained personal, husbands and wives, or jealous lovers.

In that time I saw the old lady twice, but I saw some other people first, because it turned out that the old lady was only one of several. On Geary Street, among lots of old men walking their dogs, there was one old man who had a three-legged mutt. It looked like a wiener dog crossed with a sick hamster. The man dressed in wool suit and top coat on the sunniest days. His face was cratered and twisted, the way sick men, and addicts, and alkies get in the last stages. He slowly limped in one direction while his dog limped in the other. They made a crooked pattern of movement along the sidewalks. One time, as I stopped to pick up passengers, I heard the guy say, "Chaos, stay!" The dog did not sit, but it stood motionless.

And there were other old men and women. I learned to spot them. Old people were pretty much everywhere, and lots of them had companion dogs. Most all of them were perfectly normal. Perfectly nice.

Occasionally, though, unusual ones showed up. Always with a mangy mutt. Always dressed against cold, as if the slightest San Francisco mist would blow right through them. For one three-month period I actually held my own investigation, kind of tracked them down. One dog was named Despair. The other names were worse.

So I met the old lady two more times. The first time was in a wretched little park sandwiched between California Street and a nowhere lane of forgotten asphalt. Jill was with me, and it had been a lot of years since Jill met the old lady. Jill understood what I did not.

"She's not real. No one that old walks around. Dogs don't live this long. She's a hallucination." Sometimes Jill's brand of crazy comes up with truthful stuff. This time, her smooth forehead wrinkled with something that wasn't exactly fear, but surely wasn't confidence. Still, she tugged me forward. I tugged back. She won.

"Are you real?" she asked the lady. "If you are, then am I? Why are we here, and doing this?"

I expected Jill to ask after the Meaning of Life, but she must have missed a cue. Jill is narrow and leggy, very good-looking, and she stood hand on hip like a cowgirl about to grab a shootin' iron. Lousy acting. Jill was still Jill.

"I serve a sentence," the lady whispered, "but it's kind of you to ask." At her feet the dog seemed poised for attack.

"Sentence? Like in jail?"

"That's a fair description," the old lady said. She wiggled the leash, looked down at the dog, and tried to smile. Her face was so twisted the smile turned out crooked. "I keep Torment leashed. There's power in that, but not a power anybody would want."

"But are you real?" Jill can be a genuine pain when she sets her head on something.

"Torment is real," the old lady said. "Once in a while he gets off leash. Perhaps you're still too young to understand."

At the time, Jill was pushing forty. Old enough to play Shakespearian tragedy. Unskilled though, and so she wasn't gonna.

"When he gets off-leash I get a year added to my sentence," the old lady said. "Don't ask how. I don't know."

"How long are you in for?" Dumb question, but I felt I had to say something before Jill stole the whole scene.

"In a few years the twentieth century will pass," the old lady murmured. "If he stays on leash for a few more years…." She seemed taken with a chill, or maybe she figured she'd said too much.

"Why?"

"You don't want to know," she told me. "If you ever do know, then you may walk for a century." She wiggled the leash. The dog clicked its worn teeth, made that fire-rushing noise.

"One does get weary," she whispered, "tired of being needed. And now we must go."

She moved away most slowly. I thought to follow. Jill stopped me. "Epiphany," she said, "don't screw up the dramatic moment." I didn't know what she meant, and neither did she. Or maybe she did. She seemed scared.

Something came between us after that. Jill grew remote. We still walked sunny streets. We still strolled the parks on Sundays. We still embraced, but distantly. I knew that a gulf was opening between us, partly because my dreams caused sadness.

I dreamed night after night of irrigation crashing white spume beneath sun. I dreamed of tall buildings, naked and needing greenery, ferns, trees. I dreamed I could fly, could cast growing things across bare landscapes, turn deserts into gardens.

I quit driving bus, and drove cabs. It came to me that I was no longer young. The little Japanese garden in the rear of our apartment turned scruffy. No matter how much attention I gave it, something went wrong. Somehow or other, my eyes had lost their ability to judge proportions. The garden looked like it stepped fresh from the pages of Sunset magazine, something rubber-stamped.

In other cities across the country there were riots, bombings of abortion clinics, assassinations. I found myself muttering, "Chaos must have gotten off leash." The minute I said that to myself, I knew it must be true.

And, almost right away, some guy proved to me it was true. The fare wanted a cab from airport to business district, and his destination stood near that park I'd landscaped so many years ago. A crippled old man led a three-legged wiener dog between green hills of grass. My passenger muttered to himself. I said "What?" He said, "How in hell did that man get here, all the way from Miami?"

"You're sure?"

"I'm not sure of much these days," the guy said, and he was grim. "But I'm damned sure I saw that man and mutt in Florida."

"Or else you saw a ghost?" I just suggested it; sort of had to suggest it.

"Could be," the guy said. "What the hell do I know?" He looked ahead, searching for his address, and became all business.

Jill decided that actors were troubled people, and directors were saints. She stopped the walk-ons, and turned motherly. Her little theater group depended on her for counsel, and for suggestions on set design.

Jill said, telling of the group, "If everyone would do exactly as I say, they would all be happy." Quite a mouthful, but the group put up with it. They allowed her to direct a farce. It wasn't a good production, but it wasn't awful.

"You really shouldn't ask," the old lady told me on the last time we met. "I keep Torment leashed. I'm a protector of dreams."

She stood shivering beneath noonday sun, her fur jacket wrapped tightly over the velvet dress. Along the busy sidewalk people passed intent on business, or lunch, or a love affair... people intent on raising kids, or scoring a high; all the things that people do. The dog clicked its worn teeth.

"And those other dogs, Chaos, and Despair? Those old men?"

"They, too," she said. "Those old men pay their debts. Sometimes they fail. Their charge, their creature, runs loose."

"Debts?"

"We pay for our failed dreams," she whispered. "Once in the long ago I wished to be a dancer. I suppose I did not want it enough to make it happen." Sorrow, like no sorrow I have yet known lay in that whisper. It was the sorrow of lost years, failed ambitions, paths taken because they were, if nothing else, easy enough, and practical. Sorrow.

"And so we rein in foul creatures. We try to protect the dreams of others." She tugged at the leash, turned away, and entered the hurrying crowd only to disappear like blown mist.

I'm not going to tell Jill about that. I'm not going to tell Jill that yesterday I saw Torment, still on leash. But this time an old man, dressed in thin robe beneath heavy greatcoat, was in charge. Our old lady's sentence has completed.

No, I won't put that kind of fear before Jill's eyes. It's bad enough that she frets over me these days, and there's not much she can do. She joins in a drink before dinner, or maybe a couple of them. They blunt whatever needs blunting.

Because no matter what I do, I know that one of these days an old man, or an old woman, will step into my cab. They will have a creature named Sorrow on leash. When they leave the cab, Sorrow will remain. So will the leash.

The Best Left Neglected
Library of Dry Facts

I COULD HAVE BEEN LITTLE MORE THAN TEN, AND SCARCELY out of pinafores, when child-wandering led me to the Best Left Neglected Library of Dry Facts. It was not in those days—or in these—actually known as such. It is called, when it is called at all, The Document Archive of Boston Towne; and it is a curious building that nestles like a cellar above ground. The foundations are stone, but walls display centuries-old brick. The Archive sits between brick row houses on one of the last sleepy streets of Boston. Brown leaves cluster in yew hedges that hide the building from the street. The leaves crackle and blow in autumnal bursts, even in spring and deep summer.

At age ten I did not yet recognize much difference between rich and poor, or men and women; but I did know myself as a New Englander. My father, a gentle man though stern, carried the name of Justice John Tilton. My mother was Prudence Glade Tilton, of the New Hampshire Glades. They each lived eighty-nine years, and tenderness dwelt between them; although it was tenderness a young girl only guessed. My parents were not cold, but they were New Englanders. Their hearts were carried elsewhere than on their sleeves.

Dark clouds scudded before a dark wind on that day of my childhood. As I wandered home from school, wind came wrapped in the smells from storms at sea, or in nuances carried to eyes and nose from a waterfront where cloth and cordage and rum went aboard steamships bound to Australia or Zanzibar. If, in fact, I was ten, the year would have been 1924. Today I am seventy-six.

Even to the eyes of a girl from Boston the building seemed threatening. In other, less solemn places, children might have been terrified. They would view barred windows and heavy oaken doors as having to do with jails or schools or prisons. They might see the copper roof, all green with tarnish, as proper shelter for the balding pates of judges. The normal child, being imaginative, is a first class revolutionary against stuffiness; and normal children would imagine horrible crimes of law being perpetrated on free spirits.

I loitered a long while on that first day, waiting to see pirates dragged away in chains, or fallen women branded, or a hooded and black-robed Inquisitor step through the doorway and pass by to enter a Duesenberg or Pierce Arrow. The waiting produced nothing except the dry rattle of leaves, and the movement of wind among ivy covering much of the old brick. In the hubbub of Boston town this small corner sat in unperturbed silence.

I thought, while gazing at dusty windows which seemed to gaze back in studied indifference, that a shape moved within. Each time, my heart fluttered; not with terror, but with awe and question. At age ten one is sometimes overwhelmed by the irrational power of the adult world. Children wonder how they will come to fit in such a world, because, of course, children do not believe they will change. They will only grow bigger.

I did grow and change. So did Boston town. But, in my heart of hearts, it was clear that I changed more than Boston. As I grew to adulthood and understanding, it became certain that Boston lies in the shackles of the past. It carries pride in its aristocracy, and pride because it is the seat of the American Revolution.

It does not deny, although it does not celebrate, its enduring darkness. In Boston, two hundred and ninety-eight years ago, the Reverend Cotton Mather troubled over the use of 'spectral evidence' as he fed the fires of the Salem Witch Trials. Nineteen people were hanged, two dogs were hanged, and Giles Corey was pressed to death as weights were piled on his chest.

In Boston, only a hundred and thirty five years ago, the best and the brightest of Boston collected money to support the abolitionist butcher, John Brown. These facts, and many like them, seemed electric to the mind of a young woman, and they have not lost their voltage as that mind grew old.

When, at age thirteen and less timid, I once more approached the Archive, it seemed that my comfortable world was about to crumble. My developing body suggested differences between men and women, and I was becoming a woman. The fact was alive with potential and dread. On more than one silly occasion, perhaps in a drawing room or at a piano concert, a man's eyes would engage mine for only a moment. The man would be handsome and well-dressed and vibrant; and, being perhaps age twenty-five, would see me as only a schoolgirl. The schoolgirl, though, would begin to flutter and behave in a coy, schoolgirlish manner. Confusion made short shrift of Yankee common sense.

In those days becoming a woman was thought to carry even greater responsibility than in the past. In 1920, with the passage of the Nineteenth Amendment to the Constitution, women won the vote. The whole world seemed in a whirl, times changing, while Boston town muttered darkly against change.

I stood outside the Archive as dry leaves fluttered. A horse-drawn ice wagon passed, the iceman huge and Irish and singing to his horse. Children followed the wagon, intent on grabbing small slivers of chipped ice when the man departed the wagon to make a delivery. Behind a dusty, sun-glazed window a figure moved. On a bold and impulsive notion, I stepped onto the sidewalk leading between yew hedges to the Archive's door.

To a child, the woman who opened the door seemed old, although she was not nearly as old as I am now. Wrinkles of smiles and wrinkles of sorrow webbed her face. Smoothly brushed hair fell nearly to her waist. Her hair was a shining cape of silver. Her dress fell to six inches above her ankles, a dress of dusty rose with small lace and small brocade. Her slippers were patent leather, of a kind made for dancing and not for a practical and workaday world. In my New England experience, no one moved so easily and with such quiet self-confidence. Her movements were as smooth as that cascade of beautiful hair. Her voice the same.

"This place has proved good shelter against most storms," she said pleasantly. "Even the storms of youth. Come in." She spoke so easily that I felt qualms. In my experience, new acquaintances were always taciturn. "This is where facts spin chrysalis," she told me. "Sometimes we hatch a butterfly."

She stepped back as I entered. She would prove wise in many ways, and one way dictated that the Archive was best seen before being explained.

Overhead, timbers thick enough to be ships' keels supported

that enormously heavy roof, and darkness dwelt between the timbers. The room lay like a vast, well-lighted cavern where shelves of books, journals, ships' logs, yellowed nautical charts, and court records covered brick walls and rose into darkness. Low bookshelves ranged across the enormous room, and one might see over them; so that in a glance it was possible to view an array of facts large enough to baffle all but the most experienced librarian. Yellow lamplight glowed in dark corners, and a woodstove at the farthest corner supplied heat that was not really needed at this time of year. A tea kettle simmered, supplying water for tea, and the needed amount of humidity. Oaken file cabinets ranked along one wall like soldiers at drill. One drawer in a central cabinet seemed to bulge a little.

"We're about to get a hatch," she said. "This one promises to be a bit dry." She walked toward the back of the room where tea things were kept in an old pie safe. Her desk held neatly arranged work, and I imagined it large enough to support a game of ping pong. A small table was set for tea.

"My name is Amanda Mary Glade Tilton," I said, my voice shy. "I didn't mean to bother you."

"Mine is Elizabeth Smith," she said, "just plain Elizabeth Smith, and almost nothing bothers me. Lies bother me; and during winters one must dress very warmly in here. Except for those I have no botherations."

On the wall behind her, and under glass, a Pine Tree flag from the American Revolution hung in faded green contrast to the faded red brick. I could almost hear fat explosions of black powder cannon, feel the heeling of a small ship discharging a broadside. A variety of small arms hung on the long wall, together with tools and utensils and patchwork quilts; the quilts also under glass. Flat-faced portraits from the 18th century stared with stern, but not unfriendly expressions. In fact, a portrait of a young woman with the unlikely name of Magdalen Beekman seemed nearly ready to smile and wink.

"And I am happy to say," Elizabeth continued, "that because of my presence, few liars actually visit here. Liars, when pinioned on the collecting pin of facts, become disconcerted." She chuckled, as if sharing a private joke. "I have bagged more than my limit of such blatherskites." She glanced toward the file cabinet and the slightly bulging drawer. "Poor thing," she murmured, "to go to rest as a moth and emerge as a mayfly." She smiled at my confusion. "But you must tell me about yourself."

When you are thirteen, and someone cares enough to ask about you, the conversation will surely turn toward hopes and dreams. I chattered and rambled that day. The cavernous room somehow seemed small and private because of the woman, or perhaps because of the tea things on the small table.

My dream in those days was to fly an airplane around the world. It seemed a sturdy dream then, and seems even more so now. At the time, Charles Lindbergh had not yet flown from Long Island to Paris, and would not for another three years. At the time, Amelia Earhart was still a teacher and social worker here in Massachusetts.

"An adventurer," Elizabeth muttered with approval. "It's no surprise. I might almost guess that adventure is borne in the bloodlines." She smiled at her statement. "Of course, we have no facts to prove such a guess."

The drawer of the filing cabinet trembled, as if within a small but desperate battle flared. The drawer pushed open as much as half an inch.

"Facts are alive," Elizabeth said, "but unlike other living things they do not die. They metamorphose. Sometimes they lie dormant for centuries, but die they do not." She touched my hand, motioning me to accompany her.

We stood before the cabinet as a tiny, mud-colored beetle emerged to stand teetering on the edge of the drawer where it dried its wings. As the shell and wings dried, the insect took the sheen of old mahogany. It shone as a brilliant brown dot against the varnished oak cabinet. The Archive filled with the sounds of low rustling, and feelings of tranquility seemed warm as a feather bed. I did not understand Elizabeth's words, nor understand the value of a bug that might be squashed by the flick of a fingernail.

"Not a mayfly after all," she said. "Now it rises and reenters the world. This little fellow's value is that he will cause no change." We watched the beetle whirr upward into darkness between the supporting timbers of the roof. "It's a drafty building," she told me. "He'll find a crack or crevice, then journey into the world."

She reached into the filing cabinet and pulled forth a folder that held a badly faded document, a sort of map.

"This is the scheme of an old water system," she explained. "Our ancestors had no metal pipes. They sawed logs down the middle, hollowed them out, then joined the pieces together. They sealed their wooden pipes with tar, then bound them with heavy hoops. Through the centuries the system decays. Just now, the last particle of that old system disappeared." Inside the folder she wrote a precise note giving time and date, and which carried the comment 'returned to soil'.

I could not fathom meaning from the event. At the same time my practical Yankee assurance suffered. No one had prepared me to view a world of such implied power, or a world this intricate. My genuine fear was the fear of growing to adulthood. I desperately wished to remain a child.

"Facts are forces," Elizabeth murmured as she replaced the folder. "Forces of change, and forces of stability. Both are necessary, or the world gets knocked catty wampus." She looked upward into darkness. "That little fellow has an important but quiet role. Our sparse New England soil lies slightly enriched. It waits for plow or steam shovel, or perhaps it waits to welcome a grave." Her words were stern, but her smile matched the patent leather slippers which were made for dancing. "The whole business takes some getting used to."

Times changed. Change swept in great waves across the country. Change flooded across the craggy forehead of Boston town, and I, changing, met my share of liars.

Some liars arrived through the ether. The first radio station in our country was KDKA, founded in 1920. By 1927, radio liars across the country were in full cry. They called what they sold 'ballyhoo'. Today it is called 'hype'. The liars sold sensational news of murders and trials and seamy divorces. They sold stories of bold explorers (and some not so bold), as well as covert sex. As the blather increased my mind did not retreat from adventure, but it often sought quiet and solitude.

I believed then, as I believe now, that to have a best friend, and to be one, is one of the great glories of life. During my thirteenth year I returned time and again to the Archive. No doubt I would have preferred a best friend of my own age, but in many ways Elizabeth seemed nearer to my age than did my schoolmates. Her cheerfulness, her kindness, and her dancing feet were compelled by a soul both happy and content. Although I witnessed the hatching of several facts, hearing and feeling their gauzy presence, Elizabeth did not mind that I remained more interested in dreams. A number of months passed before I actually encountered her anger, and actually saw a wounded fact.

The fact fell from darkness between rafters on a snowy November day. Beyond windows of the Archive, giant elms lifted spectral branches in to a darkened sky. Snow piled like mounded roads along the branches. In the streets no autos moved, and precious few horses. Elizabeth and I worked near the stove. We catalogued records of 17th century sailing ships which had visited Barbados. Elizabeth's slippers were exchanged for patent leather boots and wool stockings. Although styles dictated shorter skirts, I wore mine long. I clasped its folds between my ankles as we sat, a thick wool skirt that helped deny the chill.

The fact was a broken butterfly that might once have been a hopeful shade of green. Now it lay fluttering on the cold floor. Green faded nearly to white, and the butterfly secreted a tiny amount of clear fluid.

"It left here on strong wings," Elizabeth said, "and it returns flogged by lies. It is a weary creature, ready for rest." She knelt to cup the butterfly in the warmth of her hand. "It wishes to complete its cycle," she explained. "That's the reason for the release of sap." Her hands trembled.

My mind trembled. As Elizabeth carried the fact to a dark corner I feared she would rage, or perhaps launch into the air, flying into the dark day, howling anger into the snow-burdened sky. I did not understand the meaning of the word 'fury' until that day.

She gently placed the butterfly in a box that contained dried grass, wood shavings, twigs, and thread. Then she moved toward a filing cabinet and withdrew a folder labeled, 'League Of Nations'. She made a note of date and time, and the comment: "This day went to rest."

I feared her, but, because she was my friend, I also loved her. She now moved in a nearly aged manner, and I, at thirteen, had no wisdom to give, no comfort. Mystery dwelt all around us, and in this small event were enough forces to turn me from the ways of a child, toward the struggle for adulthood.

Elizabeth stepped across the room to a heavily cross-referenced section of philosophy and religion. She pulled forth a folder and wrote: "On this date became current 'The Program Of The N.S.D.A.P'. It contains the aims of a German political party called The Nazis."

I stood in amazement, not understanding, yet knowing for the first time the awful power and weight of history.

"My reason tells me that I must not judge," Elizabeth said, her voice tense as finely strung wire. "My good sense tells me not to tamper. There are times, though, when my heart would wish for a box made of Bessemer steel in which some facts could be locked for eternity."

My feelings were so confused that I nearly stuttered. I remember saying something about facts, wondering if the facts that lay around us went beyond Boston. Did this archive shelter all the facts in the world?

"It's complicated," she told me. "Physics says that for every action there is reaction. Much the same is true of facts. Facts string across centuries, knocking each other down like dominoes. If, for example, Charles Martel had not defeated Abd al-Rahman at Tours in 732, this conversation might be held in Chinese."

At age thirteen, the abstraction was too difficult for me to grasp.

"If Israel Putnam had not been at the battle of Breed's Hill, the American Revolution might have failed. We might still bend our knee to an English king."

I almost understood, and was proud to know that the Battle of Bunker Hill had actually been fought on Breed's. In those days children still studied history.

"But you are correct about Boston," Elizabeth told me. "Whenever anything good or bad rises in American history, look for its source in Boston. You may not find it there, but Boston is a very good place to start." Anger gradually drained from her voice as she taught me, while I did not even understand that she was teaching. She gently, but firmly closed the drawer of the filing cabinet. "Do not visit here for a week," she said, and her voice was grim. "I do not want you to see the hatch from that drawer."

When I returned after a week of wishing to be with her, the Archive had suffered distress. Through nearly three centuries some cabinets had impressed the outlines of their bases in the pine floor. Now, here and there, tiny lines appeared showing the cabinets shifted by a quarter inch. Although the day twisted before the violent cold of northeast storm, the Archive lay cloaked in the memory of heat. Elizabeth seemed not herself. Wrinkles of sadness around blue eyes exceeded wrinkles of happiness. Glowing silver hair had lost some lustre.

"True witchery returns," she said. "Warlocks ride an ancient gale across the world."

"What hatched?"

"It was enormous and black-winged and strong. The wings radiated heat and caused wind." She looked toward a row of cabinets holding 16th and 17th century documents. "A thousand dark facts hatched with it. Every mindless fact of intolerance that ever spun to sleep awakened. A great cloud of facts." She looked at the backs of her hands where veins now stood prominent, hands that suddenly seemed old. She looked at my young face. "I hope I have not waited too long," she murmured, but she did not explain.

1928 whirled past, and much of 1929. Virginia Wolfe published Orlando, Amelia Earhart flew the Atlantic, Georgia O'Keeffe painted Nightwave, the first Mickey Mouse cartoon appeared, and Benito Mussolini published his autobiography.

On Thursday, October 24th of 1929 when I was fifteen, a hatch began among bank records extending to the times of Alexander Hamilton and John Jay. Elizabeth watched the bulging file, and she watched me as she made a decision. "I feel my age," she said, "which means that you must grow strong quickly. This time I will not tell you to stay away."

On Tuesday, October 29th, The Great Depression sluggishly emerged to dry its wings. It was an enormous gray moth, of a size too large for an insect. The thick body hung over spindly legs like a flatiron perched on finishing nails. Wings beat as if the creature were tired, and would never cease to be tired. Wingbeats were whispers of sorrow as it rose into darkness between beams. Gray light flooded the Archive, and even I felt old.

"There is howling and tearing in Europe," Elizabeth murmured, "and now this." She turned to me with the tenderness of a mother, but with the straightforward tones of a big sister. "Are you still an adventurer? Will you undertake the greatest adventure of all?"

I trusted her then, as I trust her spirit which still occupies this archive. By then it was obvious that one need not fly around the world to find adventure. Here, in this creaking archive, dwelt more power than could be generated by all the engines ever built.

She looked across the Archive, at rows of filing cabinets, at mementos of the past, at shelves of books rising into darkness. "Who controls history controls the future," she whispered. "Who serves history, perhaps serves the future. It's a Gordian problem, and it may be time to cut the knot."

When she looked at me she must have seen an earnest but unformed Yankee mind. She was courageous, because even now the very idea causes me to fear. "If we end up cutting knots," she said, "you'll have to know what you're doing."

The years of study began. They were years marking the world's anguish, but for me they were the happy years. We did not simply study the sweep and flow of history. We studied ways to bag a liar.

As the world heated up, the visits of liars to the Archive became more frequent. While Germany began to rage, and while Stalin commenced killing twenty million of his own people; and, while facts hatched and rose like demons into darkness, liars congregated.

The liars were occasionally historians, but were more often genealogists. Some were the representatives of politicians. They came to the Archive with briefcases and cordial smiles, and it was their intent to create an America that had never existed. They called for old records, but were selective about which records they read. A few of the liars were preachers, but the worst of all were the apostles of hatred.

And, of course, a few were not liars. It became increasingly important to know the difference.

"None of them can comprehend all of history," Elizabeth explained. "The ground rule is this: Are they here to seek understanding, or are they here to prove a point? If they're here to prove a point, be ruthless."

I watched her pinion many a liar. These were the days when hate-mongers talked about 'UnAmerican Jewry'.

"The facts are," Elizabeth whispered to one such rascal, "that Jews entered Georgia as early as the 1730s. They had synagogues in New York well before 1763. I suggest, sir, that Hebrew roots in this nation are deeper than those of your own family." She then smiled in a most friendly manner. "Review your conclusions and see if they can withstand public scrutiny. I will be obliged to refute you in the press."

It was an age of liars. Henry Ford lingered in the background as the hate-monger Father Coughlin, Priest of Royal Oak, stepped forth. By 1937, when I was twenty-three, antisemitism swept our nation and the world. Neville Chamberlain became Prime Minister of Britain, and Lord Halifax made a visit of appeasement to Hitler.

Across the world other people fought back. Karen Horney published The Neurotic Personality of Our Times, and Dos Passos published U.S.A. Marietta Blau measured cosmic radiation, and Picasso painted Guernica.

On September 1, 1939, Hitler's armies drove into Poland, and the Archive filled with wind. World War II was a monster in black with blood-reddened wings. The brick walls of the Archive seemed about to push outward. Swarms of black flies and black bees circled into darkness between the beams. The stench of putrification followed the creature when solid oak doors blew open and it flapped into the night. Half of the file cases of history opened like screaming maws.

"We must fish or cut bait," Elizabeth said. "I suppose I always knew it would come to this." She turned to me. "You are very young."

By then I was twenty-five. I responded by saying that I was getting older by the minute.

"It's dangerous to take a tuck in history," she told me. "The problems are moral and ethical. They are also practical."

It seemed to me that no nation could stop Hitler. That was practical.

"For good or ill," Elizabeth whispered, "this will be the great act of my life. It will exact a price." She stood before a neglected file in a dark corner.

"We are Bostonians," she said, "and Boston town is a prototype of America. It carries darkness and light. It is ruled by stern New England conscience." She was resolute, but for a while she hesitated. "My conscience says to leave facts alone. My logic tells me to contain them. A third alternative is to fight facts with facts. Maybe that is honorable."

She reached into the file and drew forth a badly woven orange chrysalis. "Dormant since 1917 and not ready to hatch," she said. "God help us all."

A prematurely hatched fact is always awkward. Sometimes it is deformed. When Elizabeth cupped the fact in her hands and breathed it into life, the chrysalis split to reveal an ungainly creature that gnawed at its own legs as its wings dried. "It is cruelly pulled forth," Elizabeth whispered. "We can only hope it is strong enough. This creature is the Spirit of the Russian people."

The fact rose on wings of green and gold and red. On June 22nd, 1941, German troops invaded Russia. They expected to encounter two hundred enemy divisions. They encountered more than three hundred and fifty.

Whether Elizabeth's action was correct or not, she was correct in knowing there would be a price. As the tyrant Hitler departed the world's stage, the tyrant Stalin stepped more firmly forth. In 1945 the war ended and I was thirty-one. Elizabeth was feeble through age and grave responsibility. She lived long enough to see the chrysalis of the League of Nations fly forth as the hopeful green hatch of the U.N.

"I shall become a cabbage moth," she whispered. "My soul will flutter above gardens, white-winged." By then we were such friends that we could read many thoughts between us. "The Yankee disposition is judgmental," she told me. "It sometimes forces action." This was the only defense she ever offered, if it was a defense. "I never wanted power," she said. "I only wanted to serve. Plain Elizabeth Smith."

Her coffin lies in our sparse New England soil, but her spirit sometimes darts whitely from darkness between the beams. She visited often during those years when I reluctantly carried the power to change history.

The 1950s roared onto the scene as liars congregated. Joe McCarthy descended into the madness of a witch hunt. Nixon made his Checkers speech. Television quacked its way into American homes, and hypesters learned that Khrushchev made hot copy. American troops ranged along the Main-line-of-resistance in Korea, and other Americans fought as well. Martin Luther King Jr. stepped forward in Alabama. Arthur Miller published The Crucible, and once more appeared Esther Forbes' A Mirror For Witches.

Change pulsed as the nation became a world power. Marriage and divorce rates rose, as did birth rates, insanity, and suicide. Facts hatched in such great numbers that for weeks together I did not leave the sounds and flurryings of the Archive. I became expert at bagging liars.

"Sir," I would say to some political opportunist who wished to build an America that never existed, "the first revolutionaries in our history were Anne Hutchinson who came to Massachusetts in 1634, and Roger Williams in 1636. Neither was political, but each understood political hounds. Hounds such as yourself."

In 1962, when I was fifty-eight, a shy child of about ten stood before the Archive on a chilly autumn day. Her school coat barely covered her knees, and her short dark hair snugged tightly beneath a worn scarf. Her nose leaked because of the cold, and her cheeks were chapped and red. Her grandparents had obviously been members of the Italian immigration that came to Boston town in the early 20th century. A girl from good stock, for immigrants by definition must be adventurers.

For the next three years she occasionally returned to stand watching the Archive. In those three years files bulged and the hatch increased. By 1965 bizarre insects began to rise on psychedelic-colored wings. Turmoil lived between the darkened beams, and turmoil rocked the nation. Malcolm X died of gunshot. Martin King marched from Selma to Montgomery. There were riots in Watts. However, 1965 also marked the seven hundred and fiftieth anniversary of the Magna Carta.

On a December day winds blasted young trees where once had stood mighty elms. I watched the girl walk timidly toward the great oak doors, and I opened one of them gently so she would not be frightened. "This place has proved good shelter against most storms," I said, and remembered Elizabeth. "You must warm yourself with a cup of tea."

"My name is Theresa Marie Lauricella," she said, "and I didn't mean to bother you."

"And mine is Amanda Tilton," I told her. "Plain Amanda Tilton. Not much bothers me."

She would become the child I never had, the daughter who might have been mine were it not that adventurers become absorbed in adventure. As she became comfortable at the Archive, she combined a ready smile with dancing feet. In her practical manner, she viewed her adolescence as an inconvenience. She stood amazed and only a little frightened by dark wings; but she stood absolutely thrilled at the emergence of true butterflies.

By 1968, when Theresa was sixteen, police rioted in Chicago, and Muriel Spark published The Prime Of Miss Jean Brodie. American conscience gathered dust amidst the howling, or it muttered questions while weeping over answers.

Theresa's own adventure began to incubate. It was my selfish hope that I would be allowed to remain a faithful keeper of facts. History might not force me into action.

It is true that through my career I occasionally breathed life into a fact, but it was always a fact that illuminated other facts. In the '60s I breathed life into Eastern philosophy and religion. In the '70s, as musicianship declined, I would breathe life in to the spirit of music. Sarah Caldwell would become conductor of the Metropolitan Opera. Musical groups ceased to hide behind their drummers. Leonard Bernstein gave the first performance at the Kennedy Arts Center.

Theresa need learn our history of darkness and light. She needed to take firm hold on the purity of her conscience. She must learn how to bag a liar. More than all else, she had to learn the responsibility of power. About us lay facts for the taking and the twisting. We might launch them, or house them in boxes of Bessemer or finer steel.

In the years from '65 through '79 I progressed from age fifty-one to sixty-five, and felt my movements slow. Pope John Paul II was elected in '78. He visited America in '79. Theresa grew to womanhood and beauty. Her long hair reflected lights, swinging above dancing feet that moved like song across the old pine floor. It was her firm hand that began to faithfully record the hatch of that period: two million dead in Biafra, fuel shortages, Watergate. Dark wings beat darkly between the beams where, on the gravest occasions, also fluttered small white wings.

Wrinkles of laughter and sadness appeared around Theresa's eyes. The 1980s hatched. They emerged as a praying mantis, strong claws, and wings like wire. The creature's wings screeched as it rose into darkness.

"You are still very young," I said, "yet, you have worked hard."

"Getting older by the minute."

"There are computers. New ways of lying. There must be new ways to bag liars."

She loves a humorous situation. "We might be faithful to our trust if we practice on Mr. Kissinger."

As Babel grew the nation fell before forces of arrogance. Stupidity and greed are not new in human affairs, but now they were regarded as virtues. Saber rattling increased. The nation's symbol became a mouth, as the arms race hurried rapidly toward war.

I was deeply alarmed. We might put an end to a pandering president, or to a pornographer, but such facts would gnaw away at Constitutional law. A change was needed, not only in the nation but in the world. I spent many a night grieving, many a night denying action.

Help arrived as spirits congregated. They came to me from where they fluttered above gardens. They dropped on silent wings from beneath the beams. Small white moths danced and circled in the air before my face. Whispers of conscience, and whispers of resolution dwelt among them. Puritan voices they were, but some of them were tender. I understood that America is at its best when it is just.

These were the souls of the keepers of facts. This archive has now stood for three hundred and forty years. Through all that time someone has held the reins of power. Elizabeth was not the first, and Theresa will not be the last.

They understood that a catalyst was needed. This was not a matter of minor change. This called for broad strokes of the pen across the pages of history.

When I reviewed the histories of all the nations of the world, attention gradually centered on Poland; and I felt no small amount of terror. That nation first appeared in the ninth century. It is a nation of idealism and destruction, of art and intolerance. It was the homeland of Copernicus and Conrad and Madame Curie, but also the home of the Vasa Dynasty.

Babel grew. Liars strutted while Afghanistan stumbled and the Middle East became a powder keg of terrorism. History pressed, and I controlled my mighty fear.

"This will be the great act of my life," I whispered to Theresa, "and there will be a price. When this bird flies it will shriek."

The chrysalis holding the Spirit of Poland was faded royal purple with broad streaks of white. It bulged with courage, but it also bulged with pogroms. I remembered my youth, the hate mongers of the '30s, the killing beliefs of the Axis.

"It is cruelly pulled forth," I whispered as I breathed it into life. "May God help it and all of us."

The hatching was tortuous. The chrysalis shuddered. It vibrated, resistant and thick-walled. When the creature emerged it lay helpless, more like a baby than an insect. It finally rose on scarlet wings; a crippled butterfly beating unsteadily into darkness. From files across the Archive rose gnats and locusts, but also rose broad-winged creatures of color and beauty and hope.

History churned. Great forces were generated. Dominoes fell, and there is little more to say. The Berlin Wall is down. Europe once more enters turmoil. Old hatreds surface, and new tyrants stand ready to tread the stage. I fear not for myself, but for Theresa. She need be strong. Unto her is bequeathed this fire.

And I? I never wished to take action. I only wished to serve; to be plain Amanda Tilton. My personal price is heavy. I never birthed a child, though I have helped form my dear Theresa. Facts, some of them butterflies, have warmed to life in my hands. Facts are my children. My personal price is the weight of responsibility that follows me to new adventure.

It is time to spin my own cocoon, to draw my shroud closely and enter the gauze of history. I spin my metamorphosis toward our sparse New England soil. My shoulders slowly urge their way to wings.

My soul will become a cabbage moth. It will dance white above gardens which carry their own sense and symmetry of facts. I will serve as one of the keepers of the earth, one of the keepers without number.

Yet, I will visit here often in Theresa's early years. She is afloat in waters great and deep. Perhaps, as times become terribly troubled, Elizabeth and I will meet among the dusty beams of this archive, circling down from darkness. We will drop to glide about Theresa. We will brush our wings against the air before her face. We will dance most whitely.

The Patriarch

"A HILL TOO STEEP FOR SLEDDING." SOL SAID THAT TWO DAYS BE-fore he died. "God is a character, but picky where He puts His hills."

"If you are ten years old," I said, "it is a wonderful hill." I knew what he was going to next say about God. I just wanted to hear him say it.

"A hill to keep old men alive," Sol said. "Puts sparkle in the toes." He inched up the hill, and he looked at the surrounding brick build-ings which had been standing for about as long as we had; which in Sol's case was seventy years, and in my own case seventy-three. The sunlight over Seattle seemed to flatten the red brick, and it glazed the dusty windows of the mostly abandoned buildings. My old man's feet were comfortably sweaty, for at this age sweat is a luxury.

"So being picky, He wouldn't waste a good sled hill in such a country," Sol said. "This place has no snow. Remember, this is the rabbi telling you."

I have often wished that I were a Jew. No matter how old they are, or where they are, Jews have fathers.

In mixed sunlight and shadow, in Seattle, we were spending our last day together. We both knew it, and we were giving thanks for such a day. At our backs Puget Sound lay like a blue pond, and the distant mountain range was still peaked with snow. The spring melt had not reached above seven thousand feet. It was a day to be born on, to be married on. It was a day for old men to walk in the sun. It was a day for falling in love, for sailing to India; a day for buying flowers—spice—tea—silks—a day for giving flowers—tea—silks; like old-time suitors beckoning to wives of many years.

A gift of a day, a day of gifts. A Victorian day, complete with the lace of sunlight.

"The belly," Sol said. "Think about it." He took a step that covered eight inches, then rested on his walking stick. He seemed to hover over the stick, an enormous man, but fading now. His hands were smooth, pale, and his nose was a slab, his graying eyebrows like bushes sprouting on rocky ground. His face was also pale.

"Your belly?"

"Mine will do," he said, "since it gets the operation."

"I worry about Benjy," I told him. "Jerome can maybe handle this. Sam can maybe handle this." I was naming his three sons. Benjy is the youngest, and Benjy is forty-two. "Can Sarah handle this?" Sarah is his wife.

"God is a trickster," Sol told me. "He gives me a Presbyterian belly. Don't tell me about Sarah."

"Still, I worry."

"You have better things to do," Sol said. "I'll worry for you. Quit worrying. It infarcts the belly." In the street, between the old buildings, and weaving casually uphill with its lights blinking slowly like the driver had forgotten to shut them off, an ambulance headed for the hospital at the top of the hill. We were headed for that same hospital. The ambulance stopped at a traffic light. When the light changed it rolled backward for a short distance before surging forward. A whole line of traffic rolled backward, then surged forward.

"The heart," Sol said, "is a Jew. The mouth, the tongue, all Yiddish." He stepped another eight inches. "They have all the fun. Think of the fatted calves, the wine, the loaves of bread, the cheeses. Seventy years across the tongue, down the gullet, to feed a Presbyterian."

"The rabbi is telling me."

"Because," he explained, "the belly has no fun. The heart and tongue have fun. The poor belly does the slave work. A sweat shop beneath this buckle." He patted his waist. There was no buckle. He could no longer wear a belt. His gut was swollen.

When we were younger, when we were fifty and forty-seven and first met, Sol was muscular and quick; at least quick for a rabbi. I, Louis Pegourie, was also muscular, but quicker. My quickness came from an early life spent in logging with my father's crews in Canada. When my father was killed in a logging accident, I became a reader of books. Most likely because the books held sense, and the accident was senseless. When Sol and I met, I worked at the public library.

The rabbi and the reader. Twenty years. Not a long time after all. Once a month in those years, or at least once every six weeks, we had managed to spend an afternoon together. "Because," Sol had once told me, "I get tired of only the Jews. You are a nonsectarian friend of books. You are greatly, wonderfully irreligious."

"Not irreverent," I recall saying.

"What am I telling you? Was I making words about reverence?"

It is supposed to be terribly hard to be old. I don't find it so. It is hard to be sick, to be sometimes weak. The worst part is that the world treats you as if you were stupid. This man beside me, for instance, had written a larger number of books than many people have read. I have done my share as well. Yet the world hollers at you and ignores you; and that is what is wrong with being old. The hills grow steeper, yes, but old men still walk those hills. Young men do not have the time. We stepped forward, and I wondered how a concrete sidewalk could be laid on such a steep hill. Surely the wet concrete would run downhill before it set. What is hard about being old is that there is less time to learn, and to think about what you learn.

"Sarah," Sol said, and stepped further up the hill. "1934. New York. Depression."

"I was twenty-three."

"I was twenty, but she was seventeen," Sol said. "Her father was a practical man. All starch. I won a bet." Beside us a street tree was just coming into leaf. It was only a little stick of a tree, and to protect it the street department had placed an iron grate around it. The grate stood like a little fence. Sol tapped the grate with his stick. "No consideration for dogs," he said. "Suppose you are a poodle with a bladder that feels like a Great Dane. Suppose you come along here, your eyes swimming with pee, and they've put up this grate."

"You'd pee."

"But think of the compromise. A world without honor." He turned to look back down the hill. "We are progressing," he said, "and I am in no hurry." Out on Puget Sound the sea traffic was heavy. A blue and white Alaska ferry looked like it was shaving the bows of an outgoing tanker, although of course it was not. A small Navy craft, maybe a minelayer, was a black dot beside the larger ships. A hundred or more sailboats were like snowflakes on the water.

"Her father did not want her engaged to a scholar. The Great Depression. Even practical men could not get jobs. So who needs a scholar?"

"You bet with him? Practical men don't bet. I have it first hand from Montaigne. I have it first hand from Thoreau."

"Montaigne," Sol said. "I have my doubts. What does a French politician know, him and his phony tower?" He turned back up the hill. "I bet myself," he said, "that I could get a job. If I lost, I lost her." He tapped the sidewalk twice with his stick. "Romance. Of course, I was younger then." He stepped upward a bit more strongly. "Among the Jews," he said, "a father is no joke." His belly was hurting him. If you know a man long enough, you learn to read most of the different ways in which he smiles. "Still," he said, "I made a joke. I went to her uncle, her father's brother, and borrowed ten dollars...." We were near the corner where the ambulance had stopped. Traffic lined up behind a stop light.

"The first stop lights in New York," he said, "were installed in 1928. They had a bronze statue on top of each one. Before that the police directed traffic...of course, that has nothing to do with the joke. With the ten dollars I bought a job from a man who was selling jobs. 'Can you cut flank steak,' he says. I say, do you want the ten dollars? He says, 'report for work' and sent me to a restaurant. On the way I stop at my aunt's flat because my aunt has the brains of the family. She—one—two—three—teaches me how to slice any kind of meat. I mean, here, even, pig's knuckles." He watched the traffic light. "We have to get across this side street," he said. He stared at the sky, and deadpanned. "A little shove there, God. Let's have a little shove."

He was starting to make me angry. Sol always could do that.

"Don't die," I said. "Such a humorist. Such a loss to the world." He did not answer right away. We were busy crossing the street. It was a narrow street, but the crossing was all uphill.

"In two years I was head cook," he told me. "Don't worry about Sarah. Sarah has sons. This business about Sarah. Do you think the Book of Ruth is a joke?"

"You are the humorist."

"The joke was," Sol said, "that Sarah's uncle had to borrow the ten dollars from Sarah's father." We stood on the corner, not yet ready to tackle the last long block. That next block was the steepest part of the hill. My legs hurt, especially the one that had been broken once when working in the woods. Still, if he could haul that belly I could haul a couple of hurting legs.

"I courted," Sol said. "Ah. Oh. I bought flowers at a secondhand flower shop on 34th. I swore to myself that someday she would have a house and I would raise flowers for her. To this day I don't really know how much she likes flowers." He looked into the street. "Uh, oh, poor Benjamin. The fix is in."

A large, new car pulled into the side street and stopped. It parked illegally, and Sol's son Benjy climbed out. Benjy is big, like his father, and he wears expensive dark suits, dark like his shiny car, silk ties, a diamond ring. He walked toward us looking for all the world like a little boy trapped in grown-up clothes.

"Papa," he said. "Hello, Louis," he said.

Sol leaned on his stick. Waited. Benjy was actually blushing. "Your brothers sent you," Sol asked, and his voice was kind.

"They are waiting at the hospital. They are worried because you are late." Benjy's voice was a whisper of embarrassment.

"The hospital has been waiting for seventy years," Sol said, and his voice was still kind. "You go along now, Benjy, and we'll be there soon enough."

"Papa, I can give you a ride."

"This is your father speaking."

"Yes, papa."

"But later, you will drive Louis home."

Benjy, a big man, Benjy, and yet he walked back to his car and did not look big at all. He was too embarrassed. Sol turned, to look up the last long grade. "This is getting serious," he said. "I expected that it would." He looked across the street at an abandoned house. "They had fine workers in brick around this city. A pity for the buildings. So misused." The second floor of the house still had windows. The sun lay like golden satin across the dusty windows.

"So it's serious," he said. "All right my friend, we proceed." He stepped upward a short pace, and then another short pace. "We go to rejoin the Jews."

"We are meeting your family."

"Don't be fooled. Before this is through, half of my last congregation will come through that hospital." He looked further up the hill, where the hospital rose tall and white in the sun. "Temple builders," he said. "Physicians need temples. It makes them secure about their balls."

"Why are you doing this?" It was a fair question. The man was dying. The operation would simply kill him a bit sooner.

"The family has hope. The family believes in miracles." His face was even paler, if that was possible. "Miracles. Strange." He rested on his stick, then turned once more to watch the water and the mountains. Dark patches lay here and there across the water, shaded patches from high and scattered clouds. He turned back, upward.

"My first congregation met in a store front. Then the store front was torn down. We met in the storeroom of another store, like old-time Quakers in living rooms. A long time ago. Now there are babies in my last congregation, who I don't even know their names. Babies. It continues, but the congregation is too large. It needs to split and regroup. Hah. Try telling them that."

We stepped for a while in silence. I wished that we could weep together, but Sol was not the weeping type. We were both too old to rail against this, and death itself is only one more adventure. Death is no problem, but dying is frightening. I thought of my first wife, Jenny, who died in childbirth. I have no sons, no daughters.

"My friend," he said when we were halfway up the block, "do not be fooled. I am no Moses. For more than forty years I have led my people, but Moses was denied. I have never been denied. The rabbi is luckier than Moses."

"You have a fine family. You have a fine reputation. Sol, it is all deserved."

"I also have the Jews," he said, "and that is important. And yes, maybe I deserve it, maybe not, but I will not complain against it. Meanwhile, I have a burden for you."

"What do you need? What can I give?"

"My family," he said. "I know them. When I am gone they will require something from you."

"Whatever I can do."

"Remember that," he said. "Do what you can do. Do not try to do what you cannot."

When we arrived at the hospital, ascending the last of the hill and walking across a courtyard of white stone, his family did not come flocking into the courtyard, the sons, the wives of sons. They managed to restrain themselves and allow him that final courtesy. Sarah met him at the door. He turned back to me. He embraced me, kissed my cheek. "Go with God," he said. "Benjy will drive you home."

When Benjy dropped me off I went to my room, and stayed waiting for the inevitable phone call. I read from work of St. John Of The Cross, and a detective novel. In two days Sol was dead, a quiet death under anesthetic. That was the only bad part, for knowing

Sol, he would have been so interested in dying. I regretted for him that he had not been awake. At the same time, I was occupied with my own grief. For two more days I remained in my room, confused and sometimes weeping. I thought of my second wife, and the loss did not seem less with the years. I remembered Sol's kiss, his blessing. Then, on a spring evening, I walked a block down the hill to the Chinese store where they know me. I bought two candles, special ones that were not on the store's shelves. Religion is a joke, but St. Therese and St. Jude are not jokes.

The spring seemed to drag. It did not have the explosions of flowers that have attended other springs. The flowers bloomed, but nature itself seemed reluctant. Benjy came to visit twice that spring. He did not know what he wanted. Talking to him, it was clear that the family was not doing well. It handled its grief, but it was huddling together. Fearful. Some amorphous force seemed to be attempting to spread the family, disperse it. I could see the problem, could give no help. Sol had been so strong, that the family no longer felt the force of strength in their world. Benjy was having a terribly hard time, and his formal mourning did not seem to be helping much. A ritual that was not working.

I mostly spent the days walking in the sun. The nights were difficult. Memories. I have lost everyone, except for Sol's family. In the nights I thought of my lost wives. I have had good luck with women, but the women had no luck. My first wife was Jenny. We were married in our early twenties. We had seven happy, kid-crazy years together. She died in childbirth. The child died. I did not touch another woman until I was fifty, because of fear. Then I married Margaret, who was my same age, and who worked beside me at the library. We had thirteen quiet years, and I woke one morning to find her dead beside me. Stroke. I wanted to die and could not. Life insists. Interminably. There is no honor in suicide. Sometimes at night I recalled the burden Sol had given me. I wondered what that service was which must yet be performed.

Benjy is a fine man. Of Sol's sons, perhaps Benjy is the best. He is sensitive. When he finally came to me, in June, he was not phony. He was not lying.

"My mother is dying," he said. "I do not think I can bear this." He sat, all fine suit and tie, in my old room. He did not see the faded wallpaper, the smoky ceilings. He only saw me. "She is in the hospital," he said. "Louis, please come with me."

Naomi. The Book of Ruth. Maybe Sarah was dying, but I had my doubts. Sarah had sons, and those sons had just lost a father. Those sons had not yet gotten hold of their individual strengths. Dying, to Sarah, was out of the question, no matter how ill. However, there was no possible way to explain that to Benjy.

"You go to the hospital," I told him, "and I will be along directly." I live on the hill, not a good place for an old man, but it is near the library. When Benjy left I walked the hill to the hospital, as a testament to Sol. A trellis of roses stood behind a fence. I reached through the fence, picked two.

Sarah is a small woman. Tough. As tough as her sons would be someday. Outside her room, one of her daughters-in-law, Hannah, waited, and supervised some of the grandchildren who clustered in the waiting room or drifted up and down the hallway. Boys and girls, some of them nearly young men and women. Soon there would be great-grandchildren.

"Louis," Hannah said, "there is more trouble inside that room than you can see at first. Everyone is nearly out of control." Hannah is tall, fair-haired, and a woman to trust. A high school teacher. If a high school teacher says a situation is out of control, it pays to listen.

"Sam," I asked. Sam is the oldest son. He should be leading.

"He is trying," she told me. "He is trying so hard that he just adds to the problem."

The men were there, the women, and three of the oldest grandchildren. Sarah's bed was raised so that she was nearly sitting. When I entered there was silence, and it was pretty clear that there had been little but silence. That is no way to run an illness.

"So, Sarah," I said, "is this a joke you are making?"

She smiled. It was as if she had not smiled for a long time and was pleased because she remembered how. Her hair, nearly all gray, is getting a little thin. Her small mouth is still firm, and the smile seemed girlish. She reached to touch my hand. "Louis," she said, "a few tests, a little flushing of the system. Tell these people."

"Wailing walls are in bad taste," I said to whoever was listening, and they all were. "This is a matter of taste. You want to remember that." I looked at them. Benjy, troubled, fear in his eyes. Sam, nearly sullen from his responsibility. Jerome, a little too eager, like a man who wants to do something, anything, to help; a man to set in motion, if a direction could be discovered. The wives, Grace and Janet, the children, Jacob and Clara and Sally; the children, confused.

"Look at them," I said to Sarah. "They look like a Mormon choir. That Joseph Smith might have lived to see this. So many Jewish converts."

There was a stirring in the room. Something half felt. Like the stirring of faint hope. Jerome took a deep breath. He looked like he was about to charge back and forth, back and forth, in help or celebration. Jerome is the lean, wiry one of Sol's sons. He is quick. He is fast in reading a situation.

They needed something, and they sensed that they were about to find it. They had been so fearful, so confused, that they had not even known what they needed. They needed to know that force and strength still lived.

"My friend the rabbi," I said, "if he were here, would make a joke. Joseph Smith would run. Humorless, these Mormons." I raised my right hand, but slowly. Sarah took my left hand. Her small hand was anything but frail. She pressed my hand, a kind of confidence and reassurance; and I needed it, because it was going to take nerve and luck to pull this off. Jerome stepped to the doorway, whispered, and Hannah entered the room. The children stood, nearly afraid. My right hand floated in the air, untrembling; an old man's hand, but it did not tremble.

"Benjamin," I said. "Here beside me." He stepped forward, confused but glad. I lowered my hand, kissed him, took his hand. Sarah released my left hand.

No, Sol had not been Moses, but he had led his people. He had led these people, and when he died he had the Jews. Sol was lucky. Golden lucky.

I began to speak, and I lowered my left hand, pressing it gently against Sarah's cool forehead. The words, the old, old words, came so easily. My voice did not tremble. I felt the union, the community, the family return to itself; as steadily, ageless, I gave my reverent, patriarchal blessing.

The Priest

[*This tale was written after a year of study over the journal of George Fox.*]

In the beginning was the Word and he had known that all his life. Now, with his thick hair gray and the rough beard too often pointed into his breast, he was no longer sure that he knew enough. Rafe told himself that beyond the Word must be the thrall or the song; world without end.

Winter without end.

"Unto all of ye who somewhere dream. This is a prayer." He would chant across the ice. "To all music that yet dwells. To what heat still lies in the ice-covered hills. To the embering sun."

Sometimes in deep winter the world held a hint of shine. When he was wrapped, bundled and insulated against the cold it was possible to be abroad for a few minutes. The Diggers never came in deep winter. In deep winter the sky was orange on days of shine. Usually it was brown. The thin air made him suck hard through the net of mesh swaddled around his head.

There was padding beneath the slit glasses. Rafe's father had taught the care of eyes. To think of his father and to see...That was enough to make a man believe in all words and songs because himself, a man, was there to say or sing them.

"At the end of the world all is holy." Rafe remembered his father always.

Sometimes Rafe's words were like the air. The song was thin and disappeared beneath the grinding of the ice. Some years brought more ice than others. The towers were down. The tall buildings were stumps. On the surface of all the world that he could see there was only the movement of ice. His songs were like showers of dying sparks. Even the voice of The God was lost or distant most of the time.

The God did not expect faith. The God gave knowledge. If the knowledge was old and the experience long past it was still remembered. The God drove invisible through the thin air and above the ice, through the broken and icy rooms of the crushed buildings and across the storage pits that held the food-dead who were encased in ice. The God passed silent through the cellars and sub-cellars of those same buildings where the cold touched but did not quite overcome the dying heat of the enclosing earth.

There were cries in the dark and the movement of The God through scrabbled passages. The rats and the raccoons and the cats and the new creatures fought over a dying economy. Flesh and fur, meat traded back and forth, the numbers diminished with the years and the occasional raids of The Diggers. Screams in the dark. Pack. Hunters. The clear force of The God drove through the burrows and above the crush of life and death, above the squalling.

When the fog rose in middle winter, around the old July, a sense of tranquility paced the slow movement of The Diggers through the dead city. In old July the sun was red. The visitors came from their great burrows in strength. In old days they had come to raid. Now Rafe did not know why they came. They were men who tramped like conquerors in insulated clothing. The areaways between buildings were broad canals of slow melt. Guides led their appointed packs along the surrounding ice ledges. The movement of The Diggers was confident because of their superiority. They considered themselves the self-blessed. They were the sons of the wise and their race was perpetuated. Rafe would watch them from an obscure outpost of broken masonry that was edged with decaying ice.

"These too are holy." His father's name had been Jubal.

Rafe would watch The Diggers and try to feel love. He would try to feel sadness. He felt little of either. When a man has lived long enough and thought hard enough there is not much under any sky that can make him sad. Even when they shot at him it did not make him sad, and they had only shot at him twice on the times when he had been careless of his concealment.

The clear force of The God drove soundless through the air.

Rafe was preacher to rats, theologian to the beasts, overseer of a grotesque evolution of blind life that scampered and crawled. Creatures of the dark did not develop cones in the eyes. It had not always been that way.

"This is how the world ended." His father had been the greatest of his teachers. "It is also how another world began."

"In the ending there was fire." As a child Rafe had repeated the words as a duty.

"Such is the dogma." His father was tough and believed little. "The fire lasted for a while. There was the heat of bombs and words. There was the hot shame of expeditious governors, but it was temporary fire. There were weapons to throw and the persuasion to throw them, but these would finally mean little."

"A lance had been fired at the sun."

"Such is the dogma." His father was small and stringy and as tough as the rats. "The lance is symbolic. Lances were fired at the atmosphere, at the depths. Mountains and volcanic systems were lanced. Prairies, forests, meadows. It is symbolic."

"In the days of our fathers . . ." Rafe would begin the loved ritual.

"Four generations are passed since the fields."

"I bow to the life of the fields. I sing of the grain . . ."

In pockets here and there beneath the shattered buildings were the sacred artifacts. They were protected from teeth by vaults of steel.

". . . clothe with boiler plate."

"And the people said, 'Now has The God spoken, and now do his people turn even as scavengers unto the bowels of the earth.'"

"What that means," his father said, "is that the people saved what they could of the things they believed were Godly. It wasn't much because it took them years to understand that the things were being destroyed or eaten."

"There was great revulsion."

"You learn the words," his father said. "Think beyond the words. Yes, in their grief and fear they hated all things for a while. They destroyed many of those things."

The sacred artifacts still made Rafe tremble. There were voices and eyes and ears in those boxes if one thought symbolically. There was the tactile and there was scent. In one box was an instrument made of wood, the strings gone, the casing cracked. There was another made of brass. There were pictures and books and statues.

There were opticals. There were jujus, pieces of fabric and ribbon and crucifixes and something called leaves that were delicate and smelled warm. The leaves had once been green. This his teachers told him. "Green is this color, here on this canvas. This part is the painting. This part is the canvas."

Rafe's father died old. Rafe praised his father as he ate him and gave thanks to The God for his father's success. Rats did not polish his father's bones. Against dogma Rafe interred them with the food-dead. It was then that there was revelation. The clear voice of The God was serene with love.

The voice told what his father had taught. The race was run and life was to impart to life.

Rafe searched for silence. Away from the grinding ice. Away from the hiss and howl and tearing of the beasts. Away from the thump and occasional vibration that The Diggers caused deep in the earth.

Through corridors, through abandoned rooms. The packs followed, stalked, screamed and fell on each other. Rafe had never known heat but the calm voice of The God was green.

By revelation he knew that he was the last man above ground, and he knew further that those below ground considered him inhuman. They considered him food. In the power of the voice he knew that The Diggers were mad. He wept for their madness and for his own.

"Two sects developed." Usually when his father taught they had been in the broken upper buildings. It imparted urgency to the teaching for it was impossible to remain for very long. "The two sects were the sect of The God and the sect of The Mind. They were believed antithetical."

"So it is taught, sir."

"They aren't," his father said. "I speak heresy, but it is an old heresy of little importance now." Like all other people Rafe knew or remembered, his father's hair was coarse and long. It was pulled crosswise beneath the chin, wound backward and tied at the back of the neck. The hair then spread under the rough clothing and fanned across the back. His father's hair was a cloak. When he was little, Rafe had placed his hands beneath the hair and felt warm.

"We are the last of the sect of The God," his father said. "The Diggers are of the sect of The Mind and they will outlive us. Then they will also pass. I cannot know what is important to them. Food, perhaps. There is a knowledge called populations. It is no longer useful to us."

"But for us, The Word."

"In our sect all are priests," his father said. "There is one duty, only. Remain coherent. Learn this well, for the duty is that we must end well."

"The sister is a priest?"

"The sister will not live. The mother will not live."

"You know this, sir?"

"It is the mother's choice and it is her heresy in which I join. She deals in life. I praise her."

"I will pray."

"Above is the ice, below the disease of the rats."

"Still, I will pray."

"Forget dogma."

In the time of silence with the green voice of The God in his mind, Rafe remembered all of his father's words. He remembered his father's grief. He was sustained by his father and by his father's hope that he, Rafe, would be the great priest.

The silence was a mistake. To be alone was to suffer madness. To suffer madness was to be incoherent. This his father had taught. He returned to the beasts and to the occasional thunder of The Diggers far beneath the city.

"There are so few of us." His father's voice mixed with the voice of The God. "That is good luck. We pass soon."

"The artifacts will remain."

"In the time of the last days of your grandfather fires died. It was easy to remain civilized when we had fuel. We must not become beasts."

"Some of our people no longer see or speak."

". . . so much to explain." His father crouched during the lessons. Heat was conserved in the crouch. "Some adapt. There is a knowledge called nutrition. Few adapt."

"The Diggers have heat."

"The Diggers have hydroponics. They have fuel and the tools to scrabble deep in the earth. They have light and government."

"They will survive. I am warm by their survival."

"They do not have The God," his father said.

Sometimes there was weakness. In the years after his father's death Rafe called to The God. He asked to remain coherent. "Only in the Word," he prayed. "Take the eyes."

The God did not want his eyes and The God did not need his words and the weakness always passed. Rafe sang, chanted, clapped and danced through the corridors. He would not allow himself to mumble or whisper. Song was but one of the names of The God.

Life was another. As he grew old, Rafe disclosed to himself that hated The God. The God did not care. When life departed it was vacuumed into The God. To praise rightly was to die. The diminished generations of beasts praised rightly.

"So taught the mystics," his father said. "Our being arises from life and returns to life. Our being is only a physical manifestation of life."

"Take my eyes," Rafe prayed.

The end would be soon. He was old. It had taken so long to become old. The world changed as he had become old.

Again, as in the long past, the tumbled cellars sometimes vibrated with the actions of The Diggers. Pulses in the earth. The faraway vibrations of machinery. It was a warm thing.

Twice in the time of the last three old July's the subcellars had been broken open with machines. Lights flashed, beasts fled, were netted, stunned, clubbed. The rapid silhouettes of men chased back and forth in the flash of the lights as they gathered meat. Rafe watched each time with a passageway at his back. On the time he was chased they were afraid to chase him far. He came to anticipate the gathering of meat. When the machines broke through there were warm drafts in the passageways.

During his last year he was content. He no longer hated The God. Deep winter came and stayed and passed. The pulses in the earth were sporadic. When they came they came as occasional heavy shocks. The Diggers did new things. He was warmed by the shocks because they felt like heresy. He thought of the mother and the sister and knew that heresy was the best prayer.

"I own my eyes," he told The God.

The old July returned. Water began to seep through the passageways. He loved his eyes and took them above ground.

The world was crystal. He had never known it this way. It was necessary to proceed slowly and with caution. He shadowed his eyes. The slit glasses allowed too much light. Rafe moved with a squint. The sun was nearly yellow.

There was melt among the food-dead. He accepted this as a sign and loved them. He spoke to his father's head, spoke exactly and at length to prove his coherency. He described the crystal world to his father. In this old July there was much melt.

The Diggers came from the burrows and he was hidden beside a wet outpost to watch. They came with caution this year. Their stride was harsh and they moved in larger groups. There were more of them and it caused a great fear in Rafe's mind. He crouched in the strange light. Awed, struck dumb at their harsh movement and numbers. He was driven by terror and fled. Into the passageways, the aisles, corridors, toward the sacred. The steel boxes were wet with melt. The voice of The God was gone.

He fumbled and almost dropped an artifact. He willed his movements to be slow. The God spoke. The artifacts were Rafe and Rafe was the artifacts. From the jujus he chose a ribbon. It was long and broad and smooth and continuous. It was life. It was the voice of The God.

His fear left and he moved toward the surface. Strange sounds repelled, fascinated, finally attracted him. He moved slowly to prepare his eyes. On the surface he crouched behind a broken wall.

Fire bloomed in the distance. He had never seen fire, but he knew that it must be fire. On the thin air was a garble of shouts, cries, a babel that was distorted and confused and rabid. He slid carefully away from the broken wall to scuttle forward. Words choked in his mouth. He was incoherent.

To sing them. He could only move erratically over the clumsy footing of melt. He found no song.

To make a noise then. He slowed and held the ribbon before him and began to chant. In his ears the chant seemed like the hiss of the beasts, but the ribbon gave strength and his voice grew stronger. He walked toward the fire, chanting, chanting, the words now splendid in his mind and almost understood. He was not afraid. He was not sad. He walked with love and chanted with a green voice. He knew that in the end it was only necessary to say to them that they must stop shooting at each other, they must stop shooting.

Tearing Up the Pasture

GRANDMA'S SPIRIT TSKS AT MY SHOULDER AS I STROKE CLEANLY with my cue. A cone of light clasps the rectangle of green felt. Invisible geometric lines connect brightly colored balls. Rails of the table are brown, the cue chalk is blue, and my left hand glows white with perfumed talc designed to be spread on baby bottoms. Grandma's spirit shudders—she's been tsking over my soul for a good many years—because the game of pool layers up sin like avalanche snow on mountains. Sooner or later that avalanche will fall, and zip, another loafer is headed for perdition.

Grandma has her point. Half of the game of pool amounts to loafing. It is a terrible waste of time. It's even worse in our small town bar, because there's only one pool table. The bar top glows with polish. Our bartender, Heidi, is young and lovely. She used to be talkative, but these days she plays cowboy laments on the jukebox while loggers drink and loafers loaf.

Grandma also believes that pool players hang around with bums, awful influences. Yep.

I arrived late in life to the game of pool. The early years were wasted in dreams, ambition, hope and work. From my age fifteen, to age sixty, pool tables sat at the back of bars while I sometimes sat at the front. Reverent murmurs occasionally spread from the rear of the joint as some miscreant dropped an impossible shot. When I turned sixty, the murmurs started to make sense.

When you turn sixty, retirement is not all that far away. Mine was basically a career decision. In these uncertain times it is always best to have a second occupation, and age sixty is a little late to master art or medicine. Hope stirred in my soul as I watched pool hustlers. It might still be possible to do some good for this world. It might still be possible to be exactly like them. Grandma didn't have all the facts.

My first and greatest teacher, a retired party-goer from North Carolina, went on the wagon for only one reason: the sauce messed up his game. His name is Hen. He retains a fondness for near-beer, Snickers bars, and high-right English on his rail shots. Deep dispute (theological antinomianism, at times) continues about high vs low English along the rail. I have actually seen first year physics textbooks spread on pool tables as one believer or another illustrated faith in his version of rotational forces.

Hen is of the pragmatic school: "Hell, boy, the shot went down. Don't talk to me about college."

He stands above the table, face round as a Carolina moon, wrinkles across forehead and down earlobes. His touch can be gentle as a puppy's tongue, or precise as a rifle shot. His stroke is fluid as a southern stream. His wisdom comes from hustling sailors, tourists, punks, Makahs, fishermen, loggers, plus other hustlers.

Hen is a small town hustler. He bets on few trick shots, and nothing slick. He plays a steady, psychological game that wears opponents down to despair or rage. Either is just fine. "It don't pay to get emotional." He confronts complex shots with a phrase learned during childhood on a farm. "Hold 'er, Newt, she's rarin'."

My second teacher, Jake, was also once a farm boy. Now he runs with city slickers, mostly ladies. His lies are fabulous. Even finer; I have never before known a sixty-eight-year-old who so deeply loves a bar fight. When he's without companionship, and when his eyes are not bruised shut, Jake is a master of trick shots and razzle-dazzle. "Three rails in the spittoon," he says, and drives a side-pocket, end-pocket shot, that curls across and nails the other side pocket Shadows lie in wrinkled hands, and light glows on heavily muscled arms. His cue becomes a magic wand waving rack after rack of balls solidly into the chutes. His bald head glows beneath the cone of light. Green felt brings back his boyhood, and he sees the table as 'forty acres of pasture.'

"Jake could-of made a name for himself," Hen says, "if he cut out the fightin' and the floozies."

We generally play eight-ball until a live one comes along. Then the game goes to nine-ball, and if it's a good hustle finally to three-ball. There's fame and fortune to be made here, but I'm not making them yet.

It's only a matter of time and practice. My instructors make me lag the cueball for hours. ("No other way to get the touch.") They draw diagrams on cocktail napkins. "We ain't playing pocket billiards, here, boy. We're playing pool."

I learn the subtilties of English, carrom, jump-shots, massé. I drive twenty miles to play on the worst pool table in the county. If you're hot on a bad table you can really show off on a good one. I know the names of good pool bars all across the state—the Artic Tavern in Artic, or the Chilled Alaskan over on Gun Club Road—because pool without a bar somehow loses lustre. Largely, I suppose, because bars are places for loafers.

What grandma missed is that there are times when only loafers may serve our common cause of humanity. Everyone else is too busy.

Like the time when Heidi, the daytime bartender, went home and stabbed her boyfriend John, the nighttime bartender; we did not play pool for three weeks. Heidi figured that John was 'fooling around', and probably John was. At any rate she missed his heart, but it was still a nasty wound, and deep. Had it not been for barroom loafers, we might have had cops.

Instead, Jake practiced medicine and art. He went over to John's place and bound up the wound. Then he called a veterinary friend, claiming his dog needed a prescription for penicillin.

Jake and Heidi sat with John, and pilled him while he healed. They fought his pain, and theirs, with cowboy songs and innumerable cans of suds.

"They're young," Hen said. "Stuff happens when you're young. " I helped Hen run the bar. The police knew something was going on, but small town cops are generally smart enough to let things take their course.

Meanwhile, grandma's spirit tsks. Grandma knew a lot about life, and about the higher forms of behavior. But, she did not understand that pool is an intricate, always changing game that is only about fifteen percent luck. Pool, like poker, is a metaphor for life.

When young we are members of the 'slam and be damned' school, and the cueball jumps the table on the breaks. In our middle years we begin to catch onto the system as we perfect our follow-through and learn the value of greed. "Snap the wrist, don't turn it."

It is only in our twilight that we grow subtle with our game— "Make a deliberate scratch on this shot, if you scratch you've got him buried"—for we have perhaps earned the right to be compassionate with youth; even as we chuckle and take youth to the cleaners.

Term

Books line the walls and outside it is deep summer which does not happen often in the Northwest. Sparrows pant while dogs amble tail down. The campus is dusty with sunshine, the kids lolling and compacted and satiated with sun; and I, musing, cannot touch this sheaf of papers by my hand.

It is a rough tale written by a girl who killed herself. My curses do not pass and I imagine that original creation mindless, adrift in nothing and with no concept to test the void. Unformed and not able to define space until a pinprick of intuition wriggles through sluggish tranquility to conceive one star.

The works of man more truly define. The heart is more than a target.

Hard to explain that to these kids who loll in the sun. It is not time for them to care. Maybe this fall. For now there is other heat. The great experiment of young life continues while my hands seem stiff with my thirty-six years.

"I danced," she said. The involuntary memory cries in a fury against this place. It sobs loss and the loss is not only of the girl. Dancing was one of her ways to give form in chaos, but I do not understand that need because she was so solitary. And I? I sat before a diminishing mortality and spoke unpracticed theory.

It was not unpracticed in the past. Women and movement and force ran through my life like sporadic eruptions from young volcanoes. Until I returned to college for the degree my education came from books carried in the back pocket to construction jobs. Hard hats and the sneers of a smooth world. A fight with a dirt farmer past. Sometimes Saturday night drunk. It was not joyous, but it helped punch holes in the past and promised a future. I trusted it.

When you are young you must expect to be lonely. That first occurred to me when Kath came to my office. Blue jeans, rucksack, sloppy attire. A perpetual gaiety that was a desperate cover for hysteria. It did not override the sadness around brown, dark eyes. A Kansas smile, which is a loud smile when it is safe, louder when fearful. Small mouth, a body too tall for its slenderness.

By then I was already touching her in my imagination. I wanted to touch her hands, to impart personal value that would allow her to trust my barely concealed love of what I believe. Why did I not touch her? It would have cut the form, and the form overused is nothing but formula. By then she was in love with me. That is common among students toward their favorite teachers.

"Speak true and you can ride any wind," I tell them. "If you do not hit that fine, hard line at first you will get it later. But only if you learn to speak the truth."

After being lied to most of their lives and after being taught to lie, it is a difficult thing for them to do. The facades tighten and are meshed as hard as the chain link fences around grade schools. Fingers nervously roll ball pens on the table, for there is no possibility of taking notes on such words. In a few weeks the facades fall as they almost fearfully accept that someone cares for the young wisdom they have learned to conceal. Their ignorance meshes with the wisdom, and for a while they are content to follow this still muscular, tobacco-toothed fool with a tense face and thinning hair...but only lately a fool.

Why did I not touch her? Nothing new has been discovered about human heat since the book of Deuteronomy.

My words mix with the glare of classrooms as efficient as the bank of stainless steel buttons on the elevator. Push, whirr, click, open and shut. I grind cigarettes into unscorchable vinyl floors. A poem could not be written in such rooms, yet people in wool and tweed and cultured disdain drift along the halls. They call themselves poets and they speak in spermy voices devoid of fecundity.

From the first day Kath could overcome even that atmosphere. She was always beyond the assertive or vulgar, her narrow form a bust of frustrated but honest energy. On that first day she sat in the exact center of the room, vibrant to the point of deflection. Chairs on each side of her seemed blank. A teacher estimates a class, looks for strays and hopes for the contentious. I watched Kath and was sure she would drop out. She did not seem organized to handle the large bulk of work. Yet she had the control which gives superlative grace that only changed when she was conscious of being watched. Then, like most young girls, she became clumsy. When the class began to turn in work I was surprised to find that she had written a story. It was not the assignment. It made no difference. The control was on the page and not in her tangled life. Usually she clumped in ten minutes after the bell, rucksack of books, wool logging shirt and thin ankles that disappeared into hiking boots. Impossible that a girl could strive to be more unattractive.

Her story was about an eighteen-year-old girl who returned home from college pregnant and convinced her fundamentalist Kansas family that she was the reincarnation of the Virgin Mary. It was not a funny story and it worked.

I was stunned. The writing was bulky. She was not a natural story teller but the movement was there. The pages were full of the flat, branding heat of summer over dry fields, of thick and dull-clanging church bells; of flathead V8s roaring through the darkness on country roads, and the beer voice, sexual-frustration voice, the last judgment voice of the American middlewest. It smelled of over-heated and balding whitewalls, needle-dropping Christmas trees, and the sights were of tombstones reading Smith, the resonances of preachers howling Armageddon.

I remembered my own midwestern past and felt in my bowels the damning voices of spite-ridden and unforgiving men of God. Some of it never leaves. My first experiences with women were as much anti-religious as they were sexual. The mind-killers dictate rebellion in low places. I read Kath's story three times and fell in love. It is a matter of hope. I do not expect to be understood.

Only this:

If, in the name of some great good, we should blow ourselves from the face of this planet, and if fifty thousand years in the future the remains are visited by another race of beings, they will judge those remains not in terms of our science, our politics or our religions. They will judge in terms of our art. They will wish to know how much we dared to dream.

They should study the rest, though, for it is to our credit how much we must unlearn before we are let to dream.

Kath, Kath. Here was a great writer in the female hide of an eighteen-year-old. Fantastic disadvantage. Young, ignorant, guilt-ridden and a genius. The writer who I could never be... I have accepted that. I called Kath in to talk about the story.

By then winter was half over. The campus was clumpy grass skidding in mud. Scandinavian faces with narrow noses and thin looks appeared like blond exclamations beneath dark hoods. Between classes the sidewalks were a stream of bobbing umbrellas. The sky, heavy misted and filled with smog, hovered over the city like a force bound to muffle good intent. In the polished halls people shuffled, laughed, spoke of all things disparagingly and with analytic certitude.

Kath appeared with the rucksack in place. Red and black checkered shirt, patched jeans. I went through the conventions.

"Tell me about yourself." It was the first time in a long time that the question carried more than tranquil interest. This was the daughter I did not have, won't have . . . this was the woman genius still absent after a life of search. Ambivalence is only a word. So is incest. So is art.

Kath was making me a hero and was apologetic for conventional information. Two brothers, father and mother living, rural background and a part-time job on campus. Her Midwest and mine matched. It sounded like my autobiography.

I edged around the material in the story. It is difficult for the conventional person to understand, but I hoped she had been pregnant. It says something about nerve, the need to know, no matter the risk. Such writers have a Pilgrim morality, but to others the morals are sometimes lewd. One does not speak of life if he worries about wasted postage. These gleaming halls murmur creativity and floor wax. When a real creator appears there is a tremble in the air and a loud shuffling of annuities. Kath did not know that her bulky story and lean observation could build more than this place can ever destroy.

She backed away from my questions, covered, did not commit personal information. Her control was good. The guilt on the page was not reflected. That was professional.

I watched her, thinking; if you could capture this girl, if you could evoke her on paper, you would attain to some of her greatness.

Wet hair puffed inconveniently as it dried, and, although pulled back, enough was worked loose so that strands of dark brown touched the corners of those brown, fearful eyes. A barely concealed tremor in the narrow hands, a movement of confusion. The hair narrowed her already narrow and almost gnome-like face. A person who seemed to have sprung alive and smiling from beneath leaves, a girl who might dwell with tranquil unconcern among dragons, but who was desperate in the closing perimeters of history or life or situation or waxed hallways. Which? Practical if narrow hands. Working hands.

"Have you ever painted," I asked. Painting is much like writing.

"No." She was puzzled. Her face was not pretty, but it was more than only young. The chin tucked in too short. Teeth off center. She had vitality and controlled movement, the most precious commodities of the actress because they spell presence. Acting is like writing.

Kath was as unintentionally sexual as nakedness.

"Many good writers have tried to paint," I told her.

Her face changed. A defensive clamp on her eagerness. Too many knife thrusts and casually imposed tasks from teachers and parents. I let it hang. You have to find out how good they are. The red checked shirt was large and bulked around narrow shoulders to almost hide the tension.

"I danced," she said. She looked down, fingered the rough wool shirt, seemed trying to explain something to her boots; and I, the fool, so captured in my vision of her genius, did not understand that she was pregnant.

"Ballet?"

"Five years."

Ballet. Five years of being too tall, too narrow, the actual wrong physical shape. The valor in the young can make you want to howl and weep.

"There are other important ways," I told her. "You'll have to work harder at this than you ever danced."

Her eyes said that it was impossible.

Winter passed, the snow in the mountains changed to spits of rain, and then Seattle turned to spring. We broke classes in June, and I've sat on this campus during the summer thinking of life and death and everything, of poetry, of the pulse and heat of the young. She followed compulsions and old harms that were stronger than her genius, and I did not follow the inclinations of mine. To be father or lover. It made no difference, but it did make a difference that I never once put an arm around her waist. My mind seems held together with occasionally snapping tin wires that were once intricately soldered. I want to hit someone and do not have what it takes to begin a stiff argument.

A world of people. A world of ideas. It all passes beneath this window in the heat of deep summer, and on the distant lake sails flap and strive for an opening breeze. God is walking around in that heat somewhere, and I do truly hope the bastard gets vagged. The indecent exposure of God, creator of chaos, dreaming tranquilly a paunchy banker's dreams. Who, after all, creates what? The immortals have always been lean and star-ridden and hungry.

There are only two bad things that can happen to an artist. The first is comfort. The second is death. Madness, failure, despair and immeasurable joy all have their place. It is true that these can sometimes kill, but the bad thing is the result and not the process.

I know why I did not touch her. I will, goddamn, be honest for once. I was comfortable. There were women my own age. I could be surrogate father to dozens. Finally because I accepted the fatness of this place. I kept the door open during conferences in the best tradition of teachers. I subscribed to the proposition that for teachers there are few valid forms of love. I tried to deny that formulas only produce a sod buster in durable cloth.

Her second story was about disembodied heads that floated like propelled balloons through the air as they spoke of regret. Sometimes the heads collided. When that happened a policeman came and jailed them in small square boxes. The control was perfect, yet her shame and pleading was right there on the page. I felt the control and treated her like a professional, but she was only a kid.

"Get a guy," I told her.

"I don't need it." She got prim.

"Why are you angry?"

"I'm not." The tremor never left the small hands. The tension rose in the back of the neck and not on the brow. That was right. I invited her to coffee and we sat among the clatter of trays as people spoke of Freud and Skinner and Sophocles.

We talked of her authoritarian background, the rule of familial and fundamentalist guilt. I led the conversation instead of listening, and she listened in a way that said she believed I understood everything that ever happened in her whole life. Her lips trembled, about to speak, and then in confusion she excused herself to go to a class. I did not touch her hand.

Sitting in this office, hearing the low murmur of kids lolling in the sun. Sitting here this summer, grieving, blaming, feeling the texture of my own guilt and mental blindness. I can guess from my own history why at eighteen she could not make a moral decision to get an abortion. I can remember my own shame and loneliness and how bad it is to be broke in a seamy town where morality is determined by killings in grain and pork. I understand the pain, and the final wild surge of despair that one night made her overdose on pills with no more regard to a swelling belly.

Writing is not like life. It is life. She made it as far as Topeka . . . to end in Topeka . . . but it was as close as she could get to home. She lasted until April, wearing, one supposes, one of the bulky wool shirts. Perhaps sometimes in that rented room . . . but, I cannot allow the imagination to crawl. Yesterday in the hall I stood speaking to two colleagues.

"The kind of person," said one, "who sees a Miller play is the same bland intellect that goes to a show of Wyeth." He stepped back two paces to deliver himself . . . this is not a good place. This place is evil.

This place is like Kansas.

Outside the kids mutter and laugh. There is the hard drive of music from a portable radio. Soft drink containers tumble from a profusion of waste in a trash can. Squirrels dart from trees, examine the trash, dart chattering away at the indifferent ramble of a panting dog.

I can teach them this fall.

The radio stops and someone is chording a guitar. Laughter. Low giggles. A memo on my desk speaks of the faculty retirement program.

The books line the wall. Hemingway had to be a brute. Kazantzakis could never be Zorba. Poe had to chase love and respectability that he simultaneously destroyed.

Paton, Nexo, Faulkner . . . form and love and sense. The void filled with mind and heart. I can teach these kids. I can say that the writer loves truth alone, that the fine, hard line on the page is and must be exclusive of any exterior condition. It is only necessary to be true.

And what I would tell them is not a lie. But it is a lie if I say it. Melville wrote of good and evil, while I speak only of sin.

I dance, they dance, we dance, she danced.

112

I want to kill but I don't know who. Sophocles?

. . . and death is the other failure.

But I'm not good enough to teach it any more. I know that. I'm not good enough now, and I don't think I'll ever be good enough, ever again.

The Time That Time Forgot

... Ah, love, let us be true
To one another! for the world, which seems
To lie before us like a land of dreams,
So various, so beautiful, so new,
Hath really neither joy, nor love, nor light,
Nor certitude, nor peace, nor help for pain;
And we are here as on a darkling plain
Swept with confused alarms of struggle and strife
Where ignorant armies clash by night.

from *Dover Beach* by Matthew Arnold

I

THROUGH A RANDOM CAST OF ANCIENT HUMORS, OR THE ALmighty hand of God; or perhaps only the whim of indifferent Nature, some souls are given to wander widely while the cautious stay at home. We walk the nights, look down unending roads, and the universe stands before us cold as a harsh thought; though speckled with the stares of stars.

Thus it was in our youth when we went to war, and so it remained in this year of 1879 when we three, Charles Hare, Ephriam Miller, and I, Jonathan Light, arrived in these wet mountains of southeast America. Wanderers three, we proceeded in the name of Science, although by our natures we would, science or no, come exploring.

Rumors about time a-shifting, and ghosts, and power rose from these hills and stretched as far away as comfortable Baltimore from which we departed with mixed emotions. The greatest war in history is still vile memory. Baltimore abounds with former Confederate officers seeking new professions. Congress has failed America. It manufactures frenzies, although most of our people wish only reconciliation. No doubt it was war that originally caused rumors about this land. Some fleeing Yankee or Reb stumbled into these valleys, and stumbled away, shrieking.

When we departed Baltimore our interest was ethnology. It is a young science, much praised these days in press, but cursed from pulpit. Our subject: a people living in these remote mountains where time seems skewed and wondrous. In 1879 there exists unexplained movement in skies and forest. The movement is always seen through mist, and whether it be animal or machine we did not at first know. There also exists a civilization that, for all intents, still lives in the 14th or 15th century. And, among the natives of this land are ancients who have power. We now know that the power is fabulous.

Rumors about shifting time, and ghosts, caught the attention of Charles Hare, our captain who is wealthy and could finance this trip. Charles is usually modest enough and, during the war, brave enough. He has a gentleman's persuasion about ethnology, and an English-y face not a little like his horse. His hair is brown and mane-like, his hands nearly as blunt as hooves. When he sits his horse one thinks of fox hunts and aristocracy.

Ephriam Miller, on the other hand, is near opposite. A down-easter of lower persuasions, in his native Maine he is known as a drinker and a brawler. He is also a ship maker and sailor who lives on the bare edge of respectability. During the war he was a Bosun. He is built like a massive barrel, but the girth is muscle and not fat. He is a man too cheery for the grim coast of Maine because he laughs with joy as he fights. He stands for drinks when he wins. No one has ever seen him lose.

And I, Jonathan Light, am quiet, bookish, and a recorder of this adventure. Before the war I worked for newspapers and perhaps read too many adventure tales by gentlemanly Englishmen. While I make no great noise about it, and sometimes regret the truth; fact is that I am too large for a man of books, too strong. A circus once tried to hire me as a giant. A man of my size does not need to say "no" more than once. Unlike our friend Ephriam, I no longer enjoy battle because I've killed too many. I sometimes enjoy laughing.

These valleys are not easily found. When we arrived in Asheville and completed our outfit with stores of flour and salt and tobacco, local people denied knowledge of this place. They thought us northern intruders, or, as likely, did not wish to think of what lies in these mountains and valleys. Asheville presents a closed and aristocratic society, self-anointed. In Asheville time proceeds, clock-like, day after tranquil day. It is always respectable. It does not wind around or turn upon itself.

We departed Asheville in late April, three men, five horses and a mule. We carried .44 Colt revolvers and the new 45-70 rifles with a wealth of cartridges.

Now it is early August. One horse lies dead. The mule walks overloaded. The animals put a strain on our situation. We buy hay and a little corn at an occasional hill farm, but mostly depend on forage. Thus, the animals are not thrifty. Ephriam and I could do without them; but about horses, Charles is adamant.

Trails are few and we descend or ascend carefully. Our remaining horses snort and hesitate when entering a trail. They show the good sense of large animals in dangerous territory. And, although we are experienced adventurers we also hesitate before this immensity of forest. Streams run from every hill, crystalline and noisy. Ancient mountains rise mist-clad, round-shouldered, and worn by an eternity of weather.

The horse was stricken in the midst of storm. We had seen the sites of other strikes, but took them for the results of lightning; because, in this wet land lightning walks the hills on forked legs. Lightning here is common as mist, and mist is common as air. Only during afternoons of full sun does the mist withdraw.

There is no arguing with these storms. Thunder rolls across mountaintops, booms through valleys, and rain sheets before wind no less than in a storm at sea. We huddle in waterproofs and beneath canvas if in the field. Otherwise, we seek shelter in a cave where we have established camp.

It was at the camp the horse died. It stood hobbled with the others. The animals grazed until the arrival of storm, then moved toward each other as thunder crashed like cannon, and rain turned their hides bright.

The doomed mare stood in the center of the little herd. Suddenly, surprised, she fell as silently as night wings. The other horses screamed, edged aside, moved through mist like slow specters. The mare lay with smoke rising from a furious wound. Even with wind, ozone tainted the blowing mist. The carcass lay still. No burns appeared on the other beasts. Worse, no thunder followed. This stroke of light, or lightning, walked in silence.

"Thunderation," Ephriam said. Then he said, "Damn." Then he said, "Goddamn." He stood beside us in the mouth of the cave. Behind him the cave stretched far back in darkness. Ephriam stood in the cave's entry like a man framed in a shadow box. "Chums, it's against nature. Where? What? Smell the stink."

Charles stepped into the storm. "Unfortunate beast. Poor animal." He walked through driving rain to the horse, knelt, and touched the searing wound. He drew back his hand and blew on burned fingers. Then he rocked back on his heels heedless of rain and became a detached observer. His scientific interests are wide. While all three of us have inflicted hot wounds during the war, none of us, and doubtless no one else, had ever seen this kind of wound. It ran through the beast like a scorching razor.

The carcass was not halved. Rather, the strike hit directly from above. It struck between neck and shoulder, so that the head twisted awkwardly away. Bone gleamed hot and flesh cooked. Stench rose and rain pounded. We three stood beside the animal and fought justifiable fear.

"Think carefully. What did you see?" Charles, who is sometimes fastidious, sometimes finicky, wrinkled his nose at the smell of burned hair and bone.

"When lightning strikes," Ephriam mused, "there is always sound. There's a crack or a thump. There's always thunder. I didn't see nothin'. The important part is I didn't hear nothin.'"

"We have witnessed hot damage elsewhere," I said. A week after departing Asheville we began seeing broken trees and broken rock holding the imprint of fire.

"Make complete notes," Charles told me. "Be assiduous."

My notes partially read: 'Light flashing like a bolt from Jehovah or Zeus. Bones sliced shear. Flesh instantly cooked.'

When the rain stopped we towed the carcass fifteen rods from camp. The horses wanted no dealings with the dead mare. They shied, but Charles is completely attuned to horses. Our tow left the dead mare near an animal trail. Scavengers would take care of the carcass.

These hills roll endless and rise to heights between five and six thousand feet. When standing on a high ridge one looks west and sees tops of mountains stretch to the horizon. There is history here, one worth knowing if we are to survive.

Forty-two years ago in the presidency of Andrew Jackson, peoples of this region, Cherokee and Creek and Catawba, were removed to the western territories. The removal was not gentle. Many died. Some escaped to these hills. They mixed with people already here, an odd mixture.

The resident people live in ancient ways. The refugees who fled Jackson's soldiers were accustomed to more modern ways. Before removal many Cherokee were wealthy. They owned businesses, farms, and slaves. They had a written language and a newspaper. Even though highly civilized, they still knew how to survive in these hills.

They survived because no army on earth is large enough or skilled enough to find someone hiding among these endless mountains. The very eye of God would become befuddled among these mists and valleys, among these smokes and rushing streams. And, there are spirits.

No ethnologist worth his salt would deny the presence of ghosts. For, although one may not believe in ghosts, one must accept that others do. Thus we walk in a fantastic land where the people we study have a great mythology. It is a mythology of ghosts and spirits and witches.

And, one must admit, although a few men may not believe in ghosts, it does not mean those men are not haunted. Each of our party carries memories of war. The dead and dying drift through our dreams; of which, perhaps, more later.

On the day when the horse died, and before disposing of the carcass, we returned to the cave as the storm slackened. August heat returned and the forest steamed. Giant trees formed a canopy holding heat to the ground.

"Reduce our knowledge to elements." Charles stripped wet clothing. He knelt quite naked as he searched his pack for dry gear. Charles appears gawkish without clothes. His upper body weighs heavy, his lower body light; like a workhorse on legs of a racehorse. To me, Charles said, "Make a written note." He did not say a record would be wanted by others if none of us survive.

My notes further read:

The Land
Wet with eternal mist
Movement in the sky but only in the mist
Movement on the landscape but only in the mist
Electrical storms of frequency and strength
Dense forest
Much game
Destructive strikes of light
The People
Reclusive
Matrilineal
Hostile. Doubtless warlike.
Primitive, but with occasional modern weapons
    acquired in aftermath of The War of the Rebellion.

"Ain't likely the natives throw lightning bolts." Ephriam does not enjoy mysteries. "Seems like what happened ties to storm."

"Examine all possibilities," Charles told him. "It may tie to mist. It may tie to neither."

"As I understand it," I suggested, "our first problem asks if these strikes are random, or planned. If planned, we face an unknown and dangerous opponent."

"Random, surely," Charles said. "Planning supposes a controlling presence. In which case, we would already be lost."

"Because," Ephriam growled, "folks in these parts are somewhat direct." His barrel-like figure seemed vague in the dim cave. His blue eyes shifted as he looked beyond the cave into the mist. Even at rest, and in an easily defended spot, Ephriam searched the forest for enemies. "Fair question. What do they think of you?" he asked me. "With them it sets up as either worship or kill."

When we first encountered the native people they fled before me. Men of my generation rarely stand six feet tall, and certainly not seven-six. Men of my generation may weigh, bone and muscle, fourteen stone but not twenty. The native people stand small beside Ephriam, are dwarfed beside me. They fled believing I am a monster or a creature of mythology.

One who did not run was a young woman. Early in June we paused, thinking ourselves unobserved, at the foot of a trail which ended at a confluence of two streams. The young woman attended a fish trap. She removed a catch of trout.

She dressed, as do all the ancient people, male and female, in deerskin apron with single strap across naked breast; the apron with numbers of carefully sewn pockets. People here carry their livings with them; flint, tobacco, pipes, knives and other small tools. In winter they cloak with furs.

"Beautiful sight," Charles breathed. "Nature's fair child."

"Beautiful fish," Ephriam muttered. "I'm wearied of venison. You reckon she'd trade?"

I wondered what crossed her mind as she turned and saw three strangers sitting massive horses. We must indeed have looked like creatures of myth. Charles is of average height, but larger than the native men. Ephriam has the girth of a sound tree, and I, a giant astride a giant horse. We expected her to fade quickly into forest as had others before her.

Instead, she stood quietly and watched with the calmness of power; the calm of a woman who knew she could harm if she wished, and could not be harmed. From the forest came the crashing of a heavy body, the snort of a bear. Mist blew across the streams. Damp warmth radiated from the forest.

"We witness courage," Charles said in a low voice. "Either hers or ours. We must speak to her."

Fragments of the English language survive. A primitive sign language exists. Before our departure from Baltimore we learned somewhat of Cherokee. Given time and patience we could communicate. I give the sum of our conversation, since phrase by phrase would be tedious.

"Why are you here? I don't want you." Her voice sounded low and no more friendly than her words. Her face was not as round as tribes of the far west. Her face seemed nearly European, brown eyes, tan skin, a face that would be lovely should she smile. I judged her as being in her middle 20s.

"We come in the name of science." Charles spoke softly.

"I do not know that word. It is not necessary. Your science is no good."

"There is much lightning here."

"It is the robe of Thunder."

In the forest the crashing of the bear told that it circled us. Bears have curiosity. They will follow a man for great distance, not stalking, just watching. They walk silent when they wish, but this one did not wish, and it sounded huge.

"I want to know Thunder," Charles said. "Does one praise Thunder?" One learns of a people by learning of their Gods.

She looked at Charles as if she feared him hopelessly stupid. "You praise Thunder. You dance. Thunder laughs."

We would later understand that the natives teach by asserting the ludicrous. If, for example, a youngster does a foolish thing, he will be praised for doing well. The culture teaches with kindness, but with no small touch of sarcasm.

"Then Thunder is an enemy?"

"No."

"A friend?"

"No."

"What?"

"Thunder is."

We would also later understand that the natives accept existence of natural things without judging. To them a stream without trout pools is not worse than a stream with many pools. One is a stream with pools, one without, neither better or worse. Thus, Thunder is.

Charles looked to the skyline where round-shouldered mountains stood with tops covered by mist. Far off, in the mist, movement flashed in positive streaks of silver and orange. Orange bloomed like explosions, but there was no sound. Mist muffled sounds of forest and stream. Rapid and desperate movement came and went through the forest, as if killing forces confronted each other.

We all have memories of war. Memories of charges, battle flags flying and the screams of maddened or dying men, and dying horses. Perhaps our memories peopled the mist and the forest with soundless battle.

Charles pointed upward but remained silent. The young woman stood content with her own thoughts. Soon she would decide we were no longer interesting. These people are direct. She would simply walk away.

"War?" Charles asked.

"You go away," she said. "Carry off all that you brought." She turned to leave.

"Let her go," I told Charles. "She'll say no more. Not at present."

*

In the days and weeks that followed, as June folded into July, and then to August, we feared we would become complacent with forms and colors that moved through mist. Patterns developed. On days when mist was cut by storm, and when rain fell with violence, colors on mountain tops flared high. Because of mist, red explosions appeared as orange smears, and flashes of blue light turned silver. Sometimes ozone drifted through the rain. We would later discover a wrecked tree, seared and smoking.

On noons when mist retreated before August sun, movement in the forest fragmented. We could see figures of men ghosting from tree to tree and sometimes meeting. The figures were nebulous. No one could actually say he saw battles, but could not say he saw anything else.

We often went to the confluence of streams hoping for the return of the young woman. Instead, our adventure took a different shape. Natives concluded that while we might be demons we were not presently dangerous. We were approached by delegates of two separate camps.

The first was a warrior who appeared out of mist. He moved easily and without fear. He wore gray pants of a kind that I had seen on many a dead Confederate, and linen shirt, worn but serviceable. He carried a cap-and-ball rifle, and a steel knife. This warrior had a broad Indian forehead combined with negroid features. His skin was chocolate colored, his hair kinky, a statement of other important history.

In the American south, from the first visits of negroid and Caucasoid peoples, there has been much interchange with the native population. The ethnologist who hopes to find an unmixed culture is overly optimistic. However, because of the ancient peoples there was some reason for optimism. This warrior, though, was modern.

He was clearly an experienced man. His rifle was shouldered muzzle down. His moccasins were worn without being worn through, which showed that he knew how to move with admirable economy. Moccasins would not have lasted our party for a week. His rifle is now out-moded, but muzzleloaders were serviceable during the War of the Rebellion. Doubtless, like us, he had fought. He stood nearly as tall as Ephriam and he moved with the light steps of a man who can walk soundless through dry leaves. Such woodsmen drift like spirits through the forest.

"No need to fear," he said most pleasantly. "I'm not the Fool Killer." His English was as good as ours, but slightly nasal. It held hints of cultivated speech, the soft and often dangerous sort one finds in Norfolk. He approached three well-armed men. He actually reassured three experienced men. His confidence set us aback.

"No fools here," Charles said easily.

"The mule ain't too bright . . . but got a trick or two in his withers." Ephriam moved two steps away from Charles. If a fight was to happen it would be stupid to remain clustered.

"Next time you get to town," the warrior told Ephriam, "shop around and buy a sense of humor." He grinned openly. "You gents are serious beyond moderate." He searched the forest behind us. "On t'other hand, you've got a right. You have stepped into a hell of a fix."

"Charles Hare," Charles said, introducing himself. Then he introduced Ephriam. I introduced myself.

"Bester," the warrior said. "Albert Bester." He gave his white name. No Indian would give his real name to strangers. We were forced to wonder if Bester actually was Indian, or only had the blood. Lots of Cherokee and Catawba had abandoned Indian ways for white civilization. And, where had he acquired hints of cultivation?

". . . a helluva fix," Ephriam asked. "Which one? It looks like we got enough to fill a main'sl."

"Why are you here? I'm not just curious. Your answer is important." Bester stood casually but not at rest. He rested his rifle, but did not lean on it.

Charles explained and Bester at first seemed amused. Then a sense of unease entered the situation.

"If only you were hunting gold, or trapping fur, or stealin' children, I'd know what to tell you." Bester mused. "The people in these parts have handled such matters for nigh on three centuries." He actually seemed puzzled. "Don't you have enough trouble with your own world?"

We figured then that Bester was Indian, or at least mostly. The spirit of science is alien to Indian vision. Tools, yes. Inventions, yes. But systematic inquiry toward a nebulous or unknown end, no. One cannot understand the notion of is and inquire about maybe.

"We do have enough trouble," Charles admitted. "If we look at someone else's world we may find ways of fixing our own." His simple explanation didn't cover all the facts, but covered enough.

Bester smiled in the quiet and cultivated manner of the best southern society: here he was, Indian, negro, a rough and tumble woodsman; and yet when he wanted he could put on the ways of the white aristocrat. Quite an actor. "Tell of your success."

"We're eating well," Ephriam said, "and wearing out our boots."

"We early on understood that we would have to establish camp and wait for people to come to us." Charles watched the forest where movement had ceased with the appearance of Bester. "If we enter villages without invitation we would be seen as intruders."

"Odd thing to hear from a Yankee," Bester said quietly. There was cloaked anger in his voice. "Nobody invited Grant and Sherman."

"We explore on foot," Charles explained. "One man always stays in camp to attend the animals."

"Because," Ephriam muttered, "horses have a way of wanderin'."

"They have a way of getting stolen," Bester said. "Renegades take them. Say what you mean."

"The funny thing is . . ." Ephriam told him, ". . . I like you. You've already jumped my hide twice, and damn if I still don't like you."

"You made a good scheme," Bester told Charles. "Had you entered a village you would have been treated well, then killed on return to camp." Bester looked toward the forest. "Three forces exist here, and all three can handle you."

Bester explained that a village of Cherokee, adequately armed, held territory a few miles to the southwest. Native people, the people from whom the Cherokee had risen, held territories scattered through the mountains. Although a certain amount of tribal interchange was possible, the groups pretty much went their own ways and ignored each other.

A third force came from medicine known only to a few of the original natives, the ancient people. Such people used power rarely. "But," Bester explained, "they can bend nature to their purpose. Their own people revere and fear them, my people mostly fear them, and you would do well to be mortally afraid. Nature guards them."

I thought of the young woman we had met back in June. I thought of the crashing of the bear in the forest. A huge bear.

"And the strikes of light and fire? Are those a manifest of nature? We've already lost one horse."

"They come from the west," Bester told Charles, "and people don't go there. However, it's what I want to chew over with you."

According to Bester the strikes of fire began during the war, but never amounted to much. In these endless hills war otherwise made little impression. Life walked day by day and night by night, the unending circle of time the Indian knows. Skirmishes between small groups occasionally ended in the death of a warrior, or the kidnapping of a child. For the most part seasons rolled. Corn crops and tobacco and pumpkins grew and were harvested. Rumors of war penetrated the hills and some men walked off in the direction of battle, to return with stories of exploits that might or might not be true. And, of course, a good many did not return.

"We see dead men moving through the forest," Bester said. "Lots more lately. Strikes of fire increase. You might say things are no longer casual."

"We see them also."

"Most likely, you see spirits," Bester said. "Spirits fill this land. People live beside spirits and don't much care, because spirits only live on the edge of the world. The ghosts are a different matter." Bester tapped his rifle butt against the ground. He now seemed a little dangerous, and very sad. "A ghost is the shape of someone who made bad mistakes. Folks here live in established ways. We fear mistakes."

"Spirits on the edge of this world? Are they part of tales we hear about time? Are spirits from another time?" Charles tried to sound casual, but it was a failure. His excitement at getting new information got the best of him.

"What is your experience?" Bester asked. "Something has misfired. Something is cockeyed. What's the date?"

"August 14th, 1879," I replied. When one keeps a record, one always knows the date.

"It probably is August," Bester said, "because it smells like August. But what is this?" He fished in a pocket and pulled out a small piece of material. It was flat and hardened like fired clay, but without the graininess of clay. "Came from the sky," Bester said. "Plunked into a stream. Rattled people."

The fragment showed cracks and a burn. It measured no more than two inches square, and affixed to it was a very small, colored cylinder with soldered wire.

"A raven or a jay had to have dropped it, but what in blazes is it?"

"Came from the sky?"

"I know what you're thinking," Bester told Charles, "because I already thought my way down that trail. But only birds fly. It's either a bird or a sky god."

"Fire on the mountaintops," Charles said. "Always to the west?"

"Up until now."

"And what comes from the east?" Charles looked toward the east. "I ask, because if we look west, it pays to know what's at our backs." He let the business of sky gods pass. Time enough to inquire about superstitions later.

Toward the east the sun had cleared the mountaintops an hour after first light. Mist rolled into valleys and hollows. In two more hours sun would begin to drive the mist upward. The forest would lose some of its green glitter as mist dried from leaves and needles.

"Ghosts and Yankees," Bester said. "Dead Confederates. Ghosts come from the east. They also drift this way from Georgia."

"Have there always been ghosts?"

"Here and there," Bester said. "Lots more of them lately. They hover around men like you. And men like me." Bester turned the broken fragment over and over in his hand. The colored cylinder, orange and blue, contrasted with his dark skin. "Men like you won't believe this next, and I could give damn less, but tell you anyhow."

He told of buffalo ghosting along trails, although forest buffalo disappeared from these parts two hundred years ago. He told of Spanish adventurers in search of gold, and, although gold has been found in these hills the native people never valued it. He told of murder, rape, retaliation; told of the ghosts of history. "Sometimes," he concluded, "it's like three hundred years never passed."

"It's always been this way?"

"Only a little . . . lots more of late. Spanish came into these parts in the 16th century. Sometimes they're still here. It's like nothing is ever lost, which is unnatural." Bester looked eastward, shrugged, and presented us with an explanation. His notion seemed simple enough, but none of us had thought of such a thing. Bester claimed that in normal history—as opposed to what was going on—every time you gain something, you lose something. Sometimes you lose something good.

"You have new Springfields," he said about our rifles. "You can extract and load in two seconds. I can load in ten seconds. You gain time, but you lose dexterity." He looked toward our horses; two roans, two blacks, one with a white star. "Around here people picked up mobility when they got horses. Some folks can't live with-

out. Other people understood that they lost freedom if they adopt-
ed horses . . . which is why plenty people don't have 'em."

He was correct, of course. Horses take too much time and care.

"Which means," said Bester, "that I'm quicker than you, and
freer than you; and I live without horse dung and horse flies. You,
on the other hand, can travel further and load faster."

"I understand," Charles said, and he did. It was not a novel idea,
only sensible. "What we have is handy in war and adventure, but
limits us in everyday life. Gain and loss."

Bester looked at the fragment of unknown material which
looked foreign in his hand. He looked west. "There are some gains
a man don't need. Something showed up during the war. I want it
defeated. We can handle Spanish, be they ghosts or real, but fire
on the hills and strikes in the forest. . . ." He looked at Charles as if
wondering whether we were good enough. "Somebody has to plug
a leak in history. I'll venture it, but could use some extra rifles."

We all looked west. One rifle, or four, seemed feeble if what we
saw was what it seemed.

"Keep explaining," Ephriam told Bester. "Them explosions is
matter for comment."

"If they are explosions we'll know in time to turn back. I don't
fret the explosions. What I fret is whether you gents are causing
the leak." Bester laid a hand on Ephriam's shoulder, like friend to
friend. "You haven't been here. All you know is you've lost a horse.
I've been here, and the price of this lantern show has already gone
from a plug-nickel to six-bits."

"And you'll solve it with rifles?" Charles was intrigued. Our
sense of adventure had brought us to this place, and so far there had
been no adventure. I entertained doubts.

"For defense and for game," Bester said. "If history is skewed we
scout and find the cause. If we can't cure it we come back."

"Or not." Ephriam looked wary, like a boat thrown ashore, and
wondering what was to become of itself.

Charles looked at me, at Ephriam. "We're having little luck here."

"We got an extra horse," Ephriam admitted.

"Bring the horses, but be prepared to trade or lose them. Or trade
them now," Bester told Charles. "Shank's mare before this finishes."

"Why?"

"This is mountain country and not a field of battle." He pointed to the depths of the surrounding forest. "From lookin' at your

plunder, I expect you gents were damned fine soldiers, but stealth is wanted. It's different territory."

"I'm a sailor," Ephriam told him, and for the first time, in a long time, looked at ease. "Don't lump me with these cannoneers."

"We'll be ready in two days," Charles said. "Rendezvous day after tomorrow."

Our second visitor stepped from the forest so quietly we did not know she was there. A horse whinnied. Stomped. Then stilled. An old, old woman moved toward us. She wore copper ornaments and a cape of raven feathers. Her face, though heavily wrinkled, showed relationship to the young woman we had met at the fish trap. I would have wagered this was the grandmother. It was as if the young woman had turned ancient. The grandmother, doubtless.

She carried a polished and ornamented stick, possibly for use as a cane. Possibly ceremonial. Possibly both.

We extended full respect. This woman lived in ways made possible through the seclusion of these hills. Either that, or time truly was bent. From her world the Cherokee, far, far back in time, had derived. She was not Cherokee, but the mother of the Cherokee; an important fact. These Indians trace family relationships from the mother. A few of the women are reputed to have great power. This woman could live in ancient ways because she was so strong she needed no gun, no steel knife, no missionaries.

"You walk west," she said. "What do you know? You better know a lot."

I could nearly feel Charles' thrill. Here was a person who we had traveled far to see. This woman could tell every custom, every tale, of the world of the 16th century. This woman's world differed in no large respect from the world when Hernando DeSoto landed in 1539.

"I know a little bit," Charles said. "You know more."

If an experienced man looked at our horses and outfit with disdain, we would be alarmed. Bester, though, had thought well enough of them. This woman looked at our camp and was displeased. "Bester is plenty smart. You do what Bester says."

When he left, Bester had disappeared to the south. This old woman came from the north. It was unlikely they had met. Her opinion of our camp caused me to worry.

Our rifles were stacked. She looked at them. "You don't want better guns. You want no guns." She looked west. "Plenty guns there." From the forest came a loud snort. A bear. A big bear.

"Thunder lives there. Thunder can take care of himself. Don't go troubling Thunder."

Charles looked at me, and the look meant—don't miss a word. Document everything.

"War lives there," the woman said. "He moves this way. You stop him." Her wrinkled face remained tranquil, but her eyes belied the face. They were afire with anger. "War has plenty medicine," she told us. "I have plenty medicine. I send medicine with Bester. You do what Bester says." She walked back into the forest.

Charles stood irresolute. He wanted to follow her, and knew he should not.

"What did she mean?" Ephriam asked. "No guns. What in raging hell did she mean?"

"We now have strong evidence that time is skewed. Surely, that woman cannot be of the 19th century." Charles looked west. "Better guns? No guns? If time is misfiring, do we see the future in the west?" He shook his head, as if to relieve himself of crazy thoughts. "Impossible. Impossible. In that direction madness lies."

"No guns at all," Ephriam insisted. "What in the name of all that is wonderful did she mean, 'no guns.'"

"If necessary I will fight to defend us," I said, "and I expect I'll fight to defend her; but by all gods great and small do not expect me to initiate an attack."

I could see by their manners that my comrades agreed. In an ugly past, Charles and I stood side by side watching men fall before our cannon. At long range we loaded shot, and as range closed we loaded canister. When we ran out of canister we loaded broken glass, rocks, and horseshoe nails. Our field piece was like a giant scattergun.

When overrun we met bayonets with clubs and knives. Ephriam, although he does not discuss it, had waded through scuppers running with blood, had seen blood splash so high that it discolored sails.

"The man is a Reb and dangerous," Ephriam said about Bester.

"And I'm a Northern and dangerous," I told him.

II

That night after the old woman left was a night of dreams. Charles took the first watch, I the second, and Ephriam the chill hours of night to dawning. The forest seemed alive with movement, and our fire at the mouth of the cave drew cold air from within. Chill circled our backs.

When I settled in the dreams began. I once more saw men run through smoke from our guns, saw the twist and fall of bodies, heard Rebel yells sharp as the call of eagles. I relived my own most horrible event of the war.

It happened on a wet day in mud. Rain had stopped. Sun glared hot as a forge, and muggy heat pressed white smoke from black powder to the ground. Smoke clung to earth like thickest fog. Rebel yells sounded an attack, and our supporting riflemen fired into the smoke as we loaded canister. Out there in the smoke men died by hundreds and we were glad. We saw little. Mostly, we only heard them dying. What we saw was smoke, and mud as liquid as a hog pen.

Tongues of flame leapt from our guns, and we had occasional glimpses of falling men, like spirits in sweltering mist. Mud threatened to silence our cannon, foul the fuse, and our cannon kept trying to bury itself on recoil. Mud sucked at the gun as I lifted it. Only my great strength kept it free and pointed.

Further down the line came the sound of a breakthrough and Rebel cheering. Then, through smoke, we heard the panting of attacking men. They were not yelling now, but sloughing through mud with bayonet and sword and pistol. They pressed forward in the face of canister, and canister swept holes in their gray and tattered line. One by one our guns stopped firing, felled either by mud or Confederates.

Then the Rebs were on us. An artillerist's hell. Charles stood with pistol and sword, and I emptied my rifle. A man jerked and fell, his face twisting in astonishment. There was no time to reload. I used the rifle as a club.

A boy, hardly more than a child, appeared out of smoke. He was small, tow-headed, with brown and excited eyes. He wore a red rag at his throat, a lucky piece probably torn from a scarf made by his mother. In his right hand he carried a cavalry saber. His left hand spurted blood; fingers gone. The boy was not yet aware that he was wounded. He stumbled from the smoke, stopped amazed when he saw me, and for a moment, hesitated. In the dread heat of battle I must have looked like a giant risen out of smoke and ancient tales. He was entitled to run. He was fourteen, at most. He was too brave.

I struck with the rifle butt, slamming it sideways against his left arm. He spun, nearly dropped the saber, nearly fell from the blow. He staggered, looked at his left hand, and looked at me in disbelief. He believed it was I who had wounded him. The wound pumped blood that spattered and mixed in mud. He was already as good as dead but seemed not to know it.

He staggered forward with saber pointed, a dead boy trying to kill a still living man. With the butt of the rifle I broke his skull and saved him having to watch his life flow away into mud.

A boy. Fourteen, at best. A boy no doubt dead because of cheap romance. He had imagined he would excel in war. He had imagined himself a victor. A boy, and not a very big one. Nothing to be done about it then. Nothing to be done about it later. Men running through smoke, ghosting through smoke. It was war; and may Abe Lincoln and Jeff Davis, and all abolitionists and slavers, and all cotton men and industrialists, roast in everlasting hell.

When I awoke, jerked out of dreams by terror and no small guilt, the sun had not yet walked the top of the eastern mountains. My head hurt. I watched my companions. Subdued. No one talked about dreams.

I almost trust Charles, almost. His judgment was sound during battle, and surely it was sound on this occasion. Ephriam almost trusted Charles. Neither of us trusted Bester.

Charles had allied with Bester, and Bester was a Reb. Perhaps Charles could forgive the war but I could not. Hard to tell about Ephriam . . . likely, with Ephriam, it was the same.

And, Bester, part Indian and part Afric, was not necessarily of a mood to cherish the company of Yankees. It would be hard for him to forgive the rapes and fires and total destruction of the war. Besides, Bester was an enigma. Why would a man of his race have done battle in behalf of the south?

It was with large suspicion, and larger misgiving that I spent the day helping to cache supplies in the fond hope they would not be stolen. We then loaded a bit of salt, sugar, and flour on the horses. We packed a few items for trade, steel knives and, more desirable, flat files to keep knives sharp. We struck south to the Cherokee village where we were first greeted in sullen silence. When the purpose of our visit became clear, the Indians professed friendliness which we knew was a lie.

We traded for Indian tobacco—strong as a drug and used as medicine—and for other medicines. We returned to camp knowing that each would carry only a knife, a rifle, a revolver, a blanket, Lucifer matches waterproofed with paraffin, coffee, a little tea; a pot or a skillet. Additional gear would be packed by mule, but we did not know how long we would own horses and mule.

"And so," Charles said at sundown, "we commit to chance, or God, or a Johnny Reb who may be saint or rascal."

"You can commit to him all you want," Ephriam told Charles. "Me, I'm still figgerin.'"

"Rascal, no doubt," I said, "but no damned saint."

The fire before the mouth of the cave glowed with small but positive energy. From the western hills came the rumble of Thunder.

In the second night of dreams strange beasts appeared, winged and fanged and unlovely; beasts of the apocalypse. Hordes of people fled along trails. From the depths of forest came echoes and strange cries, the sound of weeping, wails of such high pitch one thought only of wounds.

Disembodied faces appeared, fleshy, smooth-shaven, speaking harsh language. Jowly faces with cruel eyes. Then the faces grew bodies and uniforms, generals and tyrants, epaulets and medals dangling; those symbols of ribbon and brass that power awards itself, symbols intended to persuade the foolish that there is merit in much that is damnable.

I awoke to the sound of a heavy body crashing in the forest. My first thought was of the horses, but knew that Ephriam would be alert and attending. The heavy sound seemed somehow comforting. I stirred coals and rebuilt the fire; venison, biscuit and coffee. Charles and Ephriam packed remaining gear for the long road. Not much said. We listened to occasional crashing in the forest and stared into mist.

"If we go to defeat war," I said, "then I'll play the game." I did not explain why I said it, and my comrades did not ask questions. "If this was just a pleasure jaunt I would not." They still did not ask.

Bester appeared from the forest as naturally as a stream runs. We heard no sound. The horses gave no alarm. He still carried the muzzleloader but was now dressed in deerskin. We, having no deer-skin, had packed waterproofs. He looked over our gear even before greeting us. Bester was not a man given to wasting words.

"An old woman visited." His was not a question. He squatted before the fire, refused food, accepted coffee that was boiled and black. "Panther piss," he said with satisfaction, and by way of compliment.

He seemed less a creature of mist or history. These woodsmen are practical fellows, but their stealth often makes them seem in-substantial. "The old woman said what?"

"She sends strong medicine with you," Charles told him. Charles searched the forest. "I don't understand medicine. Do you carry it, or is it with that bear?"

"If you saw it," Bester said, "it would likely look like a bear. I think you'll never see it."

"Medicine?"

"She commands nature," Bester told us, "and don't ask how because I don't know." On this day his voice did not sound like the white aristocracy of Virginia. His voice held the same quiet, but with little accent. He sounded like a man wise in his job, but also wise enough to use caution. I wondered how cautious he felt he had to be around us.

"She said don't take better guns, take no guns," Ephriam told him. "Do you know about that?"

"You'd be amazed how much I don't know. What that woman understands was lost by everybody else two hundred years ago. Hang onto your rifles."

We followed a west-running trail. In these parts the lumbermen have still not struck. Giant trees rose in protected hollows and along streams. The broad trail skirted the base of mountains. In these hills are trails, paths, and great trails. Important to know the difference.

A path is well worn, short, and leads somewhere; a confluence of streams, an Indian ballfield of rough and dangerous games, or ceremonial site. Trails are different. Some trails follow the paths of animals, then extend beyond those paths. Some trails are made, hacked out, walked over, brush pushed aside; easily overgrown if not used. The trail we followed was a great trail used for war or trading. We moved without stealth, following Bester's lead.

We felt that we moved through a timeless landscape. We stood guard through nights of owl-call and the ticking of death-watches; and whether those death-watch insects existed in the night, or only ticked in our memories, none could say. We trekked, camped, slept, woke, trekked. Twice we waited as Bester reconnoitered an Indian camp, and twice we skirted that camp. Indians scouted us from the forest, and we could not know if they were alive or spectral. Bester remained alert, as did we all. We were soldiers moving through strange terrain.

A week into the forest, and with Thunder booming in the west, the trail crested a small rise and descended into a shrouded valley. Nature, herself, seemed to change and grow dark. Orange smears of fire flashed in western hills.

Mist covered the trail. Ravens sat silent on low branches like black smudges on mist. The birds did not call, or chortle, or shriek.

"Soul catchers," Bester said about the ravens. "Spirits. You never get a squawk from them until some fool goes to glory."

Deer bounced across the trail and chipmunks clung to trees, watching. The chipmunks did not scold. A panther stood silent beside the trail. Our horses saw nothing, or at least did not respond. They passed the panther as if it were not there.

"Nary a snort," Ephriam said to Charles, and it sounded like a question.

"Because the beasts can't smell or see it," Charles said. "I can't smell it. I doubt my senses."

"Soul catchers?" Ephriam said to Bester. Ephriam did not sound scientific. He sounded like a sailor, and sailors are almost always superstitious.

"Hang tight to what soul you've got," Bester said. "Those birdies don't jest." To Charles, he said, "Spirits aren't our problem. Trouble lies t'other side of yon hill."

In the next valley a south-running stream crashed overfilled and dangerous because of August storms. Water tore at banks. Water backed up, and young poplars stood in water. Trees bent before current. We would have to move north, or south, in order to find a place to ford.

As we waited on Bester's lead the horses made small snorts and caught the jitters. The mule flat-out brayed.

"Hunker down," Ephriam said as he headed for cover. We automatically put our horses on tether between us and the hillside. The horses tried to shy from the hill. The mule went wide-eyed. During the war, mules had a reputation for frenzy in combat. This mule lived up to it. It tried to shake its load.

"I'm puttin' trust in not much these days, but I trust horses." Ephriam took his rifle off half-cock as he knelt behind a massive oak.

"Raiders," Bester muttered toward the hill. "They want the horses and rifles. I reckon they've got more'n their share of surprise coming." He turned away from the hill and toward the stream. We heard his weapon cock.

While Bester covered our rear we faced the hillside. Blood churns hot and fast at such moments. It's hard to stand easy, but it pays nothing to court excitement. We heard the report of Bester's rifle at the same moment we heard a flat explosion, almost a pop.

Bester knelt and faced the stream. Ephriam continued to scan the hillside as, at the report, Charles and I turned to Bester. On the tree behind which Charles had knelt, a black rock hit, then fell harmless to the ground. There were lots of such rocks around, and in all sizes. They were smoothed by rolling in the streams.

From across the stream a small puff of smoke showed where our assailant had been, for surely by now he had moved. I turned my rifle toward the stream.

"Find him," Ephriam said over his shoulder, "because you'll be looking at one dead Sadducee."

Charles reached down, feeling for the rock that hit the tree. He kept searching while watching the forest on the other side of the stream. His hand felt here, there, and found no rock. He turned back to the hill while we continued to face the stream.

"Already dead," Bester told Ephriam, "and he's been just that dead for at least three hundred years." Bester did not relax but he took his time reloading. "Keep a watch for anything ornery," he told us, "though likely all you'll see is smoke. We'll soon be watching a skirmish."

"You shot at what?" Charles did not lower his weapon. He kept it pointed across the creek.

"I saw movement that might have been alive," Bester said quietly. "A picket is a picket."

"Rocks," I said, "not shot?"

"Maybe from a wheel-lock." Bester sounded tired. "You can't hit damn-all with them, but you can load anything that fits in the barrel. And make that a massacre, not a skirmish." He looked to the hillside, then across the swollen stream. "If they were shooting rocks they were out of shot. Meantime, those raiders are among the living. They're after us, but they're about to catch a case of the dreadfuls. They'll scamper like hares."

I wish I could say that what followed was a mere tableau, the carefully constructed scene, and the short vision so popular in society these days. Instead, this became one more lick of fire from the Devil's furnace.

Across the stream a small band of men appeared among trees and through mist. They dressed in light armor held together by rags, and they were no more than a dozen. Some were barefoot. They were a lost scouting party, or adventurers at the end of their adventure. Spaniards afoot in mist that rose from the hot forest; they looked like a walking museum of misery. They seemed to consult, argue as in pantomime. They were insubstantial, but more real than the sliding away, ghostly forms we had earlier seen through mist. They formed a disjointed line facing the stream. When Charles fired in the direction of the hillside, the line of men across the stream took no notice.

We turned to see Charles reloading. A horse stomped, cried, and Charles spoke to it like one friend to another. The horse quieted.

"No sense firing," Bester told Charles. "They're from the past. To them, you're from the future. They do not see you."

"Movement on the hill," Charles said quietly. "I shot as a warrant in case anything there is living."

"Just like that Spaniard across the stream who let off a random shot," Bester muttered. "He tried to scare the men who are going to kill him."

From the hillside savages appeared and they were as spectral as the Spanish. They cavorted and jeered. They tumbled down the hillside in a mob, not seeking cover among trees. They gathered near the banks of the swollen stream, actually prancing. They seemed an unlikely war crew of old men and boys. The savages carried clubs, staves, short spears. From across the stream came another puff of smoke, but no savage fell.

"Can't hit the back of a barn." Ephriam probably said it, but all thought it.

"Old Indian trick," Bester said about the cavorting Indians. "They draw attention to themselves. The real war party will come in from behind. Watch what happens in yonder forest."

From the forest behind the Spaniards, movement in mist became warriors. These were no cavorting savages, but skilled men. They moved upon the Spaniards with stealth, then fell on the backs of surprised men. They clubbed and they used stone knives.

The Spanish turned to their enemy. Lances thrust, swords flashed, and not in vain. A warrior fell, and then another. Faint cries echoed through mist. The Spaniards were overwhelmed, clubbed backward toward the stream. All but two died of wounds. The other two drowned.

"What happens if we fire into that fuss?" Ephriam had finally turned from the hillside.

"Nothing," Bester told him. "You can't change history, only put up with it. It's like a blasted play. Acted over and over. Century after century." He turned away. "Move out. There's no sense watching what's going happen to those corpses."

We turned quickly aside. During the war all of us had seen dismemberment, and worse. I thought of my own savagery during the war. I was only a little less savage than those ghostly warriors, now hacking away with stone knives. We departed that scene of ancient carnage.

Over the next ten days, and eighty westward miles, we spoke little and observed much. Harness, which had been well-oiled, began to squeak for want of care. We were never exactly wet, yet we never felt completely dry. For a while, even Bester was puzzled. A pattern emerged. We would see a congregation of spirits, especially soul-catchers. We, or rather Bester, would sense the presence of raiders. We would tether our horses and take positions of defense. Movement would begin in the forest. We would witness battles through mist. Indians, whites, Africs. Whenever ghostly battles appeared, living raiders disappeared.

"Those gents are molded, but never baked hard," Bester said about the raiders. "It's usual."

Since the war, scattered bands of men roam the south. Known as raiders, they are also marauders. They are mostly former soldiers who know about murder, but know little about soldiering and nothing about honor. They are cowards, scamps, violators of women, and burners of cabins and settlements. They will not go face-to-face with a real man. They are backshooters.

"It's not something that's just-minted," Bester told us. "In these hills it's gone on since always. Only the Almighty knows how long."

Before the war, and even now, Indians raid back and forth. They steal women and children, and they kill. Revenge and murder and low deeds are not exclusive to armies.

"But what's baffling," Bester said, "is how the enemies keep changin'. We get half-cooked whites and negras, then we get maverick Cherokee. The only common bond is cowardice."

After ten days we had seen enough to understand that we progressed through history. Spectral Spaniards gave way to spectral Englishmen, and Indian weaponry now included bow and arrow. Then Indians obtained guns. Flintlock pistols appeared. Africs came onto the scene, as slaves, or as adventurers, or raiders. Sometimes we did not witness a battle, but an assassination. Sometimes we saw small settlements burned, or single cabins despoiled. Weapons continued to improve. Woodsmen carried Kentucky rifles which were flintlock, but no longer smoothbore. When cap-and-ball rifles appeared, we became uncertain.

"I already sailed through hell. I'm damned if I want to walk through it." Ephriam said this to Charles, and Ephriam's words sounded like an accusation.

We were suddenly more afraid of each other than of any enemy. We made camp when the sun already stood in back of the hills. Charles tended the horses in declining light. Nobody said a word about losing horses, but the trail was playing out. I privately thought "good riddance." The horses had grown thin and weakish. Only the mule prospered.

Somewhere ahead the trail would narrow and then disappear. I supposed Charles already felt the loss of horses.

"You may get a second helping of hell." Bester knelt above a small cooking fire. He looked toward the horses. "We're walking into something. If the trail was still useful it would be open. Something mighty dead lies westward."

"Talk this out ahead of time." Charles had followed Bester's lead, but now he tried to take charge. "Weapons keep improving. History closes in. We'll soon relive our own sorrows."

I had not thought, when agreeing to this adventure, that I would have to relive the War of the Rebellion. Now three Yankees and a Reb walked toward their recent pasts.

"Get it sorted before we have a spat," Bester told him. "Gravel in your craw. Spit it out." Bester still knelt before the fire, but he suddenly seemed tuned to action. Our rifles were stacked, but our revolvers were right at hand. Bester spoke quietly, as bespeaks a confident man.

"Start with this," Ephriam said, and he was equally quiet. "Why would a man of your complexion stand with the Confederacy?" Ephriam always signals his willingness to fight with a small laugh, as though indifferent.

"And why in the name of Old Ned would a man of your complexion march into another man's house, and burn it?" Bester's anger sounded dangerous. He shifted his weight, but lightly. His position changed and he could now get at his sheathed knife, as well as his revolver.

"I understand," Charles said. "Men defend their homes. We all understand that."

"You understand horseshit," Bester told him. "I had a place. Had to kill a man to get it."

"Not original," Charles said easily. "We've all killed more than our share."

"Difference is," Bester said, "the gent I killed thought that he owned me. I even owe him somewhat. I even halfway liked the bastard. He brought me up as a house nigger."

And that, I thought, explained why Bester, when he wished, could act like a southern gentleman.

Bester was not done with Ephriam. "Your sojer boys burned me out. Be glad for them that I had nor chick, nor child, for I would have tracked them even after I sent them to hell. As it was I left three rotting in the weeds." Bester paused. He was clearly trying to hold his temper. "So why does a man of your complexion come barreling into another man's business?" he asked Ephriam. Then Bester turned to Charles. "Are you forgivin' me? Because don't. I'm not particularly forgivin' you."

"Forgiving is for priests. Don't get me started on blackbirds and their rosaries." Charles actually chuckled, and that broke some of the tension.

"You were in the goddamned Navy," Bester said to Ephriam, "and you're ready to talk to me about slavery?" He sounded more peaceable, like he too was about to laugh. Then he did laugh. It was a harsh laugh, but allowed space for argument.

And Ephriam, who is no fool, saw the foolishness of anybody ever trying to enslave Bester. And, Ephriam thought of the Navy; of filthy rations, flogging which was supposed to have ended in 1844, scurvy, and death so slow and painful that hanging would be a mercy. And Ephriam also laughed. A little. Tension began to abate, but all of us remained aware of weapons kept handy.

"There were no statesmen," I told them. "There were soldiers, and villains, and slave holders and Massachusetts industrialists, and bad generals and bad politicians and stupid presidents. We four were soldiers. Don't shove politics or memories onto each other." For once I was glad for my size and strength. Big men can command attention if they wish.

"Soldiering," Charles said. "We were all good at it. Hold on to that. Put memory on the shelf."

Easier said than done. Soldiering means battles, and battles mean unspeakable acts. In battle, all of us had cursed some of our fellows even as we cursed the enemy. All of us had fought beside men we loved and respected, but we had also fought beside men so foul and wild-eyed that the only cure for them was a Minie ball. Not all death in battle is caused by the enemy. An army cleans its ranks of certain kinds of filth.

As tension eased a thought occurred. I knew the quality of my comrades. Any fight between us would be face to face. At least no one had to worry about turning his back. A good deal of respect came with the thought, and a good deal of comfort.

And so we had avoided a fight, but we had not avoided suspicion between ourselves and Bester. We trekked for three more days. Black smoke rose from valleys. We heard the roll of drums, and distant Thunder. Cannon echoed through the valleys. I kept thinking of the young boy I'd killed. During the war I had seen things so obscene that the mere killing of a lad seemed pale. The difference was that I had seen those things, but not done them; well, not exactly; well, not all of them.

But, I had killed the boy. I had watched his eyes, had seen startlement and fear when he looked at remnants of his hand. I had felt his skull crush beneath my blow. Pondering, I forgot to pay attention. I cannot imagine allowing myself to be so stupid.

Toward sunset we unsaddled nervous horses in a grassy glade. From the forest came crashing of a heavy body. Somewhere ahead lay an end to the trail. We feared what we would find. I, who was comforted by the crashing sounds in the forest, was surprised when we were attacked.

"Soul-catchers are about to make a catch." Bester yelled as he sought cover.

Charles and Ephriam grabbed rifles and headed for shelter

among trees. Mud exploded between the legs of my horse, and the horse jumped sideways and shrieked. The horse banged against me, and mud from the shot splashed my leg. I held the reins, and staggered like a drunken man while fumbling for my rifle. Then I fell and rolled. Charles had one horse on long tether, one on short. Two horses fled. The mule cried, stomped, became crazed and would actually have rolled, but Charles ran to it. He used it as shield while he calmed it and secured its lead. From the forest across the glade came whoops and hollers, but not the whoops of Indians. These were renegade white.

"Take our front," Bester told Charles. To Ephriam he said, "Drift to the left." He moved quickly to the right and into the forest, silent as a ghost. Ephriam shrugged, gave a low laugh, and looked almost happy. He rolled to the edge of the glade and found thin cover behind leggy rhododendron. I turned from the yells and covered our rear.

The glade was a circle of grass. I wagered to myself that yells from across the glade were another trick, and that attack would come from behind us. I would get first shot. I got the second. Bester's rifle sounded. From cover a man rose, staggered, fell, flopped around for a moment and lay quiet. He was red-haired and wearing dirty linsey-woolsey now flushed with blood.

My shot caught a second raider in the face. A 45-70 is a dreadful weapon. The man's head did not disappear, but most of it did. This raider wore filthy store clothes, and one could not tell much about him because of the missing face.

Silence. Yells ceased. Movement ceased. From somewhere in the trees came the chuckling call of ravens. More silence, as if we and the world waited and wondered. Then ravens flocked above the dead men. They hovered in trees.

"Thin pickings," Bester said about the ravens. "They wait for the souls to depart." He still scanned the forest as he searched for the enemy.

The ravens descended in a flock but did not alight. They flew in circles no higher than two feet above the dead men. They called as they flew, and then, dropped. They covered the corpses. I could swear, and I am not a mystical man, that the dead man with the red hair uttered a curse. His lips moved, his dead eyes rolled as sounds of crashing came from the forest.

Then Thunder exploded, not from the west but from above.

141

Thunder boomed stronger than massed artillery. It pounded onto the forest, and the very side of the hill trembled. Thunder rolled about valleys and hollows, and wind rode the Thunder. Wind rose among trees, and small branches flew all around. Yet, there was no rain.

Sunlight pinioned the dead men across the stream. Wind moved red hair of one, blew against blood and gore of the other and tore at clothing. Ravens rode the wind as easily as kites on a breezy day. Then they rose with the wind and disappeared over the forest.

Wind wrapped around us and forced us to ground. Sunlight seemed brighter, and where there should have been rain, and should have been lightning, there was only Thunder. We yelled to each other through crashes of Thunder, and our voices were like spirits calling across distance, like echoes across time.

And all of it happening in sunlight. When Thunder stopped as quickly as it began I found myself lying not far from Charles. The tethered horses were crazed. The mule stood drooping, beyond madness, broken and stunned.

"Good shooting," Bester said, and I did not know whether he spoke of his shot or mine. "Pretty good dust-up." He emerged from the forest and stood beside me. He looked toward Charles, looked at the horse. "I figured," he told Charles, "we'd end up trading horses, not losing 'em. Let's chew this over." He watched forest across the glade while I watched forest behind the dead men. "I heard six men," Bester said. "We got the two who weren't yelling. There were eight, all told."

"Free the remaining horses, keep the mule." Charles did not like what he was saying, but then, Charles is fond of horses. "Better the raiders have them than they fall as prey." The horses were domesticated beasts. They were unlikely candidates for life in a forest of predators.

It made sense. The trail was playing out. If raiders had horses, they would have to go back along useable trail, not forward.

"Strip all gear and cache it," Bester said. "Make it plain what you're doing. We'll lay a trap." Bester gave a low laugh, and it was neither humorous nor kind. "Somebody will get the horses, never fear." He continued to watch the forest. "Thunder," he said, "that's what the old woman sent. That god-blessed bear is Thunder."

Charles calmed the two remaining horses. We left them unhobbled in the glade. It's a tribute to Charles that they grazed, because a short time before they had gone mad.

We cached saddles and harness, tossed saddlebags onto the mule, then trekked into the forest. We walked for a good half mile, then tethered the mule and turned back.

"One volley," Bester said. "That's all we'll get."

By the time we returned to the glade two raiders sat astride our runaway horses. The man in command was well groomed compared to four others who were at the cache retrieving saddles. The commander sat his horse in the style of an aristocrat. Although he was not a large man his presence was forceful. He dressed in brushed gray coat and clean trousers. He gave quiet orders that were obeyed immediately. I thought at the time that it would be of some note to kill this silken gentleman. In these wet forests it seemed that one mostly killed riff-raff.

The two men Bester and I had shot lay like discarded rags. They were ignored by the living raiders. Since the departure of the ravens the corpses looked shrunken. The red hair no longer glowed. It looked bloody-brown.

We took cover at the edge of the forest. We had a clear view of the glade.

"Take the horseman on the right," Bester whispered to me. To Charles and Ephriam he whispered, "on my signal." When he was satisfied that all was in place he gave the command to fire.

Both horsemen were dead before they hit the ground. The leader's chest exploded. He jolted up and back. Some dying instinct flung him backward as he tried to clear stirrups he didn't have. The horses wheeled and once more ran. The second corpse lay trampled. Two men at the cache, shot by Ephriam and Charles, had been carrying saddles. They staggered beneath the heavy bullets: .45 caliber, 70 grains of powder. They fell, then one tried to rise and run. Charles finished him off, while the other gasped blood and then lay motionless. Two other men fled into the forest.

"Prayers do get answered," Bester said. "I got to figure that nearby, some women have been prayin' for widowhood." He rose and spat toward the corpses, then walked away without a second glance. Ravens chortled in the distance. I took satisfaction in hearing them.

We trekked for another day and then the trail played out, but not the way we had supposed. We found ourselves on a high ridge looking into a barren valley. In the midst of mountains covered with dense forest, we viewed naked ground. Smoke from fires showed where downed trees still burned, and a clear stream turned into a dark flood as it rushed through the valley. Stench of putridity rose on a breeze. The remains of a broken cabin lay scorched beside the stream. At the head of the valley another cabin sat gutted and smoking. This had once been a settlement.

Guns lay tumbled, and bodies in ragged gray lay scattered. Bodies dressed in sturdy blue lay in waves across the face of the hill. We walked toward a battlefield of a too-familiar kind.

"... difference between spirits and ghosts ..." Bester whispered. "You can generally smell the ghosts." For the first time since we met Bester we saw him hesitate. He probably tried to guess our minds, as we were trying to guess his.

After losing the horses and killing six raiders, I hoped any differences between us were past. We had stood beside each other in battle. We had relied on each other.

"This is the past," Charles murmured. "Hang onto that, gentlemen. It's been said and done."

"Agreed," Bester told him, "but we walk through it, not around it." He looked west where a sky dark as ravens was cut by hot streaks of light, and illumed by orange glows of fire. "Not because we want," Bester added. "But I figger there's no god-blessed avoidance."

We descended into the valley, and we were as heavily laden with memory as the mule was laden with gear. The animal grew increasingly skittish, though broken of spirit. It still walked well. A well-found mule is one of the strongest of living creatures. Some even have character.

I remembered thinking that if we moved toward the future, nothing the future would have to show would be worse than walking through this valley. Then I wondered how, if ghosts of Spaniards could not see us because we were their future, could we see our future in that orange-glowing west? For a dazed moment I had the sense that we not only walked through the past, but toward it. And that made no sense.

Dead men and dead horses lay all around. Stench covered the battlefield like a blanket, and small animals moved among the dead. We walked with care. Grotesque faces, men and horses, broken and twisted limbs, even oddly fashioned deaths... one cannoneer leaned against a blasted stump, and his death had not come from shot. A piece of wood pierced his throat, wood exploded from his cannon's carriage.

As if mesmerized we followed the blackened stream. The mule seemed ready to bolt. The stream tumbled around corpses, and even the running water carried stench. When we passed the first broken cabin I looked inside and wished I had not. A man's head peered with ivory-blank eyes. Only the head. Long-haired. Teeth curiously shiny, the lips more smile than grimace. The body had been exploded.

Charles grunted like a man hit. Bester snarled. Ephriam made no sound. I recall thinking that we were passing through the worst of this particular battle. The going would get easier.

The going did not, and I wish that a clear record of this part of our adventures did not have to be made. We passed the depth of the valley where the stream curved away and ran toward a distant river. At the bend sat the other cabin we had seen from the ridge. This cabin had not been under direct fire from the battlefield.

As we approached we heard tiny cries echoing from the cabin. We knew full well that we dealt with specters, yet the cries sounded authentic. We had to look.

A corpse lay beside the doorway. It was dressed in rough and torn garments. A rusty pistol still lay in its outstretched hand. This was the remains of a settler, a three-for-a-penny farmer.

Bester stood above the corpse. "You ignorant fool," he said to the corpse. "You should have taken your folks and fled. You doubly-dammed fool. Did you think an army wouldn't pay its respects?"

Charles stood in the doorway. "For his sake," Charles said about the settler, "I hope he died first."

And Ephriam, whose experience had been limited to men killing each other at sea, leaned against the door post. Ephriam knew about dead men but not about land warfare. He looked sick. Then Ephriam walked away to stand beside the stream. He stared into the sky, like a man looking for a God that he could curse.

In the cabin a girl of ten or eleven lay naked, broken, obviously raped. She had been barefoot and one ankle was twisted, broken, and she had thus suffered greatly. She had then been murdered by knife and scalped.

A young woman, also raped, lay disemboweled with her foetus torn from her belly. A small boy lay with his skull caved in beside an old woman who had been bayoneted. Her blood lay like a thin carpet across the dirt floor of the cabin. In the old woman's arms lay another boy-child of perhaps two years. It had crawled to the arms of its dead grandmother. It wailed, and the cry was weak from starvation and want of water. Its eyes were crusted and closed. Thus had it lived the last days of its short life, thus had it died.

"Cherokee don't scalp," Bester murmured. "Your northern boys bagged themselves another Confederate." Bester knelt for a moment before the torn foetus. It was almost a child. The eyes were formed. It had rudimentary fingers. "Brave men. Brave men. A young nation's pride." He walked away from us, and did not say another word for the rest of that ugly day. And we had nothing to say to him.

But Ephriam had something to say to me. He drew me aside. "I reckon that was unusual?"

"No," I admitted. "A man could wish that it was."

"T'wasn't manly," he said. "Don't mention that, and manhood, in the same breath." And, from then on, Ephriam barely hid his disgust for us.

III

Strikes of light grew frequent as we moved west. Trees usually shattered and smoked, but sometimes the air only sizzled with heat. Thunder walked nearby in the shape of a bear; or so Bester claimed.

We saw amazing changes in weapons; new smells to the stench of battle, new shapes to the sounds of war. Smells of burnt powder grew sharper. Smoke from cannon and rifle turned pale and gray instead of thick and cloudy. Cannon no longer gave flat reports. Cannon cracked sharp as a slap on the face of the world.

Stench of the dead remained the same. Razorback hogs still fed on corpses, while raccoons and rats competed with the hogs. The battlefields were hurry-scurry with movements of feeding beasts.

We skirted battles, but might have walked through the middle of them. Ghostly weapons exploded, and ghostly men fell. We walked unharmed, except in our dreams.

Ephriam kept to himself. During the war Ephriam had ordered the corpses of comrades, or pieces of corpses, tossed over the side after battle. He had directed men as they drew sea water and washed gore from decks. But, he had never seen raping of children and the murder of babies. When he spoke at all, Ephriam spoke to Bester. He treated Charles' mild suggestions as unwanted orders, and scarcely honored Charles with a reply. He treated me as an accomplice. I did not respond. I had my own troubles.

We felt immersed in new weapons and old miseries. We at first believed we heard one of the new Gatling guns. When we finally identified the weapon we found it was far smaller than a Gatling, like artillery reduced in size. It sprayed shot too quickly to count.

"We have surely passed into the future." Charles said this as we camped beside a stream. August heat had given way to September mist. Westward, the sky glowed with fire and sundown. Surrounding mountains already lay darkened, the mountains still verdant but with trees in beginning change. We had progressed well and game remained plentiful. The mule proved sure-footed but weakening. It was a large, black animal with a hide that had once glistened in the sun. Now its flesh was thinning, its spirit broken. We lightened its load. We kept all of our salt and tobacco, a little coffee, a little tea, and most of our ammunition.

"I recollect one evening," Bester said, "when our boys sat at a fire like this and admired the better shooting of the enemy." Bester hunkered before the fire. His dark face seemed to absorb and reflect, at the same time, the fire-glow. He whetted his skinning knife on a pocket stone. The blade reflected the fire, dull red. "One of the reasons you gents took such pains to lose good men was because you were too disciplined."

"I like a joke same as the next man. Too disciplined?" Ephriam did not understand what Charles and I knew to be true.

"Take a lesson from the raiders," Bester told him. "Never make a frontal attack when you got other ways to jump. If the damned general says t'otherwise, shoot the damned general. Your lads didn't shoot the general." To Charles, he said, "I don't figure we walk in the future. If we do, there's no sense to it."

"It isn't only time, but place." Charles sounded pettish because he had lost control of our party. Ephriam ignored him. I looked to Bester, because Bester was the woodsman. Charles was in no position to argue, but was not ready to concede his notions. "During the late war there were no major engagements in these hills."

"But we've seen them." I, too, was puzzled. "And we see strange and frightening weapons. We see a panorama of war."

"Displacement, maybe." Bester looked at orange glow to the westward. "You early on lost a horse from one of the strokes of light. But ghosts can't see us or harm us. It figures that sometimes we're reading the past, and sometimes the present is reading us." He examined the knife blade, shaved a bit of hair from his arm, and satisfied, sheathed the knife. He pulled from a pocket the small piece of hardened clay and wires that had fallen from the sky, and which he had shown us when we first met. He studied it like a man studies terrain before a battle.

". . . somewhere east of Eden in the land of Nod. . . ." As Ephriam muttered he looked at Charles, as though he searched for the mark of Cain. He hunkered beside Bester, and those two strong men looked diminished in the gathering darkness.

"If the future can kill a horse, and strike trees, then it's part of the present." Charles spoke easily enough but he seemed edgy. "If the future can survey us then we're ghosts ourselves."

"As, someday, it seems we will be." I was not entranced with that sort of afterlife.

"We came adventuring." Charles mused to himself. "We came in behalf of ethnology, and now we engage in defeating war." He looked at Bester. "Time is a-whirl?"

"The war didn't braid this nation. The war knotted it." Bester's face was as studied as our own. "Nothing that came before, and I reckon nothing that comes afterward, will get it total unknotted." He rose from the fire and faced the western hills. Thunder rolled in the distance.

"The war deeded an attack on settled ways," Bester told Charles. "War tried to make everybody the same."

"It was war on behalf of commerce," I said. "Northern cotton men wanted to control the supply. Southern growers bound themselves to English mills to lift the price. It was war between men with different ideas about money."

"You boys think the Confederate soldier gave one whoop or hosannah about slavery? You think wrong." Bester seemed to be answering me, but in a way I could not understand.

"I think so," Ephriam said, and he was grim. "Otherwise, why were we fussin'?"

"Things got unsettled," Bester told him. He turned the piece of fired clay and colored cylinder over and over in his hand. "We're in a place where all kinds of men have brought their ways. These hills took them in and changed them, or killed them. Then war invaded. It wanted to missionary us heathens . . . and still does . . . make us into little Lincolns and Sumners. Slavery was its grand excuse."

"Damned good excuse."

"No one's denying it," Bester told Ephriam. "There were white slave holders, and negra slave holders, and Indian slave holders. But that's not the point." Bester then spoke directly to Charles. "Maybe you actually do want to learn about folks and not change 'em. If true t'would be refreshin'."

"Unsettled," Charles said. "The ancient tries to preserve, and the future tries to overwhelm."

"I'd almost wish for more raiders," Ephriam muttered. "At least a man's shooting at somebody who can shoot back."

"You won't get 'em," Bester told him. "Cowards won't walk through what we're about."

Next morning, and well before sun rose above the hills, the mule turned up missing. Ephriam had hobbled it with rope, and Ephriam's sailor-knots do not slip unless he wills it.

"Maybe I mistook about raiders. Strayed or stolen." Bester searched a wide half-circle around our camp and found no sign. He crossed the stream and found no sign. An animal that large would have left a track. There was none. For a wild moment I thought the beast had faded and become insubstantial, like mist.

"Who would have ever figured," Bester said, "that a man would mourn a mule." He divided our remaining plunder into lots for pack and carry. Since my strength was large, even if diminished from the long trek, I chose to haul the cartridges. We still had most of them, and they weighed more than enough to make a man mourn a mule.

Then time turned tortuous. Our declining fortunes hovered like night mist. We struck westward at a slower pace, and we found that although we were sure-footed, we were not as agile as a mule.

Since we made slower progress we saw gradual change. Repeating rifles accompanied repeating cannon. Great coils of wire fenced off trenches. Soil exploded upward, and in the midst of explosions men turned to vapor; explosions so hot that not even blood remained. Hand-thrown bombs bounced down hills, or into crevices where rapidly repeating guns chattered in reply. Huge balloons floated high above as men with spyglasses directed cannon fire. Massive machines propelled themselves across the land, but were not steamers. We gazed astounded because the things could move without the use of horses.

"And nothing different except the weapons." Charles probably said it, but all of us thought it. We looked at our own weapons, and were filled with doubt. We became accustomed to sprawled corpses that lay beside every sacrilege man has ever wrought.

And all of it the same except for weapons. Then something changed and our minds recoiled. We heard a buzz, like a water-powered sawmill, but the buzz came from above.

"There's your sky god," Charles murmured to Bester. "Are we believing what I'm seeing."

We stood dumbfounded, as a kite-like apparatus flew above the hills. A man tossed a small object from the kite. It tumbled as it fell, and it exploded near a trench.

"End of the world," Ephriam whispered. "If they can do that, nothing anywhere is safe." He looked at Charles, at me. "Women and children first." He turned away.

Sometimes the panorama changed. Hills faded into the back-ground and it seemed we walked the streets of broken cities. Only the streets remained. They were filled with smoking debris, and, inevitably, the dead: old men, old women, children, pet dogs, while pet cats ran feral; our world, a charnel house.

For a space of many days we trudged forward as if dreaming. Memory turned to vision, and vision performed dramas in our minds. We could no longer tell if what we saw was spectral or real. Worse, we were visited with our most terrible memories. We were no longer as strong as we had been. While sleeping we sometimes woke screaming. When eating, we carefully divided and shared deer liver against illness and scurvy.

In my visions the young boy I'd killed walked beside me like a son beside a father. He offered a name, Tom, and he offered sights he had seen and remembered: He showed me a small, tributary-cruising steamboat a-glitter in bright paint and brass . . . a one ring traveling circus . . . a haying. And he remembered a pretty country lass who to me seemed ordinary enough, but to the boy she was the essence of mystery and beauty.

"Why did you kill me?" he whispered.

"Why were you there?"

"I run away to jine up."

"Your folks?"

"Pa got kilt early on. I left, though Ma said don't." He thought back through his scant past. "Her name is Susy," he said about the country lass.

"Pretty name," I lied.

I walked sobbing, and my companions were kind enough not to notice. They dealt with their own visions.

This dream-state occupied us so we scarcely knew how many miles were passed. All we have is the written record, because, of course, I was scrupulous. It looks like this:

"Fifteenth, ninth month. Followed small river five or six miles until it bent south. Went westering approx two miles straight up, and two miles straight down. Spied an amazingly large woodpecker. Hills not as gentle as they look."

"Eighteenth. Sorrow fills camp. Last night each man woke. Ephriam had watch. We lay in silence for rest of night, and dog tired all day. Silence of sorrow worse than sorrow . . ."

And, of course, I do not understand the meaning of all that I wrote. How can the silence of sorrow be worse than sorrow? Yet, it was true when written.

We only knew that we trekked, made camp, slept, and sometimes woke with throats raw from moans or choking. September sun could not defeat chill breezes that began to blow from hollows and valleys. Days grew shorter. My record of the trek shows that we walked through most of September, but none of us remember the passage. I do not even remember making entries. My record shows that I spent some days thinking only of warm kitchens and cherry pies.

Then we returned to sanity because it seems that time twisted. At any rate, it gave us something we could lay a hand on. I know now that Ephriam, wiser than the rest, brought us out of that fog of memory. He did not order events, but his awareness that we were trapped in memory somehow altered time.

We crossed the side of a low mountain where massive trees blocked sunlight from the forest floor. In parts of these hills pine forests are impenetrable, but in the presence of these giant poplar and oak the forest lay open as a tended grove.

From the morning mist we heard the crack of a rifle. A shot exploded in a tree beside Bester, and Bester fell and rolled for cover. A weapon began to chatter like a gossip telling tales.

"Two of them, anyway." Bester hunkered behind a giant poplar. "An outpost, maybe."

The weapon searched through the forest and we watched, stunned and voiceless as the thing cut down smaller trees. It hammered, fell to silence, hammered. We had huge trees for cover, but not enough undergrowth to move without being seen. We were held in place by a weapon that chattered like a devil with ague.

Worse, we had the low ground. From somewhere at our backs, and above, came a roar and not a buzzing. A silver machine flashed above the forest, and an oblong-shaped object fell in the direction of the chattering weapon. Light bloomed in the forest and trees exploded. A bit of bark, flung like shot, caught Ephriam alongside the cheek as he peered around a tree and looked for a target. He brushed away small bleeding, the injury minor but real. Ephriam actually seemed glad. He cocked his weapon and searched the forest. The enemy out there was corporeal, and could harm. And, it could be harmed.

At our backs shouts came from the forest. Then came a second rushing above our heads, and something exploded in the forest. The chattering stopped.

"Got the dumb-shit," a voice yelled from somewhere behind us. We turned.

"They're not shooting at us," Bester said. "They're shooting at each other. Stay low." Good advice, but not needed.

"Okay for the gold-brickin' Air Corps." We heard the rapid approach of many men. We saw the first one just as the voice said, "Boys, we've got infiltrators or hillbillies. Three medium size and a big'un." The voice now sounded almost conversational. To us it said, "Drop the popguns. Do you bastards speak English?"

The man who appeared from the forest was lean, spare, and clothed in brown uniform. He wore a large helmet and carried an odd-looking rifle. The chevrons on his sleeve were small, where the Union's had been large, but they spoke the same thing. The man was a sergeant.

"Fan out," he told the men with him. "How often I got to tell you yardbirds not to bunch up? Two of you cover these guys, the rest cover the perimeter."

"Be cautious," Ephriam said softly, "about who you're calling a bastard. I don't take kindly." He chuckled. Two men had their rifles pointed at him, but they stepped backward.

"Three whites and a nig," one of the men said to the sergeant. "They brought their minstrel with 'em."

"You are overmatched and about to get scalded," Bester said, and his voice was even more quiet than Ephriam's. "You get one chance to leave before I act. Good advice says, 'take it.'" From some-where in the forest sounded the crashing of a heavy body.

"There ain't nothin' more common than bullshit," the sergeant said. "Swing away."

Wind rose from the west. It started small but grew quickly. Darkness stood like a great cloud behind the wind. In the dark-ness green glows appeared, then began to strike like green light-ning. Lightning flashed above the forest, striking through the wind, although it seemed not to strike trees. It crashed against the ground, and the familiar smell of scorched soil sailed on the wind.

"Bastardly weather." Bester had to yell to be heard. "Name-cal-lin' weather." He turned his back on the rifles and looked into the forest where broken tree limbs rained to the ground.

Wind hit and we staggered. We found that we could not stand, but had to hunker down. Wind put us on all fours and it seemed there was no lee. When we moved behind a tree, wind followed. I knelt and wind ripped at my clothes. I thought the fabric would tear, and I closed my eyes against the wind. Then I shielded my eyes with my hands and peered between fingers. All of us were down, my companions and the soldiers. All except Bester.

He stood, although in such wind it was mortally impossible to stand. He watched the forest, then motioned to us by placing his fingers in his ears. We knew that Thunder would soon arrive. The sergeant and his men did not know.

It came rolling out of the west, and it carried the sound of all the cannon ever fired in all the history of the world. Thunder held darkness in its maw, and darkness seemed a stage on which green lightning danced. Wind swept the floor of the forest, and we lay flat to keep from being carried away. Pressure in my ears was so great that I screamed into the wind and pounding Thunder. Around me men lay balled up, holding their ears, and open-mouthed, showed that they also screamed. They continued screaming for long mo-ments after Thunder ceased.

The cloud of darkness still enclosed the forest, and from the darkness the young woman we had met at the fish trap emerged. She walked without hurry, and with the confidence of complete power. Low light, a green glow, surrounded her. It framed her against the darkness.

Men lay all around, still gasping, and my head ached from the pounding of Thunder. No one reached for a weapon. Our weapons were like toys in the face of such power.

Bester still stood. "Grandmother," he said in a normal voice. "If that's what you want. . . ." He turned to the soldiers. "She just saved your sorry hides. I bid you gents goodbye."

The sergeant and his men rose, and stepping forward, must have stepped across time. One moment they were there, and the next moment they seem to have walked between layers of time, like time was an open door. They simply walked through and disappeared.

"Grandmother," Bester said to the young woman. "It is good that you are here." Then he lapsed into a musical language, part Cherokee, and part something else. Vowels sounded liquid as a running stream, warm as sunlight.

The young woman spoke to Bester. She looked briefly toward us, then turned away. Her look was not unkind. More than anything else, she seemed mildly interested.

Charles, on the other hand, could hardly restrain from questions. He watched as Bester and the woman made signs as they spoke. Their hands moved casually. Bester sounded more comfortable than he had sounded in quite a while.

"Grandmother," Charles whispered. "He called her grandmother, and yet that cannot be."

"Take his word for it," Ephriam snarled. "After all that's happened, take the man's word."

"And is he a man?" I could not explain how Bester could stand in wind so strong that other men had been forced to ground.

"I'm blamed sure of one thing," Ephriam told me. "You can't lick him and I won't. If you're thinking fight, don't think it."

Ephriam had given voice to thoughts I tried to avoid. The war had placed a gulf of fury between us. Anger dwelt deep in all our hearts and bones. We had narrowly avoided a fight when Ephriam asked Bester why a man of his color stood with the Confederates. I remembered when we discovered the foetus ripped from its mother's womb, and the child crying in its dead grandmother's arms. We had wisely said nothing to Bester. And, Bester, equally wise, had not said much.

The gulf was there. We would be fools to pretend it did not exist. We watched as the young woman turned from us without a glance and walked into the forest. She disappeared among the trees.

For a short space we stood voiceless. Then Bester turned. "She tells that all the time that ever was, or ever will be, is happening all the time. What do we make of that?"

I looked around. There were no broken trees, no smells of burning soil, no indication that a skirmish had been fought here. The forest towered above us unchanged and silent.

"She says," Bester continued, "that the hard part lies ahead." He began to collect his gear. He glanced west and for the moment seemed exhausted, the way men look after battle. "I kinda regret havin' tugged you citizens into this."

Charles murmured. "Make camp. Puzzle this out. Get the lay of the land. Start tomorrow fresh." He did not mean to embarrass Bester, but he was clearly trying to regain control of the party.

"I got the lay," Bester told him. "What I don't have is understandin' it." He sounded puzzled. "I think I just stood in a time when no wind was blowin', and you were in a time when wind was. And take a lesson on what happened to those sojer boys." He dropped his gear, sat on his pack, and rested.

"I'd think," I said, "the woman might have warned us before this."

"Listen to the man," Ephriam told Bester. "He may not be smarter, but he's bigger."

"I reckon she just figured it herself," Bester told me. "The old people see time like a circle. This 'all the time that ever was or ever will be is happenin' all the time' . . . would be new."

"You called her 'grandmother.' She can't be more than twenty-five." Charles, I remember thinking, was more interested in his damned ethnology than in getting out of this fix. Or, maybe he tried to exercise authority. I also remember thinking that I had completely lost confidence in Charles. And how did the woman know that things were going to get worse?

"If time is a circle," Bester said, "then she just steps across the circle. These old people are practical." He sat head down, and weighed with thought he was not ready to discuss. "If she needs to travel she crosses the circle and steps into her body when it was young. Try traveling when you're ancient and stove up. What she does ain't nothin' but practical."

In the days, then weeks, that followed we walked across a darkening land. We saw fewer battles, but more remains of battles. We saw terrible machines broken and torn. Huge, winged things flashed overhead and screamed, or thundered. Litter of small wires and colorful cylinders became common. They were like the one Bester said had fallen from the sky.

Bester examined a few of them. "T'ain't magic. They're parts of something. Flying machines explain the strikes of light, and I maybe see why we're wanted here."

"Strikes of light must come from lenses, like in a lighthouse," Ephriam said. "Arrange enough lenses and you can cast lamplight seven leagues." He looked to Bester. "That doesn't tell why we're wanted here?"

"I reckon war was moving east, and we're pushing it back. I wonder how far it's gotta be pushed?"

We saw corpses that seemed milled into the machines, like grain ground between stones. It became no longer possible to say which was metal and which was bone. We no longer saw the dead as having once lived.

Overhead, odd looking things flew without wings. They gave sounds of chip, chip, chip and whir above the forest. It was interesting at first. But, we became more and more aware that the final product of war is boredom. We were more concerned with our boots, which were wearing out, than with flight or death.

By the third day of November the orange glow had completely disappeared. A red horizon rose just beyond the next mountain, and silver machines sailed through the sky like bolts of lightning. Strikes of light came from the machines. Sometimes one of the machines exploded in a gush of fire.

Finally, Bester halted our trek. We bivouacked beneath a ledge of rock beside a stream. "We're not robed for winter," he told us. "I reckoned this job would be done by now, but it ain't. Get ready to spend a month."

"A month?" Charles sounded absolutely disgusted.

"Takes that long for tanning."

"We could press on," Ephriam said. "Get it over."

"I've been told what we oughta do." Bester looked west. "Beyond yon hill we'll get into the thick of it. We'd need robing, even t'was midsummer."

"The old woman told you. You're under orders?" Charles' disgust now included the old woman.

"I'm under good advice," Bester told him. "If the old woman says robe, we robe. I'll try to discover beaver, but trust in deer. We'll build dead-falls if we must."

"If a man can build boats," Ephriam told Bester, "he can build shelter. I'll put together a pole cabin." Ephriam actually sounded eager. After the uncertainty of the long trek, he now had a job that fitted.

"You aim to tan hides?" I knew nothing about tanning, except that it smelled like Satan's armpit.

"We got a little salt, lye from wood ashes, and we can use the brains of deer for tanning. Don't know why that works, but the old folks use it. I'll bring in the game."

"Bear," Charles said. "Bear is warmer."

Bester looked toward the forest and actually grinned. "You wanta try? Better study on it." To me he said, "Build drying racks and a big circle of fire rings. Weather ain't with us." To Charles he said, "Take charge of fish. I'll show you how to build a fish trap." Bester spoke most pleasantly.

Charles, on the other hand, went silent and angry. Charles could walk through the blood of battle, but turned squeamish before the gutting of fish. Either that, or the job was beneath him. . . .

Back during the war, when bivouacked between battles, men became ill. No one got sick in battle. After battle, though, and when men let down, disease stalked the army as a vengeful presence. And, the moment we let down, it stalked us.

First Charles, then I, fell like men slain before the hand of disease. Charles lay rolled in blankets, gasping like a man in the final stage of consumption. I held out for three more days, illness grasping toward me. I weakened while hauling stones for fire rings. Ephriam built a cabin, using the cliff and ledge as a back wall. I pulled in massive amounts of wood, and told myself to conquer the disease. Then, in spite of all effort, I collapsed; racked with choking and nigh breathless.

A blank space exists in this record. I grew hot, then cold, and lay wrapped a-tremble in blankets. I recall babbling, calling the names of women long ago betrayed, of comrades long dead; and I talked to remembered faces of men I had killed.

Charles the same. Charles babbled the names of horses, and he called to the memory of his mother in the same way he spoke to horses. Sometimes his mother was a horse, or so it seemed in his mind. Sometimes Charles cursed. Unusual, because Charles does not curse. Yet, when I gained a few lucid moments I heard him out-swear a sailor. And it seemed, he too, had betrayed loved women, but done even worse with women; and had murdered prisoners. In my delirium I wondered if what Charles babbled was true or only make-believe.

We owed our lives to Ephriam, to Bester, and to Indian medicine that Charles had traded for back in August. Ephriam and Bester were heroic. They kept a stout fire going, night and day. They forced bitter medicine down throats that tried to close. When we fought against the medicine they forced our jaws open. Ephriam spoke to us, crooned to us, even joked to us. When I was so dazed that a comfortable slide into death held certain beauty, Bester pummeled me, insulted me, invited me to be angry at him; enough anger to propel me back into life.

The illness crested, fever broke, and I began feeble movement within the small cabin. Ephriam did not speak as kindly after my illness, as during. No doubt I had babbled things best left unsaid.

I had lost the date. "How many days?" I asked Ephriam. And he said, "Too many. Maybe ten all told."

Thus, while time might move all around us, my sense of time become provisional. Entries start with apologies, as for example: "18th day 11th month, or perhaps the 17th, and certainly no more than the 20th, 1879. . . ."

Even worse, time grew frantic. It jumped like Mexican beans. We heard the soft tramp of horses in the forest. We heard the cries of men; commanding, swearing. At other times we saw creatures resembling men, but not fully. And, sometimes, music sounded through the forest, brass bands playing oddly syncopated rhythms, or church choirs singing. At other times, only a great depth of silence.

We recovered slowly. My huge frame seemed to me, thin. For three days I could take little food, and that mostly broth boiled from deer bones. Charles suffered worse. After a week he became able to feed himself, but was not able to walk for another week. When he once more stepped from the cabin an ice-filled wind blew through the forest, and the rushing stream had dwindled. Ice formed along its banks. Snow lay tramped, and showed where Ephriam and Bester had searched for wood.

When I tried to thank Ephriam he said, "Seems like in battle the first man killed is always the ship's doctor. A sailor learns how to make do." His voice was not cordial.

I have always been stronger than other men, and have taken strength for granted. If not Herculean, I could at least pick up and reset a cannon while other men could not. Weakness had been un-known, but now I sat dumbly and scraped hides. I was good for noth-ing else. The shale scrapers crumbled as I worked; shale a poor sub-stitute for flint. As strength gradually returned I knew I would never again be as strong. I reflected on the difference between humiliation and humility. I am not the first bookish man to have done so.

While Bester and Ephriam worked, time flashed. Sometimes we woke, only to discover dawn turning to dusk. Entire days scam-pered away, then other days would repeat: the same weather, the same incidents in forest or stream, all of it the same; repeated.

Charles remained close to being invalid. He walked timid as an ancient man stepping on cobblestones. Ephriam cut a stout stick for Charles, and throughout December Charles hobbled.

Christmas came and went. I noted its passage, more or less, but the glorious event failed to inspire. Bester hummed to himself, but it was not a hymn. Ephriam spent most of the day alone in the for-est. Charles murmured about Christmas ham.

The New Year arrived. Approximately. The year 1880 did not look promising.

We huddled near the fire as red glow flashed in the west. Snow covered the ground, melted, returned; then came ice. Freezing rain formed on trees and great branches crashed to ground. The stream dwindled further, froze, and we melted ice to gain water.

"A month more," Bester said. "Gain strength. We'll make an end to this in a month." He and Ephriam laced together cloaks using strips of scraped and tanned hide. "Not too tight, sailor," he told Ephriam. ". . . must be a bit of give or they'll bust."

We sat in the cabin before a small fire. Smoke wound its way along the back wall, up the ledge, and through a trough that Eph-riam had hacked from the limestone. "What lies yonder," Ephriam asked. "What lies beyond these hills?"

"Tennessee," Bester told him, "or Kentucky, if north. Due south ought to be Georgia."

"Flatland and big rivers," Charles murmured. "Steamboats. Trains. Commerce. Civilization." Charles' voice held yearning that said, even he, had a bellyful when it came to ethnology.

"Or, maybe not." Bester's dark skin no longer glowed beneath firelight. His fatigue was great, but he only allowed it to show after the day's work. "I won't even declare we're in North Carolina. We should have got beyond these hills a good while back."

"We're in Purgatory," Charles murmured. "Don't talk to me about North Carolina."

The month passed. Each evening we looked toward the west where red turned to orange, and then orange turned to a sullen combination of silver and blue. Snow and ice covered the forest, but westward looked even colder. Only one noteworthy thing happened. The lost mule either stepped through time, or wandered into camp.

On a cold morning, with silver mist hovering above the stream, the once-vanished mule scavenged thin forage. It was still hobbled, and while we were thin, it was gaunt. The animal's hide was dull and patchy, its withers obviously weak, its ribs prominent.

"Shoot the creature," Ephriam said. "T'will be a mercy."

That was not to be. The appearance of the mule breathed new life, or at least hope, into Charles. "It is my mule," he told Ephriam, "and we'll not shoot it."

"It is your mule," I admitted. "You financed this adventure." I knew Charles well. He would not stay with us much longer. Bester and Ephriam did not see what to me was obvious. They likely thought that when we broke camp the mule would be freed to find its fate.

Charles stayed for one more week, and he spent that week finding forage for the mule. Then, on a gray and silver morning when mist seemed frozen on the mountaintops, Charles spoke to Bester. "We'll break camp, trek south into Georgia."

"We'll not," Bester told him, and Bester was calm. "We have a duty."

"I have a duty," Charles said, and he sounded plaintive. "My belly has digested enough roots and venison and varmints. I've got a duty to get warm and clean." He looked toward me. "And ethnology can go to the Devil."

"Take a robe," Bester told him. "Don't catch a chill." He turned away in disgust.

"Go on," Ephriam told Charles. "Ride all the way to hell if that's what's pleasing to you."

I had nothing to say. I could only wonder if a Yankee headed south was a lesson to the mule, or to Georgia. The last I saw of Charles was his thin figure astride a starved animal that plodded southward. He was, after all, a man who loved horses.

IV

With Charles departed, a sense of ease, or even accomplishment filled our camp. Ephriam did not whistle or jest, but he no longer seemed displeased with every word I spoke. Perhaps my choosing to stay, rather than fleeing south, caused Ephriam to see me as separate from Charles.

"Pitiful," Ephriam said, and looked in the direction Charles had taken.

"He was capable during battle," I told Ephriam. "He was an officer, I a gunner." That was as much explanation as I was willing to give.

Thunder rumbled from the east. Without our noticing, Thunder had moved from west to east, and now it urged us toward the west. If we had thoughts of retreat, we could forget them.

Westward the orange sky had long ago faded, and the sky now glowed in tones of blue and silver that made one think of ice. Charles might fail his duty, but we could not fail ours. At the same time, one could not help but shiver when looking west.

For two more days we paused because Bester balked. He seemed undecided, although he did practical things. He cleaned his weapons. He rolled and unrolled his pack as he decided how much he might carry. Bester was so meticulous that anyone could see he delayed while making up his mind. Finally, on the second night, he decided.

We huddled in the cabin. We had used extra skins lashed with rawhide to cover outside walls. They attracted varmints but protected against wind. In this early February, with ice skimming the land, the skins did not stink. Warmth inside the cabin was seductive. We did not relish a trek into winter.

"We leave Thunder here," Bester began. His brow wrinkled. Firelight softened his dark skin but the wrinkles were shadowed and black. "No. Thunder leaves us." He hesitated. He did not want to say what he knew he must say. "Beyond yon ridge we leave everything: forest, old woman . . . I know not what else."

"The old woman told you?"

"We can choose to see this through together, or we can go our separate ways. As near as I can figure, we're looking at a different kind of battle."

"We've come this far together."

"Problem is," Bester told me, "there's weight between us. We got to get it settled. We got to be together in fact, as well as name. . . ."

"The war is over."

"You're dreamin," Bester told me. "North will never respect the south, and south will never get done despisin' the north. The war will never get over."

"I didn't burn cabins," Ephriam said. "I helped burn prizes to the water when we had no prize crews left. I fired on blockade runners. I killed men, but I never burned no cabin." It was not exactly an apology.

"If the war is never over, why in the name of Old Ned are we talking?" I didn't challenge Bester. It was an honest question. "You soldiered," I told Bester, "and I soldiered. I don't know what you did, and you know damn-all about me." I looked to Ephriam. "And you don't know either."

"You told tales whilst sick." Bester was grim.

"You were present at the telling, but not the happening. You weren't there."

"Damn good thing."

"What tales might you have to tell?" I asked.

They sat quiet, and they thought. For the space of some minutes neither spoke.

"I can see how a man might have had his reasons." Bester yawned, but the yawn was forced. He pretended he didn't care. "You in or out of what comes next?"

"I'll think about it," I told him, then paused. The other choice was to go it alone. That seemed awful. "I'm in. Someone has to watch over you gentlemen."

Ephriam chuckled. "In," he told Bester. "If only to view the show."

Thunder stood at our backs like an encouraging hand. We left the cabin and most of our equipment. We walked heavily robed. We carried light packs, bedrolls and weapons. For the moment, Thunder seemed a friend, or at least an ally. It rumbled like a giant clearing his throat as we climbed to the western ridge.

A tortuous climb. Once, in the long ago, I could lift cannon. Now it seemed almost impossible to place one foot before the other. My boot soles were thin as paper, my breathing shallow and forced. If it had not been for the strength of Thunder, I could not have pressed forward. My comrades the same. Ephriam huffed and puffed. He had lost weight and was no longer shaped like a barrel. Even Bester seemed thin. He led, but slowly.

Once on the ridge we looked down onto a landscape of a thousand smokes. Sunlight pierced gray mist, was swallowed by mist. Chill rose through the sunlight like the cold of a grave. It was enough to make the strongest heart turn back. Sunlight funneled into mist, like milk in a churn.

Struggles went on down there, but of what kind and quality I could not say. It seemed that smokes from not a thousand, but many thousand fires rose black through silver mist. Although cold rose from the valley, red flashes glowed hot as anthracite.

I thought of turning back and dismissed the thought. I could not fail Ephriam and Bester. Then I told myself to be honest. The long trek down to an empty cabin seemed more awful than being swallowed by mist.

Our descent produced layers of dread. If Thunder had not mumbled like a sleepy animal, the descent would have been impossible. Thunder then faded, and was gone.

"We're on our own, gents," Bester muttered. "I figger we're headed to a place where no one rules."

Dread arrived during the first thousand yards. We did not know where we were, but it was certain it was not the Great Smoky Mountains. Or, anywhere else frequented by living man. Of the dead, though, there were a-plenty.

"A cloak, a cloak." The voice quavered like that of an ancient man, but I saw no man. At the same time, the voice sounded familiar, if haunted. Ephriam turned, bewildered, looked all about. Bester shook himself, like a dog shaking water from its coat. He looked confused, and Bester was never one to be confused.

The voice rose from a scorched landscape and the voice surrounded us. I feared I would actually breathe it in, and tried to slow my breathing. "Poor him's a-cold, poor him. A cloak, a cloak."

Fires burned here and there, and wrecked trees smoldered. Yet, the voice complained of cold. It grew faint as we passed downward. Cold wrapped the side of the hill, a cloak, no doubt, but a cloak that told of ice.

"Trickery, trickery, dickery, dee. . . ." It was a child's voice. A waif skipped past singing. She stopped and turned. "Me lights was blowed out an' I no longer see." She was blind. And skipped.

Bester sobbed. Caught his breath. Choked. I could see no reason for it, but he momentarily slowed.

"Mad?" I questioned about the child.

"Lunatic," he said, but spoke not of the child.

Then a woman's voice. It murmured through mist, and then it wept. And then it rose in anger. And then retreated once more to murmur. Betrayal seemed to live in the air, and I remembered women, and the promises I had once made. And broken.

This voice I could not remember. All I could understand was its immense grief, and from that I recoiled.

"I'm not understanding much," Bester said, his voice subdued. "But this is a time like no other time. Like a time that time forgot."

"I feel almost alive. At the same time, fairly-well not." Ephriam pulled to a slow halt. He studied. "All the time that ever was is happening all the time?"

Beneath our feet smoke drifted from burned soil. The stench of death was replaced by the stink of burning peat, yet frost covered the ground. From the gray and silver mist came the sounds of water breaking against a shore, a distant rush of water.

"If you wish to return to life," the woman's voice whispered to us, "do not falter. Retreat is an acceptance of doom." The voice carried little hope, and no trust.

I could not tell from whither the voice came. And what did she mean, "return to life"?

Ephriam made a decision on the strength of that voice. He walked toward the sounds of breaking water. We followed, and we advanced toward a distant shore. Low surf murmured as we walked. An iron gray sea swelled around rocks, and not far offshore a barkentine carried torn sails. Fire climbed the aft mast. The vessel rode so low that burning sails seemed to rest on the surface of the sea; a hull about to take its final dive.

A second vessel, a brig, stood close-hauled in a dead calm. Sails drooped and the commission pennant hung lifeless. Men worked to clear decks after battle. They said little: a distant curse floating across water, the cry of a man wounded, the faint slosh of sea water cast on decks to clear away blood. A marksman, rifle slung across his back, climbed to the crosstrees.

"A cloak, a cloak. Poor him's a-cold." The voice came from one of two figures standing before surf. The one that spoke was old and hunched and thin. It trembled as it stood, and its call went across the surf and to sea; and its call went landward. I did not understand how such a feeble voice could cover such distance.

The second figure was equally old, but it stood erect and at ease. It was still muscular and barrel-shaped. I knew before it turned who I would see, and Ephriam knew as well. He also knew who he would see when the thin figure turned. We stopped, stunned and for the moment, voiceless.

"The time that time forgot," Bester murmured after a long pause. "Is that what's happening?" He watched Ephriam as Ephriam watched two versions of himself as an old man. Ephriam grunted, like a man hit. "Uh, uh, uh. . . ." He looked seaward.

Men from the sinking barkentine were in the water, while other survivors rowed two small boats. They attempted to rescue the swimmers. As they approached each swimmer, a rifle sounded faint across the swells, and a puff of smoke issued from the crosstrees of the brig. The swimmer would shake, the water would turn red, and the man would disappear beneath waves. Ephriam groaned.

I looked toward the brig. In the crosstrees the sniper sported. He chose swimmers about to be rescued. His shots moved ahead of the small boats, searching for men, denying life. From the deck of the bark sounded a familiar laugh. Too familiar. Ephriam choked, made odd sounds in his throat. Finally: "I had charge of the deck. I could have stopped that." He unslung his rifle. His face twisted with loathing, but the loathing was for himself. He looked at the rifle as if he tried to understand its use. I thought, perhaps, he would shoot at the man in the crosstrees. Then, for a moment, I feared he would shoot himself. Instead, he threw the rifle from him as if it were a thing diseased.

"It's not a time like you said," he whispered to Bester. "It's a time of choices. It's not a time that time forgot, but a time when I can act like the man I should have been." He looked at the two standing figures; the wailing old man and the stalwart old man. "Do I become old and simple, or old and of use to the world? Gentlemen, I rejoin my ship."

He kicked off his boots and shrugged out of his furs. "Should you chums ever drift downeast to Maine, and if I'm there, we'll drink and tell tales."

"We'll cover you," Bester said, but sounded doubtful as he unshouldered his rifle.

"Don't," Ephriam told him. "Whatever happens is what's supposed to." He walked into surf and disappeared, like he stepped through a doorway of time. When we turned, the two figures of Ephriam had disappeared as well.

"We should have stopped him."

"You know better. Think on it."

We turned away from the sea, Bester and I, and as we turned the sounds of surf disappeared. Wails drifted through mist, and wails were like silver blades. Hurry and scurry carried on around us, and sometimes we could see movement of men. We could sense dread, resolve, horror. Mostly we trekked.

Cold days gave way to colder nights and fires gleamed before crouching men. It seemed we walked through a bivouac of ghosts and ghostly fires, the fires burning but cold.

"I'm understanding more than I want," Bester told me. "I thought the old woman wanted me to take your party away from the hills."

"She didn't?"

"She did. What I didn't figger was she wanted me gone as well. She's practical."

"I don't follow."

"Men protect their homes," Bester said, "but it changes 'em. Once the fracas is over, nobody wants what they've become . . . can't blame her for gettin' rid of me."

". . . you've been listening to preachers. I'd think better of it."

"T'isn't that," Bester told me. "I figger we brought war with us. It would never have moved eastward without us. We drew it like offal draws flies."

"More preacher-business."

"Don't be a fool." Bester sounded about to lose patience. "We can't forgive each other because we can't forgive ourselves. That's what Ephriam discovered. He's forgivin' himself."

Bester peered through mist. Stink from black powder was so ordinary that I no longer smelled it. Stink of fire was common as well, but the stink of burning that lay heavy in the air was like a bonus of sorrow. "I don't know about you," Bester said, "but I'm walkin' into something. Something lies just ahead."

The terrain gave way to rolling foothills where scorched trees leaned toward smoking earth. Campfires glowed through mist and through night, but the fires were small compared to what we saw and smelled from the distance.

The horizon was alive and red with fire. As we progressed Bester began to tremble. "What you'll see," he whispered, "neither man nor devil would wish." His walk slowed as he thought on his words. "No, a devil might wish it. You could say a devil did . . . a devil with hell in his heart."

Fire bloomed through and above a cabin roof, and a twin fire bloomed above a barn. A plowhorse stood tethered, having been stolen from the barn. Squawks of fowl swept through the night, while, standing before the fires, a group of soldiers wrestled with a squealing hog. They cut its throat, and before it was dead cut away the hams; were prepared to leave the rest. Firelight silhouetted them as they packed meat into a cotton sack.

Small plunder lay about, skillet and pots. Blue uniforms shone black in firelight. A soldier kicked the hog carcass. "You're emancipated," he told the dead hog. "Oh, Lordy you are free."

A rifle popped from the darkness, and a small tongue of flame leaped, accompanied by a curse. The soldier toppled forward. He fell across the dead hog as if he embraced a lover.

From the darkness came a yell that would curdle blood. It was Bester's voice, and it carried all the fierceness of the Rebellion. The other soldiers fled quick as cats, heading into darkness; all but one who did not avoid a second shot. This soldier was hit low in the spine. He fell forward, and began screaming.

"Satisfactory outcome," Bester whispered. "If only it had stopped there."

What followed was like a magic lantern, a stereopticon. Bester stood beside me. The two of us watched the spirit of Bester ease from darkness into light, then step back into darkness. Flames crackled and sparks rose above the burning cabin like dots of hate. The screaming man moaned, fell silent, then screamed.

We watched as the spirit of Bester once more stepped from shadow, then stepped back just as a rifle shot sounded from the direction of the fleeing soldiers. At least one man remained. The spirit had deliberately drawn fire.

The cabin burned, the wounded man gasped and moaned. For a space of minutes nothing moved, and firelight illumed the corpse of the man lying across the butchered hog. Then, from a distance, the spirit's voice screamed curses. The voice moved further and further away, then fell to silence. For the moment, the lantern show paused.

"I euchred the fool." Bester stood beside me as the sounds of his past disappeared into the forest. "It was good soldiering." He put a hand on my arm. "I take satisfaction in what happens next. The fool thought I had fled."

From the edge of the forest a shadow appeared. It moved slowly, and as it moved it whispered to the wounded man. "I'm here, Johnnie. I'm comin' to getcha." The soldier edged toward his wounded friend.

The pop of a rifle from darkness, and the soldier folded forward like a collapsing tent. He grabbed at his groin. He screamed. From the darkness Bester's voice spoke, this time quietly, "Like castrating hogs . . . I reckon you'll sire no more bastards." His voice was lost in the dual screams of the two mortally wounded men.

The lantern show moved. The first paling of dawn gathered above a frame house standing at the edge of a broken town. In dimmest light, shattered buildings stood along a dirt road. From some of the buildings came sounds of weeping. The frame house stood unmarked by battle, and from it came the snores of men.

Beside me, Bester trembled. "Stop it," he muttered, and he talked not to me. Then he turned to me. "I tracked them there. I waited the night. They became drunken."

We watched as the figure of Bester appeared from behind a broken building. The figure carried sacks of black powder and a makeshift torpedo. Bester's spirit moved almost casually, as if it had all the time in the world. It circled the house with a line of powder. When it ran out of powder it made another trip. The torpedo was installed at the front door. It bulked like a dark thought in the growing dawn.

Beside me, Bester groaned. "Seven were there. I'd gotten three. Three should'a been satisfaction aplenty."

Sounds began to issue from the nearest broken building: a child's awakening cry, a woman's hushing voice that was as dark as Bester's skin and as troubled as Bester's furrowed brow. A second child spoke querulous and was hushed by the trembling voice of an old woman. The quiet voice of an ancient man reassured the child.

The family emerged from the building and stood in the gathering dawn. They looked up and down the road, deciding in which direction to flee. The woman was thin, high-rumped with a baby at hip. She was darker than Bester, splay-footed in the way of field hands. The baby was not quite of walking age. A girl of seven or eight stood beside her grandfather and grandmother. The couple stooped, moved with pain, and watched the road as if it would spit forth sorrow. They were a family that had never before traveled ten miles away from home and plantation. A family lost.

The spirit of Bester knelt with flaming torch above a trail of black powder. It watched the family, hesitated, made motion to deal in fire and explosion, hesitated.

The family began to move slowly away from the house and the snoring. Bester touched flame to powder, and a trail of fire encircled the house just as the girl child turned. She ran toward the broken building, for something left behind, a corn cob doll perhaps. She ran toward the fire, and her mother followed screaming. She was still screaming when she and the baby were felled by the exploding torpedo.

The little girl fell, holding her face, rolling in dirt as the two old people hobbled toward her. The old man knelt beside the girl, while across the road flame engulfed the house. Bester ran forward, crazed, and did not go near the child. He stood with rifle at the ready, covering door and windows. One man staggered toward the street and died yelling as Bester's rifle popped. The house burned like hellfire. The lantern show moved.

Bester stood beside me, and held my arm as if he would fall. We watched the little girl roll in the dust and clutch her face. He looked at the lifeless figure of the woman, at the dead baby. "Blinded, and orphaned," he said, but not to me. "Hell of a day's work, and it still early."

"It's past," I said. "You acted a little too fast. A mistake, but it's past."

"It can't be," he said. "It must not." We watched as the scene faded. We stood together on smoking ground. Bester clutched my arm like he was afraid he would fall. There was no strength left in me, or so I thought. I had nothing to spare. Somehow, though, we both stayed on our feet.

Bester shrugged out of his pack. He laid his rifle across the pack, dropped his revolver beside it. "What did Ephriam say? 'Whatever is gonna happen is gonna'?" He looked back the way we had come. "I'm backtracking. Somewhere back there I'll come on all this again. Somewhere back there is the man I could have been." He grasped my arm once more. "Go with God's blessing, and go with mine." He paused. "A'course, mine may be a devil's blessing."

"You'll want help. I'll follow."

"I'll want help," he said, and he was grim. "But that's not to be. This gets done alone." He turned from me. "The old woman knew that the only way to defeat war is to defeat it in yourself."

I watched him walk away. I stood and watched for quite a while, until he faded into distance.

And then, it was, that my torment began. I had been among comrades for the best part of a year, and now, alone, I felt a different kind of fear. Fear tasted like corroded brass. Fear partly arrived because of weakness. My legs persuaded me that they could not support my pack. For the space of a day, perhaps, I sat beside a cold fire in the same manner that a thousand men sat before cold fires. I chewed dried meat and used my knife to cut away part of my bedroll. Strips of hide from my robe served to bind cloth around my feet. Chill lay all around, and the fire became a mockery of cold.

It was a woman's voice that moved me along. It was a voice of sorrow, of anger, of loss. "Forward," it whispered, "or we are lost."

We? I remembered her not. The voice was not kindly.

A survey of the terrain showed that foothills were lowering. There seemed a promise of flatland, perhaps of fields and easier going. When I stood it seemed impossible to even stagger. Too much weight.

Cartridges weighed heavily in the pack. Without cartridges the weapons were useless. It seemed possible to carry either weapons or food, but not both. I cast the weapons from me as had Ephriam, and Bester.

Hours or days or months passed, or perhaps only minutes. I walked in a haze of thought and memory, but also in clairvoyancy. My mind followed Charles, watched him formally dressed and handing a fine lady into a fine carriage. I saw him standing before a stable of thoroughbreds, and saw his proud satisfaction in ownership. I saw Charles addressing his private club of gentlemen, as he lectured on 'My Solitary Sojourn and Adventures Among Red Men of the Forest.'

Time seemed suspended and I only know that I walked. The landscape changed. Foothills gave way to flat land. Farms abounded with split-rail fences down, barns burned, and the rotting carcasses of beasts dotting farmyards. Field crops stood overgrown in weeds.

Farms gave way to prairie, and I scorned myself for thinking that I once thrilled at adventures told by stalwart Englishmen, conquerors of savages in jungle or desert. Then I thought of a better kind of Englishman, and lines from his poem: *For we are here as on a darkling plain/Swept with alarms of struggle and flight where ignorant armies clash by night.*

But why remember words that spoke of "we"? Charles was gone, and Ephriam, and Bester. The land rolled immense and dark before me. Long grass had been burned, and wind swept fire across the horizon. I walked among cold embers across a flat and dreadful land.

"Find him," the woman's voice whispered. "You dare not falter now."

I did not understand, and I found no one. Fires smoked through the mist and souls wandered. And, it was while I hunkered beside a fire that the boy found me.

"Mister?" His voice came from the mist, and then he appeared. He was as small and frail as a spirit. He still wore the red rag at his throat. His other rags barely covered him, and his torn hand hung limp at his side. He approached timidly. And, although he feared me, I feared him more. "My ma sends me," he whispered. "Looks like we still got dealin's."

A woman's sobs, disappearing.

"Tom," I said. "That's your name?"

"So, 'tis."

"Wrap yourself," I told him. I passed him the blanket from my bedroll. "Are you alive or am I dead?"

"Can't say," he told me. "In these parts it don't spell much difference." He hunkered before the fire. "You're a growed-up. You're supposed to know."

I watched him and remembered that he had been too brave. In small light from the fire his cheeks were sallow, his hair ragamuffin dirty, and his eyes swollen from weeping. He wiped his nose with a tattered sleeve, squared his shoulders, and pretended he had no fears. In the distance cannon rumbled, or perhaps it was only thunder.

"Bin waitin' for you," he murmured, ". . . one snaky hell of a long time."

"You're somewhat young to cuss."

"I figgered I was growed-up," he said, and he sounded like he thought he gave an answer. He looked at his torn hand. "I was fixing to be a drummer boy. You could say that part's over."

"I lived in a big city," I told him, "and wrote pieces for newspapers. Then newspapers yelled for war. . . ." I looked over the flat and dying land. "Don't care for that work anymore. You could say that part's over."

From the east, and far away, cannon or thunder rumbled, then diminished. The boy trembled with cold. He clasped the blanket close, and it seemed he yearned toward me. Or, perhaps I only imagined such. I told myself that he had been too brave for a long, long time.

"Ma claims I got to get somethin' figgered. Can't do it 'til I know what 'tis."

"Looks like we both have the same job," I whispered. I thought back on the long journey, the war, the forest, the old woman, the trek. All of it seemed pointed toward a meeting with this child.

I felt a need to touch the boy. Hesitated. Felt the deep fright that he so sternly controlled. No boy so young should have to own so much control. I leaned toward him, then drew him to me. He came willingly. He snuggled against me the way I had once seen a two-year-old cuddled in the arms of its dead grandmother.

The Englishman's poem kept running in my mind. . . . *Ah, Love, let us be true to one another. . . .*

It must have been written for a loved woman. Yet, with the boy snuggled in my arms I thought it might well have been written as a father to a son.

"We'll see this through together," I told the boy, as silver light lay cold in the west. "We'll get it figured out. We'll walk together, westward."

The Troll

A TROLL LIVED IN THE CISTERN. SHE HAD KNOWN IT FOR A long time, but (except once to her grandmother) she did not confide the knowledge. He was a green troll with three legs because he had lost one in an accident, but he was friendly. She did not believe any nonsense about trolls who ate billy goats.

When it was possible, as it sometimes was in that September of 1939 to slip out for a few moments after dark, she would hurry to the spring house and fetch a saucer of milk. She would place it by the pipe leading from the roof to the cistern. The milk was always gone in the morning. It proved her knowledge about the troll.

When the man came to clean the cistern the troll spent a very bad day huddling elongated in the pipe. He only escaped into the cool, bricked cistern with the setting of the sun. She hovered about the cistern all day, tapping gently on the pipe to reassure him with her presence, although occasionally her mother chased her away on errands.

"I'll be back," she would tell him. "I'll be back, I'll be back." Then she would go running, her bare feet over the still-warm earth to the mail box, to the neighbor's house, to the woodpile behind her own house where kindling for the cookstove was stacked.

The mountain behind the house remained green until late in August. The small stream that had bounced, baltering about her feet and chilling them in the spring, became a trickle. The trickle still ran rapidly. To her the stream was acting with hurried care, the abandonment was gone. Later it became swollen with the autumn rains.

She knew where there was a huge fish who was trapped below an eddy. She did not confide that knowledge, either. On afternoons when the sun was hot against the persistent coolness of the forest, she ventured to the stream to speak gently to the fish who was very wild. Later, coming to know her, he would often hover in the prison of his pool, idly carried here, then there, by the jumping trickle of the stream. He always hid when she placed her hand in the water. She worried that the fish would be killed when the cold weather came.

"You worry too much," her mother often told her. "A pretty girl . . . a girl we expect things of. . . . You fritter away your time with a sick kitten. You needn't worry. The cat can take care of her kitten."

Her father always sided with her mother. He would look up from his work or reading. "Study hard this year. You did so well last year. Keep your good start going."

Her father always got the weekly paper. One night he laid it carefully beside him and said, "Damn." Then he said, "Goddamn."

"Hush. Don't swear." Her mother had been put out.

"This whole year. These past years. Depression. No work. And, now this coming. It is coming."

"I know."

To her the biggest difference in the year was in the way her parents acted.

It was the year in which her father spent most of the winter clearing the level acre of woodland left from her grandfather's farm. On Friday nights they did not visit the neighbors. On Saturdays they did not go in town. In the winter they made snow cream. One morning, when breakfast was late, her father's face looked funny. He rose from the table and walked to the barn, although no horses or cows lived there. There were not even any pigs, except in the next door neighbor's shed.

"Finish your breakfast," her mother said. Then her mother went to the barn.

That evening her parents took her to town for ice cream. They laughed, talking more to her than to each other. They did not seem quite the same. Her father bought a new picture puzzle. After it was put together they took it apart and traded to the neighbors for one they had not done.

"I got a fit. I got a fit!" she exclaimed each time she found a piece that matched. Once her father said, "So has the whole world."

She did not understand. Later, in the spring when there was talk of war she did not understand that either.

She went to fly a kite. Once she had owned an airplane but it had broken. It cost ten cents. She thought the kite much better. It only cost a nickel for the string. Her mother made it from lath, paste, and Christmas paper. It was red and white striped. The tail was made from an old yellow dress.

The kite field was by a grove not far from the school. The town road ran past the field. Often, people pulled off the road to talk and allow their children to play, or rested there before returning home from town. She did not think that it was Saturday. A great number of people would be there. She only thought it would be nice to show her grandmother the new kite.

There was no one at her grandmother's house when she banged the screen. She did not worry. Her grandmother would be next door up the road talking to a neighbor woman. While she waited she looked in the pantry and found a cookie. Then she found another.

Her grandmother returned and fussed about the cookies.

"As big as a house. . . ."

"See the kite," she said. "See the kite." Her grandmother went with her to the kite field to show her how they flew kites when she, her grandmother, was a little girl. People were always showing her how they did things when they were little.

And, they did not realize that she was no longer little. She was very grown up, taller than most children in her class, with brown hair nearly over her shoulders. She felt she could have flown the kite all alone. When they arrived at the kite field it was crowded. In the end she was glad her grandmother was with her.

Remembering that spring, as she did once or twice in the year she was seven, she had the feeling but not the thought that perhaps she was not so grown up after all.

The kite went up, twitching and stuttering along its tight bow in the April breeze. It sailed high over the grove. She and her grandmother sat on a grassy bank by a parked car and a wagon to watch. She talked to her grandmother. Then she talked to the horse. There were several men leaning against the car. The kite tugged and dived. Her grandmother said she needed more string. She said she thought so, too.

"Grow grain," a voice said. They turned to look. The men walked toward them to stand by the wagon. The horse was very thin. "Grow grain." The speaker watched the children playing. "Nothing but grain. Grow corn. Grow wheat. Oats. Pile it up. Put it in. There's going to be a market."

"Like last time. . . ." another man spoke carefully.

"Not really. Folks were different then. Everybody excited and worked up. This time I'm just thinking that I'm putting in grain."

"There's talk of soybeans."

"Well, yes. There's talk. But the Sages' boy. You know him. Went to school at the capital. He says grow grain."

"War?"

"Bound to be."

"What is war?" she asked. "War!" the little boys yelled and ran around the kite field and through the trees of the grove.

"Jobs," a man said. "God forgive me. I haven't worked and haven't worked. . . ."

"David and Goliath," her grandmother told her. "That was a war."

"Are we David or Goliath?"

Her grandmother seemed troubled and showed it in her face. "I don't know," she said.

Her grandmother's voice passed the trouble on. It made her a little afraid. Suddenly she was defiant. "We have a troll," she said. "He lives in the cistern."

"A troll?"

"Yes. And the cat has five kittens and one of them is yellow and black."

Her grandmother understood. "I lived in that house when I was a little girl. That was one of the first houses around here. The troll lived there then."

One of the men chuckled. "Maybe he's the one that gets out every twenty years." The other men laughed.

"Wind up your kite," her grandmother told her. "This is not good talk for you to hear."

They returned home to mend a tiny rip in the kite with paper and paste. A few weeks later school let out. She had passed to the second grade.

"Read this summer," her mother told her. "The most important of all is reading." On Wednesdays, before the heat settled in to bounce summer off the slate roof of the house, her mother would take her down the road and in town to the library. She was allowed to pick one book she wanted to read and one her mother wanted her to read. The ones her mother picked were always too hard.

"What is this word?"

"Pro-tect. Protect. You could have figured it out. By sound. It means that the mother rabbit is keeping the little rabbit from being hurt."

"Read it to me."

"I like to read to you. I wish I could. You must read to yourself and learn."

The summer hurried. It opened full in June. The dirt in the garden was black against the green plants. The flowers on the plants were yellow and white. Sometimes a hen from up the road squeezed clucking under the front gate and had to be shooed home. Once a pig got in, grunting and rooting up a row of radishes. She helped her father and mother in the garden, weeding and turning the black earth around corn, beans, tomatoes. One day in the garden her father spoke to her mother. He was very serious.

"I must go and try. Things are opening up a little. In the city."

Her mother seemed sad. "I suppose so. We have to do something."

The next day her father left for the city. It was lonely without him. He did not come home on the Fourth of July. He came home later, nearly a week later. He brought fireworks. That night he sent skyrockets walking up the summer wind while pinwheels fizzed and sparkled from nails on the barn.

"A job. I have a job."

"Will it last? Oh, I'm so glad. Will it last?"

"In the city. Yes, it will last. It's not the best kind of job but it is a job."

She sometimes listened to her parents talk before she went to sleep. That night, after her father came home, she was drowsy from the exciting day. Words came to her, undisturbing through the warmth of approaching sleep.

"Will we have to move?"

"No. It isn't that good a job. I hope for something better."

"But you will be away."

"Yes. It isn't far. Twenty-five miles, but, without a car. I think to come home one evening a week and after work on Saturdays. That will give us Sundays."

"She will miss you as much as I will." Had she been fully awake she would have known that her mother nodded to her room.

"She is growing up," her father said. "She cannot stay small forever. I wish she could. This is a part of her growing up."

"There was a piece in the paper. A piece that told how they get frightened with all the talk going on. A doctor wrote it."

"There are doctors to tell us everything except what we need. Will the doctor be her teacher, her friend? Will he keep her from talk among the relatives. . . . No," her father said. "The hell with the doctor. But, we will do the best we can."

"I wish you wouldn't swear."

"I wish there wasn't going to be a war. Why wouldn't a man swear?"

She came awake. The word brought her back. She crept to the door to look into the living room which centered around the cold iron of the stove that had been dull red and hot during the winter. Her father was in an old rocker before the front window. He looked unhappy. Her mother was sitting quietly in another chair. They were very still. She knew they had heard her get up.

"Do they hurt children?" she asked. "David and Goliath. Did they hurt children?"

Her mother seemed about to cry. Her father stood up slowly and walked to her. He picked her up and carried her to the rocker. He held her.

"There is something bad going on in the world," he said. "But that badness stops at our front fence. Don't worry." She found that being held was better than ever. She was more sleepy than she thought.

After that, Wednesday was book day and father day. On Thursday mornings he was gone again. She saw him very little. On the weekends she would show how well her reading had progressed. She worked hard to miss no words.

On weekdays when her reading was done she helped her mother in the garden. She ran errands. She sat watching as her mother and grandmother canned tomatoes or made jelly. The kitchen on those days was hot with huge kettles sitting on the stove.

"I wish your daddy was here to help," her grandmother said.

"Underfoot," her mother said, and smiled. "I wish he were here too."

"You were lucky," her grandmother said to her mother.

"Yes. He is a good man." Her mother smiled a different kind of smile. "He does not like the job. . . ."

"But, he does it."

"Yes, and doesn't complain. We miss him. I wish he were home more. The place is getting behind. The cistern, a gate hinge broken, the big door of the barn. . . ."

"You can hire a little bit of help now."

"I may have to. When he's home there isn't time."

Sometimes she was allowed to go to the house beyond her grandmother's to play with friends who lived there. At other times she played in the woods at the base of the mountain. Once or twice she climbed higher, exploring. It was late in August when she found the fish.

"You should meet my other friend," she told the fish on her second visit. "He is like you. He stays in one place. I will tell him to visit you." She ran home to explain to the troll about her friend. The third time she visited the fish he seemed a bit more tame. She thought the troll had come and it made her glad.

School started immediately after Labor Day. Her teacher was younger than her first grade teacher had been. She was very pretty. When she spoke her voice was sometimes like laughing. At other times it was not like crying but seemed stretched or distant. Her first teacher had been the same all the time. With this teacher she learned to listen each morning to the voice so she would know what the teacher would do.

"Reports," her teacher said. "It is something new we will try this year. I want each of you to tell about something you like."

"It sounds nice," her mother said when she heard. "What will you tell about?"

She did not know. There were a great many things. She kept a cigar box in the attic. In it was a plaster dog and some other things. Her Sunday School pin for one. She thought she might tell about the box.

"The report is tomorrow. And the day after. . . ."

Her mother interrupted. "I'm sorry. I think he won't be home until Saturday. There is a school for him at night. He will be a foreman." She pulled a note from beneath a dish on the table. "But, he will be home Saturday. We'll have a fine time." She smiled. "You'll have a whole week to tell him about."

That night it rained. She was sitting on the front porch and heard the rain moving through a cut in the mountains toward the house. A cool wind was ahead of the rain, kicking the tree branches.

A shower of leaves fluttered through the night. Her mother was inside. She could hear her moving about. Her mother was singing softly. She did not feel like singing.

During the summer she had sometimes been allowed to play in the rain. Now she jumped from the porch to get a little bit wet. When the rain arrived it was hard and cold. She was soaking almost immediately and caught a chill. Her mother sent her to bed.

The water from the cistern had always been cold. She knew it but had never been bothered. As she lay in her bed trying to get warm she listened to the hard rain against the window. There was the sound of water running down the pipe into the cistern. Without knowing why she knew that the troll was gone. Later, she understood that the reason was the cold.

It was still raining in the morning. She wore her boots and carried her mother's umbrella. As she left she hesitated by the cistern. Then she went on with only a glance. It was deserted.

In the middle of the morning they had reports. The teacher called her name. She stood up.

"I have a friend who is a fish." A boy laughed. She turned on him. "He is nicer than you." The teacher made everyone be quiet while she told about the fish. She wanted to make a picture. How the fish lay in the jumping pool, surrounded by green weeds and the shining pebbles that came tumbling clown the mountain. She wanted to show them how he looked, golden and speckled against the shadowy black rock lying at the bottom of the pool. How sometimes he swam under a ledge of the rock to sleep.

When she was done the teacher said that it was a lovely report. She asked the class if there were any questions. The boy raised his hand.

"That fish is a trout. They are good to eat. If I found him I'd eat him." He looked at her. "I'm going to find him after school," he said.

She knew he was a mean boy. She knew he would do what he said, and began to cry. At noon she was very nervous. The teacher sent her home.

"He'll not do it," her mother said. They sat in the kitchen for a long while talking. "He will not do it. . . ." It was the first time she had ever seen her mother terribly angry.

Her mother took her to her grandmother's house, then went in town. That evening her father came home. It was only Tuesday. He seemed angry. "The creek may be up. It may have risen enough in the night for the fish to get away. A fish. . . ."

"Please," her mother said, "this is important."

"A lot of things are important. I'm sorry. Yes, I suppose it is."

Her father fetched a large net and a bucket. The three of them went through the late dusk, following the creek to the pool where the fish was trapped. The fish was still there. He was very angry and flopped in the net. Her father carried him downstream to release him in deep water. She was very worried and tried to see, but only heard the fish drop into the black water with barely a splash. Then they went in town and had an ice cream.

The ice cream tasted nearly as good as usual. Her father said that he must return to the city. They walked with him to the bus station. While they walked and while they waited for the bus her father was very serious. Her mother seemed worried. Her father spoke to her in a careful, grown-up way which she was able to understand.

"You are a good, big girl," he said. He hugged her, kissed her mother and got on the bus. She and her mother walked home. On the way they did not say very much. When they arrived home it was the same as always except that the troll was still gone and sounds from the darkness told them that the neighbor's sow was plundering the remnants of the garden.

Jack Cady (1932-2004) won *The Atlantic Monthly* "First" award in 1965 for his story, "The Burning." He continued writing and authored nearly a dozen novels, one book of critical analysis of American literature, and more than fifty short stories. Over the course of his literary career, he won the Iowa Prize for Short Fiction, the National Literary Anthology Award, the Washington State Governor's Award, the Nebula Award, the Bram Stoker Award, and the World Fantasy Award.

Prior to a lengthy career in education, Jack worked as a tree high climber, a Coast Guard seaman, an auctioneer, and a long-distance truck driver. He held teaching positions at the University of Washington, Clarion College, Knox College, the University of Alaska at Sitka, and Pacific Lutheran University. He spent many years living in Port Townsend, Washington.

Extended Copyright Info